SECOND CHANCE

Jack Dillon Dublin Tale 12
Second Edition

SECOND CHANCE

Jack Dillon Dublin Tale 12
Second Edition

Mike Faricy

Library of Congress Control Number: 2023920544
paperback ISBN: 978-1-962080-83-5
e-Book ISBN: 978-1-962080-84-2

MJF Publishing books may be purchased for education, Business, or promotional use. For information on bulk purchases, please contact the author directly at mikefaricyauthor@gmail.com

Published by

MJF Publishing
https://www.mikefaricybooks.com

ACKNOWLEDGMENTS

I would like to thank the following people for their help & support: Special thanks to Nick, Roy, Julie, Mittie, and Toui for their hard work, cheerful patience and positive feedback. I would like to thank family and friends for their encouragement and unqualified support. Special thanks to Maggie, Jed, Schatz, Pat, Av, Emily and Pat, for not rolling their eyes, at least when I was there. Most of all, to my wife, Teresa, whose belief, support and inspiration has, from day one, never waned.

To Teresa
"An absolute knacker…"

PROLOGUE

The man held the door to the library open and said, "Glad you made it back to the Spanish sunshine, Amelia. He'll see you now. Let me warn you, he's not happy with the news, so best to mind yourself."

Amelia Maher walked in. Cormac Linnehan was seated in a wingback chair in front of the fireplace. He was sipping something from a crystal glass Amelia assumed held whiskey. He didn't look up as she approached but continued to stare at the empty fireplace. She stood next to the chair opposite him. Eventually, he looked up.

"Word has it, Punchy Sheehan isn't all that excited about conducting any further business in Ireland. I suppose I should tell you well done." He raised his glass toward her then drained it. "There's just one fecking problem," he said, raising his voice. His face suddenly flushed. He threw the crystal glass, and it shattered in the fireplace.

"What problem, sir? I couldn't kill Punchy since he wasn't there, but you seem to have the same result, he's not going to be doing business in Ireland. With the six bodies, I'd say the Doyle's have been put on notice to keep their fat asses in Limerick. I don't know what else I could have done."

Linnehan turned to look at her. His eyes bored holes, and after a long moment, she blinked and glanced at the floor. "All well and good, there's just one little problem. You let this wanker from the Special Branch get away. He knows it was you that did the killing. What in God's name were you thinking? Did you fancy the bastard? Was it the fact he was an American?"

She took a deep breath and spoke calmly. "It was the fact that, if I'd killed him, I never would have made it out of the country. If I'd killed him, An Garda Síochána would have traced the act to you in a heartbeat, and instead of sipping whiskey here in Costa del Sol, you'd be in hiding for the rest of your life because both the Garda and the Americans wouldn't give up until they got you. And once that was accomplished, they would go after your sons. Those are the facts, Cormac."

He seemed to think about that for a moment and acknowledged it by grudgingly saying, "Well, maybe. But we still need to eliminate him."

"I agree, but we have to wait, get some distance from this whole operation. Give it a couple of months. Let things cool down, and they'll move on. Given the work this Dillon in the Special Branch is involved in, I can set it up so there is no way in hell they'll think you were involved."

"Two months? That seems an awfully long time."

"I can rush back now, tonight if you want, and shoot the knacker. That will give you just enough time to pack a bag and stay on the run for the rest of your life. Do you really want to do that? Or, would it be a better move to enjoy the sun and some more whiskey for sixty days while I figure out how, exactly, we'll do this?"

"Sixty days, and then I want you to get that gorgeous bum of yours back into Dublin. You've a second chance to eliminate this bastard once and for all. What the hell did you say his name was?"

"Dillon. Jack Dillon."

ONE

CI McCabe, head of Special Branch, stepped out of his office and surveyed the room. "D.I. Rafferty and Marshal Dillon, a moment of your time, please," he said and disappeared back into his office.

Dillon waited for a half-second to make sure McCabe was out of sight before he shook his head. Three more reports yet to do, and apparently, he was getting called to another case.

"Let's go, old-timer. No sense in keeping the man waiting," Rafferty said and followed up with a laugh as he hurried past Dillon's desk.

"A little more respect, Kevin," Dillon replied and followed Rafferty into McCabe's office.

"Good morning, gentlemen. Take a seat," McCabe said without looking up from the pile of reports on his desk. He read for another half-minute, signed his name on the bottom sheet, and placed the file on a smaller stack just to his left.

"Gentlemen, apparently, there was a shooting out in Skerries. D.I. Suel is currently unavailable. Rafferty, you'll take his place."

"Yes, sir, it's only that I have a physical exam scheduled in three hours, and I've had to cancel twice already."

"I'm aware of that, Rafferty. I've notified Suel. He'll join you in Skerries at some point. You've my permission to leave for your physical. That said, I want the two of you making an initial appearance together. Skerries Garda has requested our assistance. Thus far, we know it was a shooting last night. The victim was an American by the name of Dennis Hickey, age fifty-six, apparently from the city of Chicago. I'd like you to examine the scene of the shooting as well as his room, a rental at the Harbour Hotel. I've been told the gentleman's room is currently under lock and key."

"The shooting?" Dillon asked. "Was it an altercation? A robbery?"

"We've no indication it was either. The gentleman's wallet containing credit cards and two hundred euros along with his passport and cellphone were still in his possession. He ate a quiet dinner by himself at the Stoop Your Head pub. His body was discovered just off Harbour Road. There is a public toilet overlooking the sea, and he was fifteen feet from that structure."

Dillon knew the area. A friend, Sean, lived in Skerries, not along the harbor but near enough. He swam a mile or more year round in the Irish Sea a number of times a week with a local group called the Frosties. They swam not far from where the body was found.

"Has the American Embassy been contacted?" Dillon asked.

"I would presume so, but I don't know that for a fact. The sooner you get out there, the sooner a number of your questions will be answered."

"Point of contact?" Rafferty asked.

"Sergeant Declan Reilly with Skerries An Garda Síochána. Here's his number. Call him en route. Anything else?" McCabe asked as he handed a post-it-note to Rafferty.

Both men shook their heads as they stood. They waited for a half-second for any final direction. McCabe returned to the stack of files on his desk, and they hurried from his office.

"I'll drive," Rafferty said. "I have a department vehicle signed out, and if Suel plans to meet us out there, you can grab a ride back with him, well, unless you want to drive yourself."

"No, I'll ride with you and keep my eyes closed all the way back with Paddy behind the wheel."

"Good idea," Rafferty said and chuckled. It took them no more than five minutes to assemble what they needed, turn off computers, lock their desks, and head out the door.

"You expecting weather?" Rafferty asked as they headed out of the Headquarters building. He indicated the tan raincoat Dillon carried under his arm.

"Well, it's rained every day for the past five days, and listening to this morning's forecast, yeah, I'm expecting wet weather."

Rafferty glanced up at the clear sky and shook his head. "We're liable to get a sunburn."

"You keep thinking that way. I'll take the raincoat just to play it safe."

"Suit yourself," Rafferty said and clicked the fob in his hand. The lights blinked on a red Toyota Corolla Cross, an SUV. The color was officially described as Barcelona red metallic. The passenger door on the driver's side was dented.

"What did you run into?" Dillon asked.

"Fortunately, not me. I'm sure whoever had it at that point tried to return it without mentioning the damage."

"I wonder how that worked?" Dillon asked.

"How do you think?" Rafferty replied as he opened the driver's door.

The drive to Skerries was uneventful. Dillon phoned Sergeant Declan Reilly in Skerries, guesstimating their arrival time. Reilly said he'd meet them at the Garda station, which wasn't too far from the crime scene and the Harbor Hotel. Once they turned off the M1 and onto the R132, Dillon enjoyed the country view. It was a thirty-five-minute drive, and fortunately, Rafferty knew exactly where he was going. He parked on the street in front of the Garda station.

The station, a two-story white stucco structure at least a hundred years old, looked more like an elegant home. A sidewalk with red flowers blooming on either side led up to the door painted with shiny blue enamel. The three windows on the main floor each had twelve glass panes. The four windows on the second floor consisted of nine glass panes. All the window trim was painted white. Flower boxes hung below each window.

Dillon followed Rafferty as he opened the door. A wooden counter was positioned just inside. Two officers, a man and woman, sat behind the counter.

The woman flashed a smile and said, "Good morning. How may we help?"

"D.I. Rafferty and Marshal Dillon from Dublin Special Branch to see Sergeant Declan Reilly," Rafferty said.

"Oh, yes, he's been expecting you, dreadful incident last night. Absolutely dreadful," she said, shaking her head.

The man next to her pushed three keys on the phone and placed the receiver to his ear. A moment later, he said, "They're here." He nodded and hung up the phone. "Sergeant Reilly will be out in just a bit."

Dillon could hear what sounded like someone hurrying down a set of stairs, and a moment later, a dark-haired man with sergeant stripes on his shirt and a neon green high visibility vest entered the room. He immediately headed for Dillon with an outstretched hand and said, "Marshal Dillon? Declan Reilly."

Dillon shook hands and said, "Pleased to meet you, Sergeant. Sorry, it's under these circumstances."

"Kevin Rafferty," Rafferty said and extended his hand.

They shook hands, and Reilly said, "Appreciate you coming out, lads. Let's head out to the scene, and then we can go to your man's hotel room. A sad state of affairs. We've not had anything like this going on two years."

"Where's the body at this point?" Dillon asked.

"Dublin morgue, transported last night. You're American?"

"Yeah, I'm assigned to An Garda Síochána Special Branch in Dublin."

"Were you involved in those shootings out at Dublin Airport a couple of years back?"

"Yes, I was. We heard your shooting took place last night around the harbor. An American by the name of Dennis Hickey, from Chicago," Dillon said, changing the subject.

"Yes, near as we can figure, it was right around 11:00. No report of anyone hearing the shots, let alone seeing something. A man out walking his dog actually found the body. Phoned us right away."

"We'll want to talk to him," Dillon said.

"Figured that would be the case. He's retired and expecting your call. Why don't you follow me? It's not more than a minute or two drive," Reilly said, and they headed out the door.

Dillon noticed a bank of clouds beginning to form. He didn't say anything to Rafferty, but he was glad he brought his raincoat.

TWO

Reilly was right. It was just a two-minute drive. They followed the Garda squad car he was driving. The vehicle was white with a neon yellow stripe running from front to back on either side. Flashing lights, blue in this case, were attached to the top of the squad car. The word 'GARDA' was written in bold blue letters on all four sides of the car. In the two minutes it took to drive to the scene of the shooting, easily a half-dozen people walking along the sidewalks gave a friendly wave to Reilly.

"Your man must be popular," Rafferty said at one point as two women waved.

"Typical small town," Dillon said. "I always liked this place."

From Quay Street, they turned onto Harbour Road and drove past the Stoop Your Head and the Blue Bar pubs. A little further on, Reilly pulled to a stop. The public toilets were just to the left. Ahead and around the corner to the right was the Life Boat Cafe & Bar. Just before that, an area in front of the Skerries Sea Memorial was sectioned off by white tape with blue lettering reading

'AN GARDA SIOCHANA DO NOT CROSS!' The words were written in both English and Irish.

Other than two uniformed officers, no one else was around. This initially struck Dillon as strange until he realized there was absolutely nothing to see. Reilly waited as they climbed out of the car and then led them up to the taped-off area. If he didn't know better, Dillon would have thought they had the wrong area secured. There appeared to be no sign that anything resembling a crime, let alone a murder, had taken place.

"This is it?" Dillon asked.

"It is," Reilly said. "We suspect your man may have walked this way last night just to view the sea. We know he had dinner at 8:00 at the Stoop, a starter and a sandwich along with a pint of Guinness. No telling how long he was here or if he used the public toilet in the harbor. His wallet, passport, and phone were found on his person. The wallet still contained two hundred euros in cash, which would seem to suggest robbery was not the intent."

"You find a shell casing?"

Reilly shook his head. "No, unfortunately, and we searched the area. There were powder burns on his skull, suggesting the weapon was fired at a very close range. Based on the fact there was no exit wound, my guess is a small caliber weapon was used. I'm sure they'll be able to confirm that during the autopsy."

"Did he have a cellphone?"

"Yes, he did. We've got the wallet, passport, and cellphone in evidence bags for you. His hotel room is locked, and other than a quick glance, we haven't searched it. Thought, since you were on your way, we'd leave that to the likes of you."

"Any idea when the autopsy is scheduled?" Rafferty asked.

"I know they were backed up. There was a car-truck accident that killed three, and that's ahead of the Hickey autopsy. I'm guessing sometime tomorrow, but I haven't received confirmation as of yet. I'll let you's know as soon as I hear."

Dillon slipped on a pair of white latex gloves. "Mind if we check it out?" he asked as he lifted the blue and white tape and slipped beneath.

Reilly shrugged and shook his head.

Rafferty followed Dillon. They spread several feet apart and slowly headed toward the center, all the while scanning the ground. "There's the spot there," Dillon said. He stopped and pointed toward an area six feet in front of them. A small amount of blood, easy to miss, was splattered on the grass. Dillon pulled out his phone and photographed the area.

They spread a little further apart and approached the area. The small amount of blood on the grass was really the only indication something had happened. There was nothing suggesting a trail through the neatly trimmed grass. Dillon glanced at the sky. The blood would be easy to miss in the daylight, and with the bank of clouds moving in, any rain would completely obliterate the scene. He circled the blood on the grass, taking more pictures.

Looking around at the lack of clues, he was reminded of the murder scene in Desertserges down in County Cork almost two months ago. An American named Dennis Sheehan and his wife. Both shot with a small-caliber weapon.

"What do you think?" Rafferty asked, bringing Dillon back to the here and now.

"I think we should check that hotel room and then talk to the guy who was walking his dog," Dillon said. They stepped back beneath the security tape and followed Reilly back to the cars.

"Parking's tight at the hotel. It'd be best to leave your car here, and I'll give you's a lift. It'll be fine. The lads will watch it," Reilly said. The drive from the crime scene to the Harbor Hotel took about a minute. It took Reilly almost as long to back the car up and turn around as it did to drive to the hotel.

The Harbor Hotel was a two-story brick structure and, at no surprise, overlooked Skerries Harbor. At the moment, there were only three boats in the harbor, all three small, private, pleasure craft. The fishing boats were out doing just that, fishing.

Reilly pulled up onto the sidewalk and parked in front of the hotel. The clouds were now over the harbor, and rain was just beginning to mist. Dillon slipped his raincoat on and smiled at Rafferty. He pulled a cap from the pocket and placed it on his head.

"Ah, for the love of, don't even say it," Rafferty said.

The entrance to the hotel was through a set of double doors two feet from the sidewalk. They followed Reilly through the double doors into a dingy lobby that didn't appear to have been updated in the past eighty years. Off to the left was a small sitting area with a couch and two upholstered chairs. A striped cat rested on the back of one of the chairs. The cat ignored the three of them as they walked past and headed toward the reception counter.

Reilly tapped his finger twice on the bell resting on the counter. A moment later, a woman, mid-forties to fifty, opened a door and stepped behind the counter. She was wearing jeans and a T-shirt. Smiling, she said, "Hi, ya, Declan. Here to go through your man's room?"

"Yeah, Mary. Shouldn't take too long. It's still locked?" Reilly asked just as the cellphone in his pocket rang

"Just as you said. He was in 204. The girls are up cleaning on the floor, but they've been told to stay clear. Follow me. I'll lead you's up." She grabbed a key from a small rack behind the reception counter. The key was brass and attached to a green plastic keychain with the number 204 in white numerals. As she stepped around the counter, she gave a nod to Dillon and Rafferty and headed toward the staircase off to the right.

The staircase was about six feet wide, with a wooden stair rail on either side. Ten steps led to a landing, and six more steps led back from the landing to the hall on the second-floor. They stepped through a door into the center of the hallway. There were four rooms to the left and four rooms to the right, two on either side of the hall. They took a left, 204 was the closest room.

The woman inserted the key, and Dillon heard the lock click. She stepped back. Reilly opened the door. "It's all yours, gentlemen," Reilly said as he pulled his cellphone from his pocket and checked the screen. "I've to get back to the station. You okay without me?"

"Not a problem," Dillon said. He reached into his pocket, pulled out his white latex gloves, and slipped them on.

Rafferty did the same thing.

"I'll just be a phone call away. Call when you've finished, and we'll pay a visit to Ultan Healy. He's your man who discovered the body last night."

"I'll be in the office behind reception. Ring the bell if you's need anything," Mary said, and she and Reilly headed back down the stairs. "So, how's it going?" Mary asked Reilly as they headed down to the main floor. Dillon stepped into the room without hearing Reilly's answer.

THREE

Rafferty stepped into the hotel room, looked around, and said, "Jaysus. I hope your man didn't think he'd have someplace fancy," Rafferty said, stepping into the hotel room.

There was a window that looked out on the harbor. Due to the slightly irregular glass surface, Dillon guessed the window was original to the structure. Heavy beige drapes were pulled back on either side of the window. It had begun to rain in earnest, and although the window was locked, the drapes were moving back and forth slightly due to an air draft.

The walls were papered with a gray floral design. The background had probably been an off-white color that had since yellowed with age and probably decades of nicotine. A four-inch section in an upper corner had curled away from the wall. The covers were pulled back on the double bed, and the pillow featured an indentation suggesting someone's head had rested there.

Dillon pressed his hand against the thin mattress and the even thinner pillow. Neither one felt as if they would have been very comfortable. A desk against the far wall had an open black suitcase with clothes still held in place by two black nylon straps. Next to the suitcase was a walnut box eight inches high with a brass plaque on top. The image of a pair of hands folded in prayer was engraved on the front of the box.

Rafferty walked over to the box, pulled the top off, and said, "What the hell is this? Cat Litter?"

Dillon stepped over, glanced in the box, and looked at the brass plaque on the lid. The plaque read, 'Maureen Hickey, June 12, 1967 - 14 February 2021.' "It's not a litter box, Kevin. It's a cremation box. Apparently, the remains of someone named Maureen Hickey. Possibly the victim's wife. It looks like she died on Valentine's day."

Rafferty took a step back and shook his head. "Why would he bring something like that?"

"Maybe she wanted to be buried here, or they had a trip planned, and she died before they went. Who knows?"

"That's really strange."

"Actually, it's pretty sad, not to mention the fact that now he's dead as well."

Dillon pulled out his phone and took a photo of the cremation box and then the suitcase. He unhooked the nylon straps holding the clothes in place. He took a photo, removed a pair of black trousers and a white shirt, and took another photo. He took six pictures in all. The suitcase contained nothing unusual, just clothes, along with a shaving razor, toothbrush, and deodorant.

He closed the lid on the suitcase and unzipped the two front pockets. The top pocket was the smaller of the two. He reached in and pulled out two boarding passes and a three-page travel itinerary from Delta Airline stapled together. The bottom pocket was larger and empty. One boarding pass was for a Chicago to Amsterdam flight two days ago. The second was for an Amsterdam to Dublin flight arriving yesterday morning. Dillon photographed the boarding passes and the flight itinerary. Hickey was scheduled to return to the US via Amsterdam to Chicago in three days.

The suitcase suddenly made sense. By the time Hickey would have cleared the airport and probably taxied to Skerries, it would have been late morning, maybe early afternoon. He checked into the hotel, probably slept a few hours, and grabbed dinner at the Stoop Your Head pub. After dinner, he walked over to the Skerries Sea Memorial to look out onto the sea or maybe view a ship passing, and he was shot. Why?

"Who in the hell would shoot this guy?" Dillon said just as someone knocked on the door. Dillon turned just as his Special Branch partner, Paddy Suel, stepped into the room.

"Don't you lot say a fecking word," Suel said.

Dillon had to bite his tongue to keep from grinning. Suel's left cheek was swollen. It had ballooned out looking like he'd stuffed half a chicken in his mouth. "So, your dentist finally had enough of you and hauled off and hit you."

"God save me. Fortunately, he'd put me out before he pulled the tooth."

"Does it hurt?" Rafferty asked.

"Not yet. They gave me a mess of pills. I'm supposed to take one every eight hours."

"You could probably sell those on the street and make some money," Dillon said.

"Don't even go there, Dillon."

"You good to give your man Dillon a ride back to the station when you're finished up here? I've got to get to a physical exam in forty-five minutes," Rafferty said.

"I suppose I don't really have a choice now, do I?"

"That's about right."

"Yeah, against my better judgment, I'll give him a lift. As long as he stays on his best behavior."

"Whatever that is. You parked out in front?" Rafferty asked.

"What of it?" Suel replied.

"Well, nothing, except it's raining cats and dogs now, and I've to walk back to where the car is parked. I was thinking I might borrow the Marshal's raincoat if you wouldn't mind."

"Oh, so all of a sudden, it turns out to be a good idea that I brought it?" Dillon said as he slowly pulled off his raincoat and handed it to Rafferty. "Only cause I'm a nice guy."

"Thanks, I'll leave it at your desk in Special Branch," Rafferty said and headed out the door.

"So, what do you have?" Suel asked.

"You sure you're okay for this?"

"Yeah, it looks a lot worse than it is. It's just a blessing to get what was left of the tooth out. I was eating pasta, of all things, and suddenly, I was spitting out pieces of a molar. Had to wait until late this morning to get in to see your man. Just glad he knocked me out."

"Better you than me," Dillon said. He glanced out the window and watched Rafferty in the rain hurrying back along the Harbour Road toward the car. He was wearing the raincoat and the cap Dillon had shoved in the pocket. "Glad we looked at the scene of the murder before this rain started. Not that there was anything to see."

"What'd it look like?"

"It looked like nothing happened. There was a little bit of blood on the grass. That's gone by now. I took some pictures. Nothing like footprints or even bent grass. Nothing. The Skerries team went over the area looking for a shell casing, never found one. Your man Reilly said, based on the wound, it looked to be close up. Powder burns on the victim's scalp. No exit wound, so he was thinking small caliber. The victim, an American named Dennis Hickey, has already been transported to the Dublin Morgue. Reilly didn't think the autopsy would happen until tomorrow at the earliest."

Dillon went on to tell Suel about the cremation box and the boarding passes. "The guy hadn't been in the country more than fourteen hours, and he's shot. There has to be some reason. I'm not seeing this as random.

Once we're finished here, we're to call Reilly. He'll take us to your man who found the body last night. Apparently, someone was just out walking a dog. After we talk to him, I'll give a call to Eric Bergman at the American Embassy and touch base. Maybe he'll know something. Let me give Reilly a call now and tell him we're finished here."

Dillon pulled out his phone and called Reilly. He answered on the second ring. "Finished already?"

"Not an awful lot to see. Could you direct us to your man who found the body?"

"I'll do better than that. I'll take you and introduce you. He was a mate of me da's. Ultan Healy. I'll be there in a few minutes, just finishing up here. Oh, the autopsy on your man is scheduled for 2:00 tomorrow afternoon, Dublin Morgue."

"Got it, see you shortly. Say, Declan, if you could bring some evidence bags with you. There're a few things we'll be taking back."

"Not a problem," Reilly said and disconnected.

"He'll be here in ten minutes," Dillon said. He returned the clothes to the suitcase and zipped everything closed.

FOUR

It was closer to forty-five minutes before Reilly returned. They could hear him charging up the staircase. A moment later, he stepped into the room. "Sorry to keep you waiting, lads. You know how it is, the phone just keeps on ringing. Then I couldn't get Ultan to answer his damn phone. Drove over to his place, and the plonker didn't have his hearing aids in. God deliver me. Oh, the evidence bags," he said and handed a stack to Dillon. "And here is your man's wallet, passport, and phone. If you'd sign this form just to maintain the chain of evidence," he said as he handed Dillon three evidence bags, each with Hickey's wallet, passport and phone.

"Thanks," Dillon said and set the bags on the desk next to the suitcase. As he signed the chain of evidence, he said, "Declan, this is my partner in Special Branch, D.I. Paddy Suel. D.I. Rafferty has some medical appointment back in Dublin he had to get to. Paddy, Sergeant Declan Reilly, Skerries An Garda Síochána."

Reilly and Suel shook hands and immediately started exchanging names of mutual acquaintances on the force. Dillon placed the cremation bin, the boarding passes, and flight information in separate evidence bags. He placed an evidence tag around the handle of the suitcase. After another look around, they headed downstairs and out the door. Suel carried the evidence bags, including Hickey's wallet, passport, and phone. Dillon carried the suitcase. Fortunately, the rain had stopped. Dillon placed the suitcase in the boot of the car, and Suel placed the evidence bags next to it. They climbed in the car and waited while Reilly had a brief conversation with Mary from reception. When he'd finished, Reilly gave a wave and climbed into his car.

"You okay to drive?" Dillon asked.

"Not a bother. We get in an accident, I've got these pain pills, so I won't feel a thing," he said. He pulled off the sidewalk and followed Reilly in the squad car.

They drove all of two blocks. Reilly pulled onto the sidewalk, leaving barely enough room for someone to make their way between the two-story stone structure and his car.

Suel stopped and said, "You'd best get out here."

Dillon climbed out of the passenger seat. Suel pulled ahead and parked behind Reilly's squad car. Rather than navigate the narrow passage between the cars and the stone structure, they stepped into the street, walked past two doors and stopped at the third.

Reilly glanced at them and said, "Your man is Ultan Healy. Hopefully, he still has his hearing aids in." He pounded on the door three times, not a gentle knock. A moment later, the door opened, and an older white-haired man smiled. He couldn't have been more than five feet and an inch or two tall.

He looked at Reilly and said, "Well, Declan. Come in, come in. You're late, by the way. Shades of your father."

"I learned from the best, Ultan. Let me introduce you to two gentlemen from Special Branch in Dublin. They're assisting in our investigation. This is D.I. Paddy Suel and Marshal Jack Dillon. Gentlemen, may I present the man of the hour, Ultan Healy."

"The pleasure is all mine, lads. Please, please, come in." A small dog suddenly stepped out from behind Healy and sniffed Dillon.

"Don't mind Lady. She's just hoping you brought a treat. Grab a seat, sit down, lads, sit down," Healy said

They stepped into a compact sitting room. A black leather couch and two wingback chairs were centered around a stone fireplace. Turf was burning in the fireplace, and it gave a pleasant warmth to the darkened room. Healy settled into one of the wingback chairs and picked up a tea mug resting on a small table.

"Can I get you's a cuppa?"

"Thank you, but none for me," Dillon said.

"Just had a tooth pulled this morning, so I'd better say no. Thanks all the same," Suel said.

"So, Ultan," Reilly said, settling in next to Suel on the couch. "Would you mind going over what you told me this morning?"

"Not at all, not at all," Healy said. "So, I take Lady for a walk every night, usually around 9:00. I'd been out to me brother's yesterday afternoon for a load of turf, had a pint with him, loaded up the car, and then stacked it all in here," he said, pointing at the four-foot pile of turf next to the fireplace. From there, Healy went back three generations explaining the location of the family farm, the neighbors, and two neighbors killed back in 1916 in the Easter Rebellion. It was close to twenty minutes before he actually returned to the previous night.

"So, after hauling the turf, having a pint with me brother, stacking the turf in here, didn't I fall asleep right here in this chair. If it weren't for Lady, I'd probably still be asleep," he said and chuckled. "She barked and woke me a little after ten. Out we went on our walk, same route as every night." He went on to give specific directions on the route for five minutes.

"Now, we'd just passed the Life Boat Cafe, only two cars parked, which seemed a bit on the light side to my way of thinking, but who knows. So we come up to the Sea Memorial. Lady always likes to sniff around and do a bit of her business, don't you know. We're walking across the grass, and I see your man stretched out on the ground. My first thought is he's gazing at the stars, but then I realize he's face down, so that can't be right. I thought maybe he'd enjoyed himself a bit too much at the pubs, so I walk over and kick him, gentle like, on the sole of his shoe. No response. I kick him again, same thing. That's when I look at the back of his head, see a bit of blood and think, this ain't right. Lady and I hurry over to the Garda Station, tell your man at the desk. Who was that, Declan?"

"Officer Mullen, Eion Mullen."

"Yes, that's the lad. Now isn't he James and Eileen's oldest?"

"He is," Reilly said.

"Funny story about the parents. This is before they were married. They decide to take the train…" Another ten minutes went by before he was back to the body.

"So, I told officer Mullen what I'd found. He gets on the radio, and the next thing I know, there's been a murder in Skerries."

"Did you hear anything like a gunshot, a scream, maybe someone shouting?" Suel asked.

"No, not a thing, but then I'd taken the hearing aids out. I got them, oh, must be six or seven years ago. Still not quite used to them. I remember…"

Fortunately, the hearing aid story was only a minute or two. "You didn't see anyone around, maybe a car driving away?" Dillon asked.

Healy shook his head. "No sir, a quiet night all around. You see, Lady and I usually head out just before 9:00. Now I was hauling turf all afternoon and then had a pint with me brother…"

Dillon and Suel were headed out of town on the R132 toward the M1.

"Not a bad interview," Suel said.

"Yeah, it only took about ninety minutes, and I learned more about turf and your man's family farm than I ever thought possible."

"Has a time of death been established?" Suel asked.

"Between 10:00 and 11:00 yesterday evening."

"So Hickey flies in from the US. Chicago, as a matter of fact," Suel said.

"Chicago to Amsterdam, Amsterdam to Dublin," Dillon said.

"Yeah. He goes from Dublin airport to Skerries. Probably sleeps a few hours. Grabs dinner at the Stoop."

"A starter, a sandwich, and a pint of Guinness."

"He leaves the Stoop and is found just before 11:00. Reilly mentioned he still had his passport and wallet. Did they ever find a cellphone?"

"That was with him as well."

FIVE

They drove for a short while on the R132. Suel moved into the left turn lane, waited for three cars to pass, and turned onto the entrance ramp for the M1 that would take them back to Dublin. He stopped halfway down the ramp and said, "Oh, will you look at this? For the love of God."

Two lanes of taillights as far as they could see and no one moving. "It'll be a cold day in hell before I spend the next few hours of my life stuck in that mess," Suel said and began to back up the ramp.

"God, look at that. It must be one hell of an accident."

"Or a plane crash," Suel said. He checked the traffic in both directions then backed onto the R132 and continued in the direction they'd been driving. They made it back to Headquarters and the Special Branch office no more than fifteen minutes later than they'd expected.

Dillon carried the suitcase, and Suel carried the evidence bags up to the Special Branch section. They set everything on Dillon's desk, and he proceeded to fill out paperwork to store the items with Dublin An Garda Síochána. He wasn't quite finished when D.C.I. McCabe stepped out of his office and came over to Dillon's desk.

"Dillon, is Rafferty with you?"

"Rafferty? No sir. He left to get to that physical exam. D.I. Suel and I finished up and drove back."

"I just received a call. Rafferty never made it to his appointment."

"Not a surprise, we saw a massive traffic jam on the M1. In fact, we took a different route back here. All lanes of traffic were at a complete standstill. No one was moving. No idea what the problem was, but I would guess some major accident. If he got caught up in that mess, he could be stuck there for hours."

"Mmm," McCabe said. "Well, thanks for the update. I've attempted to call him, but I'm dumped into his voicemail."

"Let me try giving him a call. I'll check online and see if there's any information on the accident."

"Yes, all right, do, and please keep me informed. I hope he's alright."

"Well, if it's any consolation, it looked like one of the worst traffic jams I've ever seen. Taillights as far as we could see, and everyone at a complete standstill. Maybe a truck or a bus tipped over, and it's blocking both lanes."

"Let me know if you learn anything," McCabe said and returned to his office.

Dillon thought for a long moment. He had a half-dozen cases up in the air, and now this murder out in Skerries. They'd spent the better part of an hour and a half politely listening to Ultan Healy while he rambled on about burning turf and some crazy evening a couple had on the train thirty years ago. Now, Rafferty wasn't answering his phone.

He took out his cell, looked up Rafferty on his contact list, and then called the number from his desk phone, thinking maybe his incoming call would appear a bit more official and Rafferty would answer. The phone didn't even ring. It just automatically dumped him into voicemail.

"Sorry, I'm unable to take your call at the moment. Please leave a message, and I'll return the call just as soon as possible." There was a beep a second later.

"Yeah, Kevin. Jack Dillon. I'm back at Special Branch and D.C.I. McCabe just mentioned you didn't make your doctor's appointment. Suel and I saw a major traffic jam on the M1 and wonder if you maybe got stuck in that. Give me a call back when you have a moment. McCabe is wondering. Thanks. Hope everything is okay."

Dillon's next call was to Eric Bergman at the American Embassy. His call went to a receptionist, who placed him on hold and then came back and connected him to Bergman's phone. He counted five rings and was getting ready to leave a message when Bergman answered. "Eric Bergman."

"Hi Eric, Jack Dillon. How are things?"

"The usual craziness. What's up?"

"The name Dennis Hickey mean anything to you?"

"Hickey, no, can't say that it does. Why? What happened?"

"Shooting last night out in Skerries. The man's body was found around 11:00 PM. I'm just back from there. He's American. I would guess you'll be receiving official notification shortly."

"What can you tell me?"

"Not much. He was shot. No witnesses. At this stage, no one heard or saw anything. An Garda in Skerries are knocking on doors but coming up empty-handed. Hickey is, or rather was, fifty-six years old. From Chicago. Initial examination turns up nothing unusual. He did have a cremation urn in his hotel room with a brass plaque on it listing Maureen Hickey and the date 14 February 2021. Not sure what the relationship was, wife, or maybe his sister."

"Gee, and here I was thinking it had been a pretty quiet day. You have any information on when he arrived?"

"Yeah, as a matter of fact, I do. He had scheduled a four or five-day trip. Hang on, just a moment, I've got his flight information here." Dillon grabbed the evidence bags with the boarding cards and the flight itinerary and read the information to Bergman.

"Passport number?" Bergman asked.

"Yeah, just let me glove up and get it for you." He opened a desk drawer and pulled two latex gloves from a box. He raised his right shoulder to keep the receiver in place and opened the bag containing the passport. "Okay, here's the number," he said and read it to Bergman. He paged through the passport and said, "Just checking to see where else he's been. He was in Mexico for five days back in 2018, and apparently, other than arriving in Dublin yesterday, he hasn't been out of the US."

"And you say he was shot?"

"Yeah, no sign of any altercation. He still had his wallet with two hundred euros in it. We know he had some pub grub for dinner along with a pint of Guinness. He ate at the Stoop Your Head in Skerries if you know where that is."

"Right on the harbor, isn't it?"

"Yeah, nice place, quiet, nothing crazy going on. So he left the pub and apparently walked out to the edge of the harbor. That would take all of a minute, maybe two. We think he may have just wanted to look at the sea, and for whatever reason, he was shot."

"How many times was he shot?"

"Just once. Close up. I haven't seen the body. That's my next stop. He's been transported to the Dublin morgue."

"You think he may have met someone in the pub or crossed someone the wrong way?"

"No indications of that, but I suppose anything is possible."

"All right, well, thanks for the heads-up. I'll get things started on this end and wait for the official word to come through."

"Good luck, and if you learn anything, please let me know."

"Will do, Jack. Thank you," Bergman said and hung up.

Dillon sat and thought for a moment then shook his head. It took the better part of an hour, but he filled out a series of forms to submit the various items to the property room and then gathered everything and headed toward the door.

Suel was just hanging up his phone, and Dillon stopped at his desk. "I'm taking all of this down to the property room and then driving over to the morgue. I want to take a look at Hickey's body. From there, I'm going to head home unless something comes up. McCabe said Rafferty never made it to his doctor's appointment."

"Yeah, I wouldn't worry about it. Major accident on the M1. I checked it out online. Things are moving now, but he was probably stuck in that shite we saw."

"What was the problem?"

"Car and truck accident. The truck tipped over, blocking all lanes. A fuel truck, fortunately, it never exploded or caught fire, but it took hours to upright and get people moving."

"Anyone killed?"

"One dead, two injured. Given that it was a fuel truck, we're lucky it wasn't more. Anyway, that's probably where he got stuck. I'm just glad we were able to back up."

"Yeah, you got that right. Maybe pass on that information to McCabe. I'll see you in the morning," Dillon said and made his way to the elevators.

The property room was on the lower level of the headquarters building. It took Dillon thirty minutes to enter the items and correct the mistakes he'd made on his forms. He had to list Skerries Gardai as the initial holders of the items, but eventually, he got everything submitted and went out to the parking lot.

SIX

The Dublin City Morgue is located on Griffith Avenue. It's just a fifteen-minute drive from the Headquarters building in Phoenix Park. Dillon parked on Griffith Avenue and walked past the postal building and into the morgue. He stepped into the building at the side entrance and walked up to the receptionist counter. The counter was behind a large sheet of glass with an opening for papers to be passed across the counter. He didn't recognize the woman who looked up at him.

"I'm sorry, sir, the public entrance is back out and on the opposite corner of the building."

Dillon smiled and pulled out his lanyard with his An Garda Síochána ID. "I'm here to view the body of a gunshot victim, an American by the name of Dennis Hickey. He was brought in sometime this morning from Skerries, I believe. He's scheduled for an autopsy tomorrow afternoon."

"Sorry, sir, I didn't realize you were with the Garda."

"Not a problem."

"I'll get someone to help you in just a moment."

"Thank you," Dillon said and took a seat opposite the reception counter. He placed the lanyard with the ID around his neck. The woman was already on the phone. She spoke for all of twenty seconds and hung up. She stood and leaned down to speak through the opening in the glass. "Someone will be here shortly, sir."

"Thank you," Dillon called and then waited on the couch for another fifteen minutes.

The door finally opened, and a young man Dillon hadn't seen before took a step into the room. He had a medical mask pulled down beneath his chin. He wore light blue hospital scrubs and blue latex gloves. "An Garda Síochána?" he said.

Dillon glanced around. He was still the only person in the room, and as he stood, he said, "I guess that would be me. I'm Marshal Jack Dillon. I'm here to see the body of an American by the name of Dennis Hickey. I believed it arrived here this morning and is scheduled for autopsy tomorrow afternoon."

"Yeah, arrived late this morning. I'm Noel Leonard. I'm interning here," the young man said, glancing at Dillon's ID on the lanyard as he spoke. "If you'll follow me back, please."

Dillon followed him down a hall he'd traveled a number of times before. Framed oil paintings of Dublin scenes hung along the hall between doors that led to several small offices. Toward the end of the hall, instead of offices, there were a series of viewing rooms.

"Did you wish to use a viewing room?" Leonard asked.

"No, that's not necessary. I'm guessing you've got him in the cooler. If you can just pull the drawer out, that will be good enough. He's scheduled for autopsy tomorrow afternoon, isn't he?"

"Yes, two o'clock. Did you wish to attend?"

"No, but I would like the results. I'll give you my card when we're finished," Dillon said as they walked through a security door and into a large room. The room had three examination tables. At the moment, two individuals were performing an autopsy on the table furthest away. At the far end of the room, steel doors were built into the wall. Dillon knew this was just one of a number of storage areas for bodies, but since Hickey was scheduled for an autopsy tomorrow, that was where his body would be.

The doors were numbered, and Leonard opened the door to number seven and slid the shelf out. Hickey's body appeared feet first, resting on a large steel tray. There was a tag around the big toe on his right foot listing his name and date of arrival. A sheet of white plastic covered the body. Leonard pulled the sheet down away from the face and folded it neatly below the chin.

Dillon knew Hickey's age was fifty-six, but he appeared older. His skin was wrinkled, and there was a prominent scar above the right eye that eliminated a third of the man's eyebrow. Dillon stepped over next to Leonard and said, "Would you mind if I looked at the entry wound?"

"No, not at all. Be my guest," Leonard said and stepped back.

Hickey's head was shaved. It appeared he was bald and had shaved his hair on the sides. Dillon leaned over and looked at the top of his skull. There was no entry wound.

"I thought he was shot in the head?"

"Yes, that's correct. This individual was shot just above the Lamboid Suture on the right side." Leonard reached over, turned the head slightly, and stepped back.

Dillon leaned over and examined the wound. Definitely a small-caliber round, and given the powder burns around the wound, the weapon couldn't have been more than a couple of inches away when fired.

Dillon nodded and said. "Okay, that's all I need for now." His cellphone suddenly rang. He chose to ignore it, reached in his pocket, and pushed the button sending the call to voicemail. "Thank you for your time, Noel. Pleasure to meet you. Good luck on the intern gig. Where are you from?"

"Sligo, actually. I did my schooling there at the university and then was lucky enough to get this gig for a year."

"I didn't notice an exit wound. We suspected a small caliber round. Any thoughts?"

Leonard seemed to think for a moment. "We'll know more following tomorrow's autopsy, obviously. My thought at this stage, and merely a guess, mind you, but the round will most likely be lodged behind the nasal bone. Death would have been instantaneous."

Dillon's cellphone rang again. He ignored it, and it stopped after two rings. "Well, thank you for your time. I can see myself out."

Leonard smiled and said, "Yes, and don't take this personally, but as an intern, I would be chastised for allowing that. So I'll walk you down the hall, and everyone will see I'm following the rules."

"Fair enough, Noel. You're preaching to the choir. Please show me out."

"This way, detective," Leonard said and grinned. As they walked down the hall, Dillon's cellphone rang for a third time. "Sounds like someone is desperate to get ahold of you," Leonard said.

"I'll call them back in just a moment," Dillon replied.

Leonard opened the door, and Dillon stepped into the reception area. As the door closed behind him, he pulled out his cellphone. Three calls from Suel. Now what?

SEVEN

illon stepped out of the morgue and walked to his car. He didn't run, but after the three calls from Suel, he walked at a fairly brisk pace. He pulled his phone out and pressed the call button to return Suel's calls as he slid behind the wheel and closed the door.

Suel answered on the second ring. "Where in the hell are you?"

"Sorry, just leaving the morgue. What's up?"

"Rafferty."

"What about him?"

"He was in that car accident on the M1. Somehow he swerved in front of a fuel truck. The truck apparently went up and over his car and then tipped to the side, blocking both lanes of traffic."

"How badly is he injured?"

"If only," Suel said. "He was killed."

"What?"

"Yeah, he's supposedly on his way to the morgue. I'm wondering if you'd stay there. They'll need someone to identify the body. He's got a wife and two little ones.

McCabe and an aide are on the way to their home to give her the bad news.”

“Jesus Christ. Kevin Rafferty? He was just with us earlier. Umm, yeah, sure, I’ll go back in and, umm, wait, I guess.”

“I’ve some things to finish up here, and I’ll join you. The driver of the semi and a helper were taken to the Mater Hospital. I’d like to interview them if it doesn’t get too late.”

“Yeah, I’ll go with you. Any idea how this happened?”

“It’s all a bit sketchy at the moment. Hopefully, the driver will be able to give us some information.”

“I’m guessing they’ll do a blood workup on him. Make sure he wasn’t intoxicated or on something,” Dillon said

“Yeah, that’s already arranged, standard procedure.”

“God, I don’t know what to say,” Dillon said.

“You and me both. I sure as hell don’t envy D.C.I. McCabe right now. Say a prayer it goes well, although given the situation…oh, Jesus.”

“Yeah, hey, I’ll wait until you get here, and we can identify together. I’ll send McCabe a message now and tell him we’re taking care of the identification. Hopefully, Kevin’s wife won’t have to go through seeing him here.”

“I’ll join you just as soon as I can,” Suel said and disconnected.

Dillon sent the text to McCabe telling him he and Suel would identify Kevin Rafferty's body. He stepped out of his car and headed back to the morgue. As he stepped into the reception area, the woman behind the glass looked up and said, "Everything all right? Did you forget something?"

Dillon shook his head and said, "I just got word that an officer was killed in a traffic accident this afternoon. They're going to be bringing his body here. Another officer and I will identify the body and hopefully save his wife from having to do it."

"Oh, dear. I'm so sorry to hear that. I'll inform staff, and we'll let you know as soon as they arrive."

"I'm going to wait until another officer arrives, and we'll do it together. We were just working a case with your man this morning. He had to leave and…." He stopped and sat down.

Dillon stared at the floor for the better part of an hour. He was deep in thought regarding Kevin Rafferty and actually didn't notice Suel as he entered the reception area.

"How are you doing, Jack?" Suel asked.

Dillon half-jumped. The sound of Suel's voice quickly brought him back to reality. "Hi ya, Paddy, how am I doing? I guess just lost in thought for a bit."

"Did they receive the, I mean, is Kevin here yet?"

"Not sure," Dillon said and stepped over to the reception counter. The woman wasn't behind the desk, and Dillon noted that the clock on the wall read 5:27. She'd probably been gone for at least a half-hour, and he'd remained unaware. There was a button on the counter to push for after hours. He pushed it, and a small red light flashed on. "Hopefully, this will alert someone. Sorry, I've been sitting here deep in thought and never even saw the receptionist leave."

"Not a problem. I've been thinking about Kevin on the drive over. Damn it. One moment he's there and then this. I can't believe that—"

The door suddenly opened, and a man in scrubs stepped into the room. It wasn't Noel Leonard. Dillon had met the man before, but at the moment he couldn't remember his name.

"Suel, Dillon, good to see you's. Sorry, it's under these circumstances. Your man's here. I've got it set up so you can identify him from viewing room three."

"Much appreciated, Eamon," Suel said.

Dillon smiled. Eamon Byrne was the man's name. "Thank you, Eamon," he said.

They followed Byrne down the hall. As they walked, Dillon thought it would have to be a pretty short list of people who had viewed and identified two unrelated individuals in the same afternoon. Byrne stopped and held the door open to interview room three. They walked in and stood in front of the viewing area, which consisted of a large window with metal blinds on the opposite side of the glass.

"I'll pull the blinds open in just a moment," Byrne said and closed the door as he left.

"You were in touch with McCabe?" Suel asked.

"I sent him a text message telling him we would ID Kevin. Hopefully, it will save Kevin's wife the pain. She'll have enough on her plate, and with two kids, she—"

The blinds suddenly went up, and a gurney with a body beneath a sheet was on the other side of the glass. Byrne pulled the sheet back and folded it just beneath Rafferty's chin, similar to the way Leonard had pulled down the plastic with Hickey earlier.

Rafferty's face was lacerated, and his head rested at an odd angle. The right side of his head appeared to be pushed in. Dillon and Suel were both focused on the hole on the right side of Rafferty's head, just above the right ear.

Dillon looked at Byrne and said, "Was he shot?"

Byrne put a hand to his ear and shook his head, signaling he couldn't hear the question.

Dillon made a gun with the thumb and forefinger of his right hand. He moved the thumb signaling a shot and raised both hands in a questioning manner.

Byrne nodded.

"Jesus Christ. Come on," Suel said. They hurried out of the room and knocked on the door leading into the autopsy area just as Byrne opened the door.

"Was he shot in the head?" Dillon asked.

"Yes, that's what caused the accident. Didn't they tell you?"

"No one told us anything. So you're saying the traffic accident was caused by someone shooting Rafferty, and that's why his car swerved in front of the fuel truck."

"Yeah, that's exactly what happened. I thought you knew."

They shook their heads, and Dillon said, "This is the first we've heard of it."

"I know it took quite a while to remove the body from the wreckage. He suffered a traumatic leg amputation from the crash. I've no doubt we'll find more damage during the autopsy. Are you sure you weren't informed of the bullet wound?"

"No idea," Dillon said, shaking his head.

"I'm pretty sure death would have been instantaneous. We can confirm that tomorrow during the autopsy, but that's definitely a bullet wound. I'm truly sorry, gentlemen. I was under the impression you were aware of this."

"We'd no idea," Suel said.

"That is Detective Inspector Kevin Rafferty, isn't it?" Byrne asked.

"Yeah, that's him, Kevin Rafferty," Dillon said.

"Come back to my desk, and you can sign the forms." He held the door open, and they stepped into the autopsy area. All three autopsy tables were now empty. Dillon glanced over at the row of cooler doors on the far wall and took note of number seven, where Dennis Hickey's body was located.

They followed Byrne into a small office on the far side of the examination tables. "If you'd step in here, gentlemen. Excuse me. I'll be back in just a moment."

Byrne hurried back toward the gurney with Rafferty's body and said something Dillon and Suel couldn't quite hear. He was back in the office a moment later, handing over the official identification documents for Dillon and Suel to sign. As Suel signed, Dillon looked out the door and saw a man wheeling Rafferty's body back toward an open door on the wall. Amazingly, he was placed right below Dennis Hickey's body.

They signed the forms. Byrne thanked them and apologized yet again for the failure to inform them of the cause of death, although it clearly wasn't his fault. They thanked him and headed out of the autopsy area and down the hall. They didn't speak until they were outside.

"Bloody hell. Who in God's name would shoot your man? And on the bleeding M1?" Suel said.

"It would almost have to be some nutcase wanting to kill someone, anyone," Dillon said.

Suel shook his head. "Someone with a bleeding death wish. We find out who did this…aw, what the hell is the world coming to."

"We need to talk to the two men who were in that fuel truck. You said they were at the Mater?"

"Yeah, I've got their names."

"I'll meet you there," Dillon said. "You get there first, wait for me in the lobby."

EIGHT

The Mater Misericordiae University Hospital is a Model 4 teaching hospital based in Dublin's north inner city. Dillon drove down Drumcondra and Dorset Street Lower. He took a right on North Circular Road and pulled into a reserved parking place. Just to be safe, he placed a sign on the dash stating his car was on official An Garda Síochána business. He climbed out of the car and gave a quick look around to check for anyone who might like nothing better than to damage a Garda vehicle. The hospital was across the street from the Mountjoy Garda Station, and next to the station was Mountjoy Prison, or 'The Joy' as it was referred to. The coast appeared to be clear, and he entered the modern glass fronted building.

He stepped into a large lobby, almost empty except for a man asleep in a chair and a woman seated at the visitor's station.

She looked up from the paper she was reading and flashed a smile that lasted only until she saw the An Garda Síochána lanyard hanging around Dillon's neck. "May I help you?"

"Yes, I'm here to see two gentlemen. I believe they were transported here this afternoon. They had been involved in an accident on the M1. A car and truck crash."

"Do you have a name?"

"No, I'm sorry. I don't."

She seemed about to say something then thought better of it. "Let me make a call and check. Feel free to have a seat," she said and nodded at the furnishings in the mostly empty lobby.

Dillon took a seat and placed a call to Special Branch. "Special Branch, D.I. Humphrey," a woman answered.

"Hi, Aideen. Jack Dillon calling. I'm at the Mater to interview the two men involved in the accident on the M1 today. Can you give me their names? They can't seem to locate them here."

"This is the Rafferty accident?"

"Yes, these are the guys in the fuel truck. They're supposed to be here at least overnight. I don't believe they're in serious condition."

"Hang on just a moment." She placed Dillon on hold and came back on the line maybe two minutes later. "Sorry for the delay. You got a pen and paper?"

"Just a moment," Dillon said as he pulled his notebook from his pocket. He pulled the top off the pen and said, "Okay, go ahead."

"Two men, first one is Dara White. He was the driver. The second name is Alejandro Torres. Anything else?"

"No, that should do it. You've been a big help," Dillon said and disconnected.

He walked back to the visitor's counter and said, "I have those names for you."

She nodded, placed her hands on the keyboard, and said, "Okay, give them to me."

Dillon gave her White's name first and then spelled out Alejandro Torres for her. "Yes, here it is. They're up on the third floor, Ward C. Visiting hours end at 8:30 PM."

"Thank you," Dillon said just as Suel entered the lobby.

Dillon gave him a wave, not that he was easy to miss standing at the visitor's desk.

"You know what section they're in?"

"Just got it. They're up on the third floor."

"Ward C," the woman added and flashed a quick smile at Suel.

They headed down the hall to a bank of elevators. Suel pressed the button, and a pair of doors opened immediately. They stepped in and rode up to the third floor. Once off the elevator, they followed the signs along the hallway to Ward C.

There was a nurses' station just inside the double doors. Two nurses, a man and a woman wearing hospital scrubs, sat behind a counter. The man was typing away, and the woman looked up from the file she was reading and asked, "May I help you?"

"An Garda Síochána," Dillon said, raising his lanyard so she could see his ID. "We're here to interview Dara White and Alejandro Torres. They were involved—"

"In the traffic accident on the M1," she said. "They're just around the corner in 303. Visiting hours are over at 8:30."

"That's what we've been told. Thank you," Dillon said and stepped around the corner. The door was five feet away and had 303 in brass numbers attached to it. Dillon's first thought was how convenient that the two were sharing a room. He opened the door, stepped inside, and counted twelve beds, six on each side of a center aisle. Each bed was surrounded by a white curtain. Fortunately, a name was affixed to every curtain.

The person in the second bed on the right, apparently named Riddick O'Flaherty, seemed to be groaning nonstop. Dara White was just two beds away.

NINE

Dillon gave Suel a nod. Suel stepped up and pulled back the curtain surrounding White's bed. A dark-haired man with a swollen nose and two black eyes was in the bed. Dillon pegged the man at approximately forty years old. The bed was raised, so he appeared to be sitting. He had two pillows wedged behind his shoulders. He was focused on the television hanging from the ceiling. At the moment the Dublin evening news was playing, and earbuds were in his ears. Dillon noted that there weren't any IVs inserted in him.

He pulled one of the earbuds out and said, "Doctor?"

Suel shook his head and said "No, An Garda Síochána. We'd like to talk to you about your accident."

"Don't make it sound like it was my fault. The car was traveling in front of us for a number of kilometers, and all of a sudden, your man makes a sharp turn to the left. It happened in a split second. I hit the brakes immediately, but he couldn't have been more than a foot in front. When he'd made that sharp turn, it looked like his car was about to roll over. I slammed on the brakes, but I hit it. Not a damned thing I could do."

"So he didn't pull in front of you?"

"No. I just told you he'd been in front of us for a number of kilometers. All of a sudden, he turns to the left. No brake lights, nothing. We plowed into him, went up, and then tipped over. Thank God the trailer was empty, or we all could have been roasted alive."

"Was there a vehicle passing you at that moment?"

"Passing us? There could have been, but I really can't remember. All of a sudden, he swerved, and we plowed into him. Couldn't have been more than a half-second. We were on our side, couldn't get out of the cab. Alejandro was unconscious for a minute or two, bit of a nasty scrape on the head. I think he dislocated his shoulder. At least that's what one of the nurses told me."

"What about you?" Dillon asked.

"Slight concussion, broke a couple ribs when Alejandro landed on top of me. Given what could have happened, we've nothing to complain about. Like I told yas, if we'd been transporting a full load, there's an awfully good chance we wouldn't be talking. How's your man? Did he have a heart attack or something? Had he been drinking?"

"Not sure of the cause," Dillon said. "We know he hadn't been drinking. We'll know more after the autopsy. It would—"

"Autopsy? So your man is dead, is he?"

"I'm afraid so," Dillon said.

White started to make the sign of the cross. Halfway through, he grimaced and said, "Oh, God, but that hurts. Sweet Jesus."

"We'll leave you to it, Mr. White. Wishing you a speedy recovery."

"Thanks, lads. You need anything, feel free to give me a call. Don't I know I'm just damn lucky to be here."

Dillon nodded and stepped out of the curtained area.

"Take care, Mr. White," Suel said as he pulled the curtain back, giving White a bit more privacy.

Torres's bed was on the opposite side of the center aisle and one bed over. Dillon peeked around the curtain. Torres seemed to be staring off into the distance. It appeared White's description was accurate. The right side of Torres's face was black and blue and swollen. There were several deep jagged scratches along his right jawline. His right arm was in a sling and strapped to his chest so that he couldn't move it.

"Mr. Torres?" Dillon asked.

Torres nodded.

Dillon pulled the curtain back a couple of feet so he and Dillon could step in closer to the side of the bed.

"We're with An Garda Síochána, and we'd like to ask you a couple of questions if that's okay."

Torres smiled and nodded.

"At the time of the accident, were you aware of a car in the lane alongside you?"

Torres smiled and nodded.

"Would you be able to describe this vehicle to us?"

Torres smiled and nodded.

"Oh, good. What was the color of the vehicle?"

Torres smiled and nodded.

"Oh, what the hell?" Suel said. "Torres, do you think my partner here has his head up his ass?"

Torres smiled and nodded.

"Oh, well, at least he got that right," Suel said.

"So he's not understanding a word we're saying," Dillon said.

"Yeah, pretty much."

"Thank you for your time, Mr. Torres. Speedy recovery," Dillon said and gave a wave as he stepped out into the central aisle.

"Good luck, Lad," Suel said as he pulled the curtain back around the bed.

They walked down the center aisle, out of the room, and stopped at the nurses' counter. This time, the guy looked up at them and said, "What can I do for you?"

"Just want to check on the patients White and Torres. Was there any alcohol or illegal matter detected in—"

"You mean were they taking the piss? No, nothing like that. Not sure what you're thinking, but if you're trying to hang that accident on those two lads, there was no way they'd been drinking or taking a Henry of chalk."

Dillon knew a 'Henry of chalk' referred to an eighth of an ounce of cocaine. "Thanks for the information. Appreciate you setting us straight," Dillon said and walked down the hall toward the elevators.

Once they stepped onto the elevator, Suel grinned and said, "Nice impression you made back there."

TEN

Dillon pulled into the parking area in front of his house. He sat in the car for a couple of minutes, trying to recall when he'd had a worse day. It had been a while. He was tired, hungry, and still thinking about Kevin Rafferty and his family. He stepped out of his car, closed the gates behind the car, took a deep breath, and made his way to the front door. He unlocked the door and stepped inside.

Lucifer, his dog, gave him a quick look and hurried out the door. He circled an area next to the driver's door on Dillon's car, squatted, and stared at Dillon as he did his business. Dillon left the door open and walked into the kitchen.

There wasn't a mess in the kitchen, but that was only because he had placed the wastebasket up on the kitchen counter. He opened the cookie jar that held Lucifer's biscuits. He grabbed one and then made a point of rattling the lid on the jar so Lucifer would hear. A moment later, Lucifer came back into the house. Dillon stepped out of the kitchen and tossed the biscuit to him. He refilled Lucifer's water dish and then went upstairs and changed into jeans and a sweatshirt.

He boiled some baby potatoes and fried up a pork steak seasoned with lemon pepper. He poured himself a glass of wine and settled in at the kitchen counter. Lucifer dutifully sat staring up at Dillon in the hope he would get the pork bone. Dillon finished his dinner and tossed the bone to Lucifer, who hurried back into the front hall so he wouldn't have to share.

They spent a few hours on the couch. A movie was on, but Dillon wasn't paying attention. He was focused on Kevin Rafferty's murder. That's what it was, a murder. It certainly wasn't an accident that someone had shot him while driving on the M1. Now the question was, had it been random? Or, had someone sought out Rafferty? If that was the case, intentionally shooting Rafferty, how in God's name did they locate him on the M1 returning from Skerries? Did someone have the ability to track his phone?

Had a tracking device been attached to the car? But that didn't seem to make sense. Rafferty had taken Suel's place that morning. Other than Dillon and D.C.I. McCabe, no one else would have been aware Dillon and Rafferty were headed to Skerries. Dillon thought about Rafferty through a second and third glass of wine and still couldn't come up with an answer.

He let Lucifer out, got the coffee ready for the morning, and they headed up to bed just after 11:00. Dillon slept fitfully and woke a little after 5:00 the following morning. He showered, shaved, and woke Lucifer at

6:00. They went for a brief walk, and all the while, Dillon continued to ponder Rafferty's shooting.

He was in the office at 7:00. Once at his desk, he dug into a case he'd been working on, the assault of a college student two weeks ago in the Temple Bar district. The girl, Sophie McGinn, was from County Sligo. She was a third-year student at Trinity and had been in a coma for the past two weeks after having been hit on the back of her head. Dillon and Suel had interviewed a number of people, watched CCTV footage and security camera footage from pubs, and had still come up empty-handed.

There was one bit of footage where it appeared she might have been followed, but the guy could have simply been walking in the same direction. He appeared briefly on another security tape outside a pub. He continued in the same direction, apparently not in a hurry, and although Sophie was aware of him, she never appeared concerned.

Dillon had walked the route three different times and hadn't come up with anything. Maybe the fourth time something would stand out. It was almost 9:00 in the morning when he climbed in his car and drove to the Temple Bar district. He drove along the Liffey River to O'Connell Street Bridge, took the bridge across the Liffey, and then took a right onto Aston Quay. He pulled to the curb on Wellington Quay and parked. He entered Temple Bar next to the Ha'penny Bridge Inn.

Dillon followed the route Sophie McGinn had taken, walking down Fownes Street Lower and turning right on Temple Bar. It was here that the male figure first appeared. Sophie McGinn took the next left at the corner, walking onto Temple Lane. She had walked past the Barnacles Hostel up to Curved Street, where she took a right.

The male figure had been approximately twenty feet behind her. He was dressed in black but not in a way that appeared suspicious. He wore a dark blue cap with the word Dublin written across the front in white letters. Nothing unusual. In fact, if you'd passed him, you wouldn't have given a second look. They entered Curved Street, where there were no security cameras. Eleven minutes later, he appeared walking up Eustace Street. He entered Dame street, a busy, crowded street, and disappeared.

Sophie McGinn never appeared and was found hours later, unconscious against the stone wall of an almost two hundred-year-old building known as the Button Factory located on Curved Street. She'd been hit on the back of the head and had remained in a coma ever since.

Walking at a casual pace, Dillon traversed the length of Curved Street in little more than a minute. What happened during the eleven minutes the male figure was on Curved Street? Did he chat with Sophie McGinn? Assault her? When found, she still had her purse containing her billfold. There was no sign of a sexual assault. Did she meet up with someone, and they chatted with the guy, and once he left, Sophie McGinn was assaulted? The key was finding the man in black.

Mission impossible, Dillon thought. He walked back and forth along Curved Street looking for something, anything, that might suggest what in God's name had happened. Nothing jumped out.

His phone rang, Suel calling. Dillon answered on the second ring. "Yeah, Paddy."

"Where are you?" Suel asked.

"Temple Bar. Curved Street, to be more precise."

"You're back to going over the McGinn case?"

"Still looking for an answer and not coming up with anything."

"There's a meeting in Special Branch in an hour. D.C.I. McCabe is giving an update on the Rafferty situation."

"You make it sound like he's got some information."

"Not exactly, although I think he's come to the conclusion this wasn't just some random attack. Rafferty was sought and shot. The autopsy is scheduled for later this morning. They've moved it ahead of Hickey and the two accident victims. McCabe wants us at the autopsy."

"I'll be back in Special Branch in thirty minutes. See you then," Dillon said and disconnected.

He gave a final look around the immediate area. He stood fifteen feet from where Sophie McGinn had been found next to the Button Factory. An old stone building.

The windows had been bricked over decades ago. Just the solid stone windowsills remained, indicating where the windows were. Once again, he'd come up with absolutely nothing. He shook his head, stared for another minute, and walked back to his car.

ELEVEN

Due to the number of people in attendance, the meeting was held in the Special Branch office as opposed to a conference room. Dillon arrived in time to get a coffee from the break room just before the meeting began.

D.C.I. McCabe stood just outside his office, and everyone gathered around. Since Dillon's desk was closest to McCabe's office, he sat on the edge of his desk. His desk chair was taken by D.I. Lisa O'Toole, who was in week two of recovering from knee surgery and still using crutches.

"I want to thank you all for taking the time this morning," McCabe began. "As you may have heard, one of our members, D.I. Kevin Rafferty, was murdered yesterday on the M1. I met last night with Kevin's wife, Kate. Obviously, she is in a world of pain at the moment. They've two little boys, James and Michael, aged seven and five. They've lost their father and will…" McCabe paused for a long moment, apparently deep in thought.

He cleared his throat. "Kevin's autopsy is scheduled for later this morning. Dillon and Suel, I'd like you to attend and transfer the round to the tech lab following the procedure. Carrey and Phillips, you'll head up the examination of the car wreckage. Looking for, among other things, some sort of tracking device that may have been attached to the vehicle. D.I. Rafferty's cellphone is in the tech lab as I speak. If there's anything on it related to this atrocity, they'll find it."

"Memorial service or a fundraiser, sir?" someone asked from the back of the group.

"Just a tad too soon, but I'm sure there will be both. We'll give Kate Rafferty time to make those decisions. Look for information on both within the next twenty-four to forty-eight hours. I want no stone unturned in this investigation. This is an attack on all of us and, need I say, serves as a reminder that we are all vulnerable. Be vigilant and look out for one another. Any questions?" The fifteen seconds no one said anything seemed like an hour. "All right, let's get back to work and stay safe."

The group slowly dispersed, a lot of shaking heads and sad faces. "Thanks for the chair, Dillon," O'Toole said as she stood and placed the crutches under her arms.

"Not a problem. How's the recovery coming?"

"It's going okay. Not fast enough for my taste. You know how it is. We all think we're still sixteen and things will be fine in the morning. They've got me doing a bunch of torture procedures five times a day, just in case I start to feel comfortable."

"As long as you keep at it."

"Yeah, thanks for the advice, Dad. Now any time I feel like bitching, I'll think of Kevin and do another set of exercises," she said and hobbled back to her desk.

"I see we managed to draw the short straw again. Back to the morgue in about forty minutes," Suel said.

"Yeah, you mind driving?"

"No, in fact, I was going to suggest it. You learn anything this morning?"

"In Temple Bar? Not a thing. It just made me think it's one more dead end. I'll add the Hickey case and Kevin's murder to the list, which reminds me. I want to give Reilly out in Skerries a call. Have him pull any security tapes."

"Didn't he do that? They had Hickey walking along Harbour Road."

"Yeah, but I meant Kevin. If we can get some tape of him heading toward the M1, maybe someone followed him. Maybe there was an incident, and some idiot snapped."

"Grasping at straws," Suel said.

"You got a better idea?"

"No, I'm just wondering if, after this autopsy, it wouldn't be a good idea to offer our assistance. We just go to every business along the way and see if something doesn't turn up on their security tape. It's not like we'll be looking at hours and hours. Hell, we've got an approximate timeframe."

"I think that's a good idea. Let me call Reilly now, have him draw up a list of places, and we can split them between the three of us."

"We'll head over to Griffith Avenue when you're off the line with Reilly," Suel said and walked back to his desk.

Dillon placed his call to Reilly and ended up leaving a message. Reilly phoned back a minute later. "Yeah, Dillon, sorry I couldn't take your call. I was on another line. How are things in Special Branch?"

"About like you'd expect. Suel and I will be at the autopsy in about an hour. Listen, we had an idea and—"

"Oh?"

"We were thinking we'd head out after the autopsy and see about looking at security tapes from various businesses along the route from the Harbor Hotel to the M1. We're wondering if maybe someone followed Rafferty. Maybe there was an incident and—"

"An incident?"

"Could be anything. Maybe he cut someone off. Maybe he was mistaken for someone else. We're trying to cover all the bases."

"I get it. Let me draw up a list of places along the route. You said you're attending the autopsy?"

"We are, and then we've got to run back to the office, but we could hopefully be out in Skerries early afternoon. If you could have that list ready, between the three of us, we could knock it off this afternoon. If you check the places in Skerries, we could do the establishments along the road to the M1."

"I'll draw up that list. If things remain quiet, I can cover most of the locations in town."

"Good, thanks in advance, Declan. Hopefully, we'll be out there right after the noon hour."

"See you then," Reilly said and hung up.

Dillon locked his desk and headed over to Suel's desk. Suel was on the phone and signaled with his index finger that he would only be a moment.

Once Suel hung up. Dillon said, "You ready to head over to the autopsy?"

"I am. I'm hoping we can remain in the reception room and just leave with the round. I don't need to be looking over their shoulders while they're cutting and sawing."

"We're of the same opinion," Dillon said. "We'll just let them know we're there and waiting."

They headed out to the parking lot. Suel had reserved an unmarked vehicle that today happened to be a black 2016 Toyota Land Cruiser.

"How in the hell did you get this thing?" Dillon asked.

"You just have to know the right people. But then, who wouldn't want to do the likes of me a favor?"

"Yeah, right. Okay, let's go," Dillon said.

TWELVE

T hey climbed into the vehicle. About a half-second later, they each made an unpleasant face and looked at one another. "What in the hell happened in here? It smells like the chlorine bomb they use to eliminate odor. You think someone maybe died in this thing?" Dillon asked.

"We'll drive with the windows down," Suel said.

"Can't we just get another vehicle?"

"Not in the next thirty minutes. You know what the forms are like. It would take another hour. We need to go."

"You want to take my car?"

Suel turned the engine on and put the car in gear. Dillon lowered the window and stuck his head out for some fresh air. Twenty minutes later, Suel pulled to the curb on Griffith Avenue within sight of the morgue. Dillon was out of the car before Suel had turned off the engine. He stepped onto the sidewalk and smelled his shirt sleeve. "Oh God, that's awful."

Suel climbed out of the Toyota and said, "Well, at least we made it here. I'm tempted to leave the keys in the ignition and hope someone steals it."

"Don't kid yourself. They won't last five seconds in that thing. God, my clothes reek of whatever was in there."

Maybe we should tell them we're here, and we'll just wait outside. Hopefully, we can air out our clothes." Suel sniffed the collar on his shirt and cringed.

"Not a bad idea. So much for you knowing the right people," Dillon said. "I'll go in and tell them we'll be waiting out here. Maybe you could lower all the windows in that thing. It's probably been sealed up for weeks just waiting for you to request a vehicle." Suel slid back in the Land Cruiser and lowered the windows while Dillon went inside.

The same woman as yesterday was seated at the receptionist counter. She looked up and said, "Good morning, Detective."

"Good morning. I, umm, we're here to transport the round they're going to remove in the Rafferty autopsy. We've some work to do and a number of phone calls to make, so we'll just carry on outside."

She leaned forward to talk through the opening to pass papers through. "Oh, you don't have to do that, we have—" She made a face and quickly moved away from the opening. "That might be a good idea. I'll alert the team that you're outside."

"Thank you," Dillon said and hurried back outside.

"They know we're out here?" Suel asked.

"Oh yeah. I'd say within the next five minutes, everyone is going to know we're out here," Dillon said and then went on to describe the receptionist's reaction to his smell.

Not five minutes later, Noel Leonard, the intern, stepped outside. He was in blue scrubs and wore a surgical mask. "Detective Dillon, apparently, you made quite an impression. What's up?"

"We were assigned that black Toyota," Dillon said. "It really reeks. I think someone set off one of those chlorine bombs in the thing. Now it's on our clothes and the two of us."

Leonard shook his head. "Show me. We might have something that would at least moderate the odor."

They led him over toward the Toyota. With all the windows down, they could smell the chlorine from fifteen feet away.

"Oh, God. You guys are lucky you made it here without crashing. You probably have permanent lung damage."

"Really?" Suel asked.

"No, but God, that's awful. Let me get some spray for you. You can spray the thing. Better leave the windows down. Are you driving back to headquarters from here?"

"Yeah," Dillon said.

"Okay, the spray will do the trick. Maybe park that thing and have it professionally cleaned. I'll be back in a minute."

"What was that you were telling me about knowing the right people?" Dillon asked.

"The bollox, just wait till we get back to headquarters," Suel said.

Leonard came back with a spray can. The can was black and had what looked like a chemical formula and a bunch of numbers on the label in white. He handed the can to Dillon and said, "Spray this on the ceiling, the seats, and the carpet. Keep the windows down and leave them down when you drive back. You can try to wash that out of your clothes, but don't put anything else in the washer with them. Good luck. I have to get back. They're about to start on your officer. We'll get the round out to you as soon as possible."

"Thanks for all your help, Noel. Much appreciated."

Leonard stepped back into the building. Dillon handed the spray can to Suel. "Let's take turns. You do the ceiling and the front seats. I'll do the back seats and the carpet."

Suel opened both doors on the passenger side front and rear doors and began to spray. He was finished in five minutes. As he handed the can to Dillon, he said, "Good luck."

Dillon started in the rear of the vehicle. He took a deep breath and quickly sprayed down the area, then repeated the process on the front seats and the carpet.

They waited fifteen minutes and walked toward the Toyota. They didn't pick up a scent until they were right next to the vehicle and then only a slight scent compared to what it had been.

"Hopefully, another half-hour will do the trick," Dillon said. "I'm thinking once we deliver that round to Emily in the tech department, we run home, change, and meet Reilly at the Skerries station."

"Couldn't agree more," Suel said.

Noel Leonard stepped outside forty minutes later. Even though they were outside, Leonard kept his mask on. He handed the paperwork to Dillon. Dillon signed off, and Leonard handed him the evidence bag containing the round.

Dillon glanced at the writing along the top of the bag, a .22 caliber round. "Thanks for your help, Noel. We're running this over to the tech folks. Hopefully, they'll be able to find similarities if not a match in the database."

"Good luck with that. Hope the spray worked out."

"Thanks, we'll know soon enough," Dillon said.

THIRTEEN

The ride back to the headquarters building wasn't great, but it was better than the earlier ride to the Dublin Morgue. All the windows were down in the Toyota, and whatever the spray was that Noel Leonard had given them, it had done a halfway decent job. Dillon raised his arm, sniffed the elbow on his shirt, and shuddered. Probably burning the clothes was a better option than trying to wash them.

Suel pulled into the parking area behind the headquarters building and parked the Toyota. "I'll see you in Skerries," Dillon said as he jumped out of the car.

"I'll just have a word or two with me mate who set this disaster on us," Suel said.

Dillon headed into the building and hurried down a long hallway toward the Tech lab. As he turned a corner, he passed two officers walking in the opposite direction.

"Oh, God. What the hell?" one of them said just after they passed. Dillon increased his speed and kept moving toward the Tech lab.

He pressed the intercom button next to the lab door. A moment later, a female voice said, "Yes?"

"Hi, Emily, Jack Dillon. I've got the round from the Rafferty autopsy."

"Oh yeah, perfect timing, we're all set up and waiting. Let me buzz you in and—"

"Might be better to get it from me out here. I've got to head out in just a minute."

"Okay," she said, not sounding too sure. "Be there in a minute."

The door opened a moment later, and Emily said, "You can't even take a moment to—Oh God, what's that dreadful smell? Ick."

"Yeah, some chlorine stuff. It's a long story. Here's the round," he said, handing her the evidence bag. "I'll check back with you later today or first thing in the morning."

"Maybe think about hitting the shower before you do. God, that can't be good for you, Dillon."

"Yeah, I get it. I'm headed home right now."

"Don't let me keep you," she said and quickly closed the door.

Dillon hurried back out to the parking lot. He climbed in his car, lowered the windows, and drove home. He pulled into his parking area and hurried toward the front door. He unlocked the door, stepped inside, and turned off the alarm.

Lucifer hopped down the stairs and headed toward Dillon. He stopped halfway to Dillon, shook his head, and seemed to make a face. Dillon walked toward him, and Lucifer hurried back up the stairs. Dillon grabbed a biscuit from the jar and coaxed Lucifer outside.

He undressed next to the backdoor, grabbed the pile of clothes, and tossed them out onto the patio. He hurried upstairs and into the shower. Five minutes later, he was pulling on clean clothes. He coaxed Lucifer back inside with another biscuit and then hopped in the car and headed out to Skerries.

He parked in front of the Skerries Garda station and went inside. The sergeant at the front desk recognized him and said, "Here to see Reilly?"

"Yes, I am."

"He had to run out for a moment. You might as well grab a seat. He should be back in five minutes or so."

Suel arrived ten minutes later.

Reilly returned just a few minutes after that. "Oh, hope you haven't been waiting long. Someone side-swiped a car. I just gave them a report for the insurance company. Follow me back to the office. I might have found something," he said.

They headed back to an office with four desks. Reilly pulled the chair out from the first desk and sat down in front of a laptop. "Got this from the EuroSpar. It's just beyond the Harbor Hotel," he said. "Check it out." They watched the black and white film of an empty street for ten or fifteen seconds, and suddenly there it was, a Toyota Corolla Cross with Kevin Rafferty behind the wheel. Even though the film was black and white, it seemed obvious to Dillon that the vehicle was red. The

Toyota with Rafferty disappeared from sight, and the street was empty for a few seconds. Suddenly, what looked like a silver or gray four-door BMW drove past. An individual with a goatee was driving. Dillon thought he looked familiar, but he couldn't be sure.

"You think that could be our man?" Reilly said. "I have him on three more tapes. Those are the only ones I've gotten thus far, but he's following D.I. Rafferty up past the windmills and presumably out of town."

"If we could get an image of the license plate, that would go a long way in helping," Dillon said.

"Got it from one of the other tapes. It's a 2021 model, licensed in Dublin sometime in the first six months. I did a search, and it turns out it's a rental from Enterprise Car Rental at Dublin airport. Rented on a credit card." He opened a file next to the computer. "Rented by an individual by the name of Mathew Longley. He used a Visa credit card. He's a Dublin resident, Clontarf, actually. He lives on Dollymont Park. I've got his address here."

"You check him out?" Suel asked.

"Yeah, no record, if that's what you're asking. He sells real estate and has lived on Dollymont Park for the last twelve years."

"We need to look at more tapes. The sooner we get on it, the sooner we get an answer. Your man may have been showing a house for all we know," Dillon said as he pulled out his pocket notebook. "Give me your man's name and address again."

Reilly read the information off to Dillon and Suel and followed up with the name Mathew Longley. They wrote it down and noted the time displayed on the recording as 1:23 PM. They looked at the map and divided Skerries and the route to the M1 into three sections. Reilly would take the rest of the route through Skerries and out past the B&B called the Farm Shed. Suel would take the area from the Farm Shed into the village of Lusk. Dillon would check with the businesses along the R127 and the R132 until the M1.

FOURTEEN

There was nothing from Lusk along the R127 until it connected with the R132. Once on the R132, Dillon pulled into Blake's Cross service station. There were four sets of gas pumps and a red banner advertising a 'Hand Car Wash.' Dillon parked in front of the shop and entered. There was a deli and a line of three people at the coffee machine. Dillon stepped up to the cash register and held out his ID.

"An Garda Síochána. I'd like to talk with your manager, please."

"Is there a problem?" the woman asked.

"No, just need help with something. If I could see the manager, please."

She gave him a look but then got on the loudspeaker and said, "Desmond to the front, please."

A couple of minutes later, a heavy-set guy in navy blue trousers and shirt came down one of the aisles. The word 'MANAGER' was embroidered above the pocket on his left breast. "Yeah, what is it, Aileen?"

She didn't say anything but gave a nod toward Dillon standing off to the side.

"Can I help you, sir?"

"I hope so, Desmond," Dillon said and held up his ID card. "We're working a case and wondered if your security cameras might cover the traffic passing on the R132."

"Out on the road? We've one camera that covers a bit of that, but it's actually focused on our lane leading into the carwash. The R132 is in the background, and it's a bit blurry. You're welcome to have a look. The image automatically deletes after seventy-two hours, so depending on when whatever you're looking for occurred, we—"

"This would be, oh, between maybe 1:30 or 2:00 yesterday."

"We should have that. I can bring it up for you if you want to have a look."

"Yes, please."

"Follow me," he said and headed toward the back of the store. They walked down a short hallway labeled 'Restrooms,' past the Men's and Ladies' rooms to a door labeled 'Private.' Desmond pulled a keyring from his pocket and inserted a key in the door lock. They stepped into a small office. There was a desk littered with stacks of what appeared to be receipts. A plastic tray with three-and-a-half chocolate-covered doughnuts rested on top of one of the piles. Behind the desk were two large screens, each sectioned into four quarters with black and white images. The screen on the left displayed the car wash lane in the upper left quarter.

"Tell me that time again," Desmond said as he lowered himself into his desk chair and turned to face the screens. He pulled a keyboard in front of him and began to type. The car wash lane suddenly took up the entire screen.

"Between 1:30 and 2:00 in the afternoon. Yesterday."

"Any idea what kind of vehicle you're looking for?" Desmond said as he typed in the date and time Dillon gave him. The screen went blank for a moment, and then a frozen image reappeared.

"I'm looking for a Red Toyota Corolla Cross," Dillon said.

"I'll run this a little faster. Give a shout if you see something," Desmond said.

They watched for a few minutes. A number of trucks and cars passed, but none of them were Kevin Rafferty in the Toyota Corolla. Desmond had just reached over to his desk and stuffed the better part of a half-eaten chocolate-covered doughnut into his mouth when Dillon shouted, "Stop."

Desmond hit a button and froze the screen.

"Can you forward it slowly, please?" Dillon said and took a step closer to the screen. There was a second or two delay, and the images appeared to jerk forward, but it was definitely Kevin Rafferty behind the wheel. The next car was black, and Dillon was about to swear when suddenly the gray BMW jerked across the screen.

"Could you play that back, please? The gray car."

Desmond played it back four more times. The image was blurry, but Dillon was pretty sure he could distinguish the driver in the BMW with the goatee. After the fourth time, Desmond said, "I can copy this and email it to you if you'd like."

"Yes, please," Dillon said. He pulled a business card from his wallet and set it on the counter next to the keyboard. "If you could email it to that address and this one in Skerries, that would really help," he said, placing Reilly's business card next to his on the counter.

Desmond typed away for a long minute and then turned and said, "You should have this waiting for both of you in your email." He handed Dillon a business card. "Any problem, just let me know. I've made a copy of it and have it saved in a file."

"Thank you, Desmond. Much appreciated."

"Does this have anything to do with that accident on the M1 yesterday?"

"Too early to tell. It might," Dillon said, dodging the question.

He stopped at nine other places along the route to the M1. Five of them had cameras that covered a small section of the R132. All of the images were blurry. All the images had Rafferty driving the Toyota Corolla and being followed, not too far behind, by the gray BMW. That still didn't mean much more than two people were headed from Skerries to Dublin. Hundreds, maybe even a thousand people, did that every day. But at least it was a start. Everyone gladly copied the five or eight-second tape and emailed it to Dillon and Reilly, if only to get Dillon out of their hair.

Dillon phoned Suel, and they decided to meet with Reilly at the Skerries station. They chatted for ten minutes, thanked Reilly for his time and effort, and left. Suel headed back to Special Branch, and Dillon made his way to Dublin Airport and the Enterprise Car Rental desk in Terminal Two.

He parked in front of the terminal, placed his An Garda Síochána sign on the dashboard, and turned on his flashers. He hurried inside to the Enterprise Car Rental counter. Fortunately, there was no one ahead of him.

"Good afternoon, and welcome to Enterprise Car Rental," the woman behind the counter said with a smile. "Do you have a reservation?"

"No, I don't. Actually, I'm with An Garda Síochána," Dillon said, showing his ID card. "I'd like to check on a vehicle rented from you two or maybe three days ago." He pulled out his notebook, gave her the license number, and told her it was a gray BMW.

"Oh, umm, let me just bring that up here," she said as her fingers flew across the keyboard. A moment later, she got a funny look on her face and said, "Actually, that vehicle has not been returned yet. It was due back yesterday. I'm not sure what is—"

"That was rented by a gentleman named Mathew Longley?"

"Yes, that's correct," she said in a tone that suggested, *'How did you know that?'* "The vehicle was due back yesterday. Not sure what the problem is, but it hasn't been returned yet. That happens from time to time. Is there something we should be concerned about?"

"Not at this time. Do you have a way of tracking the vehicle or suspending service?"

"Well, yes, we have GPS tracking built-in on all our rentals, but—"

"Good, could you track that vehicle for me and tell me where it is?"

"Actually, no, I can't. That's a little above my pay grade."

"Then can you contact whoever can do that so that I can find out where the vehicle is at this time?"

"Just one minute while I make that call."

She called a number, explained the situation, was transferred twice, explained two more times, and finally spoke to someone who asked her to put Dillon on the line. She handed the phone to Dillon and appeared relieved to be off the line with whoever she had been speaking to.

"Hello," Dillon said.

"Just who am I speaking with," an unhappy, angry voice asked.

Dillon waited for a half-moment and dug out his happy voice. "Thank you for taking this call. My name is Marshal Jack Dillon. I'm with Dublin An Garda Síochána, Special Branch. We're involved in an investigation concerning a vehicle rented from Enterprise Car Rentals here at Dublin Airport two or three days ago.

The vehicle is a gray 2021 BMW rented by a gentleman named Mathew Longley. I would like you to track this vehicle and tell me where, exactly, it is."

"I won't do that without a court order."

Dillon was afraid that might be the response. "Might I suggest it would be helpful if you didn't make me obtain a court order? We're working under a rather tight timeframe, and there is a situation involved that would not go well if your refusal led to excessive harm to an individual," Dillon said, thinking the excessive harm would be due to him throttling whoever was on the other end of the line causing problems.

There was a long pause, and Dillon was about to repeat his request.

"You're in Dublin airport right now?"

"Yes, I'm standing at the Enterprise counter in Terminal Two."

"If you'll drive around to the opposite side of the airport, our office is directly behind the Express Green Long Term Car Park. The office is Easirent Car Hire. We're in the Airport Business park, across the street from the commercial garage. My name is Logan Spray, and I'll be waiting for you in the lobby. Tell me your name again, please."

"Marshal Jack Dillon, An Garda Síochána, Special Branch. I'll see you shortly, Mr. Spray," Dillon said and handed the receiver back to the woman behind the counter. Once she hung up, he said, "Thank you for your help."

"Sorry it didn't go better. I wouldn't know how to track one of our cars. I just know they can do it. Word to the wise. Be careful, Mr. Spray is not what you'd call a happy camper."

"Thanks for the warning," Dillon said. He walked out of the terminal, climbed in his car, followed the road as it circled past Terminal One, and headed out of the airport. He took the first left in the roundabout and turned at the next left about a hundred yards down the road. He turned left again, headed for the Commercial garage, and there, just as Spray had said, was the Easirent office right across the street. He pulled into the narrow parking lot and parked in front of the building.

FIFTEEN

Dillon spotted Logan Spray the moment he stepped into the small Easirent lobby. He wore an open-collared white shirt with the sleeves rolled up to his elbows. He had close-cropped ginger-colored hair and a red face.

"You Dillon?" he growled.

"Yeah, Marshal Jack Dillon with An Garda Síochána, Special Branch. You must be Logan Spray," Dillon said, emphasizing the words 'special branch.'

Spray nodded and said, "You're an American, and you're with An Garda Síochána?"

"Yeah, I've been attached to An Garda Síochána for a couple of years. Appreciate you taking the time to see me. Sorry to not have an appointment, but we're—"

"Are you the American who was involved in that shooting out here a few years back at Terminal Two? It was a Russian gang and—"

"Yeah, that was me. I was hoping you might be able to trace this BMW. I've got the license number of the vehicle and the name of the individual on the credit card and—"

"That was some damn good work you did back at Terminal Two. You saved some lives."

"Yeah, fortunately, we more or less recovered," Dillon said, remembering Ann Dumphy getting wounded and now retired on permanent disability. "You think you might be able to track this vehicle?"

Spray looked at the license plate number in the pocket notebook Dillon held out and shook his head. "No, I'm afraid not. Don't get me wrong. I'd love to track that damn thing and find out where the hell it is. It was due to be returned over twenty-four hours ago. It's not unusual that a client is late returning a vehicle. We emailed the individual, and the email address came back as bogus. The credit card, listed to a Mathew Longley located in Clontarf, has since been listed as stolen. Try as we may, we're unable to track the vehicle, which means one of two things. Either it's been chopped up into little pieces and is ready to be shipped abroad or it's been destroyed, possibly driven into the sea. Whatever the cause, it's a pretty safe bet it no longer exists."

"Any chance they found the tracking device and removed it?" Dillon asked.

Spray shook his head. "Ancient technology. Nowadays, we program it into the system. There's nothing physical to remove."

Dillon seemed to think for a moment and asked, "Would you have security tape of the individual renting the vehicle."

Spray nodded and said, "Yes, we have that."

"Would you mind if I took a look?"

"No, not at all. I've been working this since yester-day. I've got it on my computer. Come on back to the office," Spray said, and Dillon followed him down the hall. As they walked, Spray asked, "So how many times did you shoot that Russian? Not the first two but the third guy, the one who shot you."

"You must have seen some security tapes. That's not public knowledge," Dillon said.

"You kidding? We've all watched them over and over again. In fact, they're part of the security course any new employee has to take when they're hired out here."

"Hopefully, they're not all carrying guns."

"No, unfortunately. A number of us would like to, but the powers that be would never allow it. Oh, here's my office," Spray said, opening a door and stepping inside.

Dillon followed him in. If Desmond's office at Blake's Cross service station with piles of receipts and a tray of chocolate doughnuts was a total mess, Spray's office was just the opposite. The desk was clear, with the exception of one file positioned in the upper righthand corner of the desk pad. Next to the file was a pen and a pencil, lined up perfectly parallel with the edge of the file and a half-inch away from one another. The desktop computer was off to the side, and the keyboard was centered exactly below the computer. Just beneath the computer was a folded silk cloth that Dillon suspected was used to clean any dust from the screen, probably several times a day.

"Take a seat," Spray said, pointing to the two chairs perfectly positioned in front of his desk. He pulled his desk chair out, sat down, and ran his fingers across the keyboard. A moment later, the screen came to life, and he began typing.

"Okay, here we are," Spray said and froze the screen. He used the mouse to roughly circle the head of the individual standing at the rental counter and then clicked a couple more keys. The facial image was immediately enlarged and took up most of the screen.

The first thing Dillon noticed was that the face on the screen didn't have dark hair. The man didn't have a goatee, either. His hair was short and blonde, no more than an inch long all around his head. If Dillon had to guess, he would have thought that the guy had shaved his head at one time and was letting it grow out. He wore glasses with heavy black frames and a black turtleneck sweater. Unfortunately, there was no sound on the recording. The man's ears had been pierced. Dillon could see the holes, but there were no earrings. There was a large bandage on his chin, maybe two inches wide, and another smaller one across the bridge of his nose. He wore gloves on his hands, which seemed strange because it wasn't winter, and it hadn't been cold.

"Logan," Dillon said to Spray. "Would it be possible to send me a copy of this tape and that isolated face image? I'd like our tech people to run it through the facial recognition database. See if anyone turns up."

"Sure, be happy to do that. I just need an email address."

Dillon pulled out a business card and handed it to him.

Spray read the business card, smiled, and then sent off the files to Dillon's email address.

"Thank you. I'll get out of your hair and let you get back to work," Dillon said.

"Pleasure meeting you, Marshal." Spray grabbed Dillon's business card from his desk and said, "We have any trouble, I'll know who to call."

"Hopefully, it won't come to that."

"Oh, yeah, of course. I find anything out on the BMW, I'll be in touch. But, like I said before, the chances of that are pretty slim at this stage."

"Thank you. I'll see myself out," Dillon said. He stepped out of the office and hurried to his car.

SIXTEEN

illon climbed in behind the wheel and locked the doors just in case Spray came out with another question regarding the shooting outside Terminal Two. He pulled out his phone and called Suel.

Suel answered on the second ring. "You coming back this afternoon?"

"I've got one more stop. I just finished up at the airport, talking to the Enterprise folks." He went on to tell Suel about the image of the individual renting the BMW. How he didn't look anything like the person they saw on the tapes actually driving the vehicle. "Oh, and just in case that's not bad enough, it turns out the credit card is listed as stolen, the vehicle was never returned, and they suspect it's been destroyed."

"Christ on a cross. It just doesn't end," Suel moaned.

"Well, I think it tells us one thing. This doesn't appear to be some random shot that killed Rafferty. It's not some nutcase who wanted to see what it felt like to kill someone. This is turning out to be a well-planned operation. You'll see it on the images they sent to me. The individual who rented the car is in disguise. The individual driving the BMW is probably disguised as well. Is it the same person? I don't know yet, but I'm leaning in that direction."

"D.C.I. McCabe wants us to meet up at 5:00 this evening to see what we've learned."

"You hear anything from anyone else?" Dillon asked.

"Not yet. That's why the 5:00 meeting is scheduled."

Dillon glanced at the screen on his phone. It was 3:37. "I'm going over to Clontarf to talk to your man whose credit card was used. See if he knows when and where it was stolen."

"Just try to be back here by 5:00," Suel said.

"Then I'd better get moving," Dillon said and disconnected. He turned his car on, set his GPS for Dollymount Park, backed out of the parking spot, and headed toward the M1. He drove a short distance on the M1 until just before it turned into the Dublin Port Tunnel, which was a toll road. He wound through city streets, as the GPS updated and brought him through Marino, onto Clontarf Road, and eventually onto Dollymount Park.

Mathew Longley's home happened to be the corner unit of four two-story attached homes on a cul de sac. The homes were all white stucco with a parking area up against the front door. Longley's place had a brick paved parking area and a concrete handicap access ramp with a brick flower box built along the left-hand side.

Dillon pulled partway onto the front sidewalk, walked up the handicap ramp, and rang the doorbell. An older gentleman answered the door. Dillon pegged him at maybe late seventies or possibly eighty years old.

"Yes?" the man said and smiled.

"Good afternoon. I'm with An Garda Síochána," Dillon said. "My name is Marshal Dillon, and I'd like to speak to Mathew Longley." As he spoke, he handed his ID to Longley.

Longley glanced at it and handed the ID back to Dillon. "I'll have to take your word for it. I don't have my reading glasses."

"You're Mathew Longley?"

"I am. This wouldn't be about my credit card, would it? Did you find the bollix that used it?"

"Yes, I'm here regarding your credit card, sir. Unfortunately, no, we haven't found the person yet."

"Well, no matter, our son canceled the damn thing, so it won't work anyway."

"Can you remember when it was stolen and where you were at the time?"

"I know exactly where I was. Please, come in. Would you like a tea?"

"That's very kind of you, but no thanks."

"Let's go into the sitting room," Longley said and stepped into the room just off to the right. It looked just like the hundreds of sitting rooms Dillon had been in, including his own. A fireplace against the far wall. Windows were looking out on the street to his right and out onto a garden on his left in the back of the room. A couch was against the wall opposite the fireplace, and wingback chairs were positioned on either side of the fireplace.

Longley gave a slight groan as he settled onto the couch. Dillon sat in one of the wingback chairs. He made a note of the eight different prescription bottles lined up on the coffee table in front of the couch.

"So, you said you knew exactly where you were when your card was stolen."

"Yes, now it's a strange situation. I was purchasing some items for my wife at the pharmacy. It's just around the corner on St. Gabriel's Road, so I can walk there. We've been going there for over fifty years. Unfortunately, the wife is confined to a wheelchair now, and she doesn't get out much. God bless. Anyway, it was right around the noon hour. I was carrying three items, a container of skin cream, a bottle of mouthwash, and a can of shaving cream. The shaving cream was for me. I was making my way toward the front carrying my credit card. You know, I was holding it like this between my thumb and forefinger in my right hand," he said, extending his right hand toward Dillon.

Dillon nodded.

"This young woman comes around the corner, steps into the aisle, and runs right into me. She knocked the credit card out of my hand. She apologized, picked up the card, and hands it back to me. She even offered to pay for the items I have. I told her I wasn't going to have any of that. She brought me over to one of those machines, you know, where you check out your items and use your credit card.

"The self-checkout?"

"Yeah, I think that's what it's called. I always avoid it, you know. Computers and I aren't the best of friends. Anyway, your lovely helps me. She did everything for me. Showed me how to tap the damn thing with my credit card, and it worked. Who knew? She placed my items in the bag, even carried them out of the pharmacy, and offered to walk me home. She was so nice. If she apologized once, she did it a half-dozen times, telling me she was so sorry she bumped into me. To tell you the truth, if I was forty years younger, well. Anyway, that's fine. Two days later, my son called me and said there was a charge on my credit card for a car rental. Why would I be renting a car? I've never rented a car in my life. My son drives us wherever we need to go."

"This was from Enterprise Car Rental?"

"The car rental? Yes, I think that's the one. My son called them, and well, it ended up we had to cancel my credit card. My son did it for me."

"So the nice woman kept your credit card?"

"Well, that's the strange thing. See, I thought she handed it back to me. I just put it in my wallet, never looked at the damn thing. My son comes over and when I show the card to him, turns out it's not my card. It's some woman's card. Hang on. I've got the name written down out in the kitchen." Longley was up before Dillon could say anything.

Dillon listened to him rummaging around in the kitchen for three or four minutes and was just about to go into the kitchen when Longley returned. "Yeah, here it is. The card was to a Madeline O'Malley. I never heard of her before. Damn thing looked just like my card, and I never bothered to check. I just put it back in my wallet." Longley handed Dillon the sheet torn from a notebook with the name Madeline O'Malley written on it.

Dillon pulled out his pocket notebook and wrote down the name. "And you didn't know anything was wrong until your son called you."

"Right. He's a finance guy, smart, obviously takes after his mother," Longley laughed. "Handles all our financial stuff. Invests for us. He's the reason we can still afford to live here."

"What did your son do with the woman's credit card?"

"He called you lot at An Garda Síochána. You weren't interested and told him to send it back to the company. So that's exactly what he did. He sent it back to the company. Then he canceled mine right away. He said he sent away for a new one for me, but I haven't seen it yet. You think your woman knows she's got the wrong credit card?"

"Yeah, I think she knows by now, Mr. Longley. Well, I should be on my way. Thank you for your time."

"You sure I can't talk you into a cuppa?"

"Thank you, but I'd better not. I've got a number of other interviews to make," Dillon said.

"Any more questions, feel free to stop by. I'm never going anywhere. Please keep me posted if you learn anything," Longley said.

"I'll be sure to do that. There is one thing."

"What's that?"

"Can you tell me what this woman looked like?"

"Well, like I said, she was a pretty young thing."

"How old would you say?"

"Oh, I don't know, maybe twenty-five or thirty-five. I'm not the best at guessing their age anymore. They all look young to me, and with the clothes they wear or don't wear," he said and raised his eyebrows.

"Hair color?"

"Her hair? Oh, she was a redhead, hair about this long," he said, waving his hand back and forth just below his right earlobe."

"Okay, well, good to know. Thank you for your time, Mr. Longley. Should anything turn up, I'll let you know," Dillon said then stood, hopefully sending the message he needed to leave.

"Feel free to drop by any time. As I told you, I'm always here," Longley said and patted Dillon on the shoulder as they headed for the door.

Dillon smiled, said 'Goodbye' two more times, and eventually headed out the door.

"Drive careful, now," Longley called as Dillon opened the car door. He smiled, gave a wave, and settled in behind the wheel. He turned on the engine and headed down the street.

SEVENTEEN

He drove around the corner to St. Gabriel's Road. A pharmacy was just a block away on the left-hand side of the road. He parked right in front and hurried inside. Apparently, he was the only customer at the moment.

He walked to the counter and repeated the line he used uncountable times over the course of the afternoon. "Hi, I'm with An Garda Síochána, and I'd like to speak to your manager, please."

The young man behind the counter looked about twelve and was wearing a red vest with the name Kevin on a plastic name tag clipped crookedly on the vest. He didn't ask if he could help or what the problem was. Instead, he pointed down an aisle toward a woman arranging bags of candy on a shelf and said, "That's her."

"Thanks," Dillon said and hurried down the aisle. "Excuse me, are you the manager?" Dillon asked.

"Yes, is there a problem?"

"No, I'm with An Garda Síochána. We're investigating a case, and I'm wondering if I could view your security tape from four days ago right around the noon hour."

She shook her head and said, "Believe me, I wish you could. We're in the process of having a new system installed, and we've been without a system all week. The new system should be up and running by the end of the day. Of course, that's what they told me yesterday."

Dillon thanked her and walked back to his car.

It was close to 4:30 by the time he headed up to Special Branch. He punched in the code on the keypad, and the door buzzed, letting him into the office. A number of people were at their desks either on a phone call or on their computers. Suel was on his phone and gave a wave to Dillon as he passed by. Dillon gathered the three tea mugs and two dirty plates from his desk and took them into the break room.

He went back to his desk and turned on his computer. He clicked on his email account and counted a total of fourteen emails from Declan Reilly, Desmond at Blake's Cross, the shops along the R132, and Logan Spray at Easirents. He quickly went through the images in the emails. He made some more notes summarizing the conversations he'd had with people today.

Suel walked over and asked, "You learn anything?"

At which point D.C.I. McCabe stepped out of his office and said, "A moment of your time, please. Let's make this quick. I know everyone is busy and exhausted. Gather around, please."

Dillon counted nine people plus McCabe. Everyone took a couple of minutes explaining what they'd been working on. Some people had checked for individuals with a known record leaving the country. Two people had worked with airport personnel regarding out-going flights. Another individual had been at Alexandra Quay checking cruise ships. Two more were in Dublin port checking ship departures. Everyone had come up empty-handed.

The initial report from the tech lab said the round that killed Kevin Rafferty was a .22 caliber, which Dillon and Suel already thought was the case. Unfortunately, thus far, there was no match found in the database. The tech lab was in the process of running the round through EU and FBI databases but had no results at this point.

Dillon and Suel explained the blurry images recovered from cameras along the route from Skerries to the M1. Dillon went on to give a brief explanation of the fact that the rental car had not been returned and that the image of the individual renting the car did not match the blurry images of the person driving the vehicle. He finished up with Mathew Longley's stolen credit card that was used to rent the vehicle and the pharmacy waiting for the reinstallation of the security cameras.

D.C.I. McCabe suggested it would be a good idea for Dillon to send the images of the individual at Enterprise to everyone. No one else seemed to have any input, and everyone returned to their desks.

Dillon phoned Emily down in the tech lab and ended up leaving a message, which wasn't surprising since it was after 5:00. "Hi, Emily, Dillon here. Sending you an email with the image of the guy renting the car we think Kevin Rafferty's shooter was driving. Please run the image through facial recognition. Hopefully, someone will come up. The car was a rental, never returned, and can't be traced. Credit card used was stolen. Call me with any questions. Thanks."

Dillon and Suel worked for another half-hour and then closed up for the day.

Dillon headed home and pulled into his parking area. He sat behind the wheel, thinking for a long moment. Something wasn't adding up, but he couldn't quite figure out what. Maybe a quiet night, a glass of wine, a nice book, or a movie would be just the thing to clear his mind. He could refocus in the morning and deal with whatever seemed to be nagging him in the back of his mind.

He climbed out of the car and closed the wrought iron gates on his parking place. He pulled his keys from his pocket and was just about to step up to the front door when a voice called, "Oh, Dillon, glad I caught you."

Dillon felt his blood pressure rise, and he turned and pasted a fake smile on his face. "Good evening, Deitora. Nice to see you." He said as he stepped onto the stoop in a final effort to escape. It didn't work.

"Just wanted to mention your front garden would look a lot better if you cleaned up the piles left by your dog, Lucette."

"Actually, his name is Lucifer," Dillon said and placed his key in the lock.

"How fitting," Deitora said. "Picking up would seem the thing to do. The rest of us are doing our bit to keep the neighborhood tidy. Basic responsibility, that's the key."

"I'll be sure to keep that in mind. Always a unique experience to talk with you, Deitora. Enjoy your evening," Dillon said as he turned the key and opened the door. Of course, this would be the one day when Lucifer would be right there. As the door opened, he bounded off the stoop past Dillon, circled twice, and assumed the position with his rear pointed at Deitora. Dillon had to wonder if it was intentional.

He quickly stepped inside and closed the door.

He peeked through the shutter in the sitting room to see if Deitora was still out front. At the moment, she was focused on Lucifer, doing his business. Dillon decided he'd leave the results of Lucifer's effort in the parking area for another day or two.

He went upstairs and changed into jeans and a sweatshirt. He let Lucifer back into the house and gave him a biscuit and a long scratch behind the ears. "Good boy, Lucifer, good boy. Thank you. Well done."

He peeked once more through the shutters in the sitting room. Thankfully, Deitora was nowhere to be seen.

EIGHTEEN

Dillon placed a chicken breast in the oven, filled a frying pan with slices of red pepper, coated them with a little olive oil, then covered the pan and placed the heat on low. He poured a glass of red wine, a Pinot, and settled in at the kitchen counter.

His intent was to check on the local news, but within a couple of minutes, he was reviewing the images of Kevin Rafferty driving past and then the individual renting the BMW from Enterprise Car Rental. He couldn't help but think the face looked familiar, but that was as far as he got. Try as he might, he could not come up with a name. The bandage on the chin and the bridge of the nose didn't help.

He ate dinner while scrolling through images of recent arrests, searching for another image of the individual, and came up empty-handed. He went through Facebook and Twitter accounts and never saw anyone resembling the image Logan Spray at Enterprise had sent, and yet….

It was 11:00. Dillon never did turn the TV on. He'd barely eaten half his dinner, and he'd had three glasses of wine. He'd spent the better part of the past four-and-a-half hours searching for a connection with the car rental image, and for all his effort, he'd come up empty-handed. He let Lucifer out into the front garden for five minutes, set the alarm once Lucifer was back in, and they headed up to bed.

Thanks to the wine, Dillon was asleep in just a few minutes. Lucifer growling woke him. He told Lucifer to quiet down several times over the next few minutes, but something was clearly bothering him. Dillon climbed out of bed and glanced out the front window. The front gates were closed. Nothing appeared unusual. He walked around the bed and looked out the back window just as the motion detector light above the double back doors flashed on. He thought he saw a shadow quickly disappear around the corner of the house, but he wasn't sure. One thing was certain. Something had caused the lights to flash on.

He opened the drawer on the nightstand, took out a 9mm pistol, quickly slipped on a pair of sweatpants, and hurried downstairs barefoot. Lucifer remained upstairs on the bed.

Dillon stopped at the bottom of the stairs and listened. Since his back garden was surrounded by a seven-foot wall, someone moving around out there was highly unusual, especially at this hour. He left the lights off and stepped into the kitchen. By this time, the motion detector light above the back doors had turned off. Dillon could see out the double doors and across the patio to the wall fifteen feet away. No one was out there. He did notice that the trousers and shirt he'd tossed out the door earlier in the day were still there, but they appeared to have been moved or, more likely, kicked aside. He went to the front window in the corner of the kitchen and looked out just as a pair of taillights pulled around the far corner of the lane and disappeared. Possibly someone coming home from the pub, but then he walked back to the kitchen and looked at the clock on the wall. It was 3:45, and the pubs had been closed for almost four hours. He went out to the entry and turned off the alarm. He returned, glanced out the window for a moment, and then stepped out the back door. The motion detector lights flashed on. The back garden was empty, and he was thinking that maybe the shadow he saw had been a cat scurrying around the corner. There were a number of them in the neighborhood, and a cat would certainly be large enough to trigger the motion detector on the lights.

He stepped around the corner of the house. Another set of lights flashed on, and the gate was open. That wasn't right. It was always closed and held in place with a deadbolt attached to the house. It could only be opened from inside the back garden. He stepped out through the gate and into the front garden. His plastic trash bins remained where he always kept them, pushed up against the seven-foot wall. It wouldn't take much to climb on top of the bin, hoist yourself onto the top of the wall, and drop into the back garden.

He looked around just to be sure no one was watching then wheeled all three trash bins into the back garden. He locked the gate, gave a final look around, and headed for the back door. As he approached the door, the motion detector lights flashed on again. He stepped inside, locked the back door, reset the alarm, and went up to bed.

Lucifer was sound asleep. Dillon slept fitfully for the next two hours and crawled out of bed just before 6:00. He ate the cold remnants of the previous evening's dinner for breakfast. He let Lucifer out, filled the food and water dishes, set the alarm, and headed to his car.

He was three steps from the house when he saw the pile that Lucifer had left last night. It had been stepped on and spread across the drive. Based on what he could determine from the footprint, whoever stepped in it had been wearing running shoes. It appeared to have been the right foot. He could only hope they spread the remnants on their accelerator and brake pedal.

NINETEEN

illon was back in the office just before 7:00. He sent an email to Emily in the Tech lab telling her to give him a ring when she had a moment. He proceeded to review the various cases Kevin Rafferty had been involved in over the past year, hoping maybe someone, somewhere, might resemble the image of the man renting the BMW at Enterprise. Once again, nothing.

Suel wandered in around 9:00. "You need another coffee?" he asked on his way to the break room.

"I'm not sure it would help," Dillon said.

"You working on Kevin?"

"Supposedly, but nothing's coming up. I'm going through the cases he worked on last year to see if there's someone or something that clicks. If that doesn't work, I'll go through the year before that."

"You get any sleep last night?"

"Very little," Dillon said and decided not to get into someone sneaking into his back garden.

"I'll get you a coffee. Let's put our heads together. God forbid we'd come up with something," Suel said.

He grabbed Dillon's mug off the desk and headed into the break room.

Dillon could hear him laughing and chatting with whoever else was in there. Suel was back with the coffee five minutes later.

"Sorry it took so long. Had to make a fresh pot. Not that it's going to be any better than what you had before."

"Thanks," Dillon said, taking his mug from Suel. Suel sat down in the client chair at the side of Dillon's desk. Dillon took a sip of coffee and shuddered.

"It's that bad?" Suel asked.

"Just the usual. So, were you able to come up with anything?"

"You mean on Kevin Rafferty? Not really, although there is one thing, bit of a long shot," Suel said.

"It sounds better than the absolutely nothing I've come up with. I keep thinking I know, or maybe met, or somehow interacted with that guy renting the BMW, but something is missing. It just doesn't seem right."

"Maybe back off for a bit. Give it some time."

Pretty much the same advice he'd given himself. "So, what's the long shot you've got?"

"Rafferty was one of three involved in the arrest of Ali Naufal."

"Rings a bell, but I'm drawing another blank," Dillon said.

"Originally from Iran, traveling on a Dutch passport. He was overstaying his visit here by two months, living in a luxury apartment on Baggott Street. Turns out he was the middleman in setting up killings. In a number of the gangland murders from maybe 2015 to 2020, he was the intermediary you'd go to. He'd get the word to take some knacker out. He'd make a phone call and assign the task to someone. It wasn't just here in Dublin. He was dealing in Brussels, Amsterdam, and down in Costa del Sol, as well."

"And Rafferty arrested the guy?"

"He was part of a team that did. Largely because this character came to Rafferty's attention, and he alerted the higher-ups, who did absolutely nothing. Eventually, Rafferty went to the powers that be, told them what he'd learned, and asked to be part of the team making the arrest."

"So they put him in Special Branch?"

"Yeah, eventually, but at the time, they go to arrest your man in this expensive apartment on Baggott Street. When he answers the door, he's wearing these trainers on his feet worth about eight-hundred euros, he's got an Audemars Piguet watch worth about forty-five thousand euros on his wrist, and he's in purple silk pajamas. He didn't put up a fight. He just let the lads in. They arrested him and started searching the place. They found about twenty grand under a mattress, more cash in a cookie jar. They found bundles stuffed in a piano, in a bookcase, and a liquor cabinet, you get the idea. All in all, they got over a hundred grand in cash. Since he's over-stayed his welcome, and he was here on a Dutch passport, the guy gets sent back to Holland, where they try him. He's found guilty of orchestrating multiple murders across the EU, and now he's serving a life sentence."

"So that gets Rafferty into Special Branch."

"Yeah, but that's only part of it. Along with all the cash, they find five burner phones, and they're able to get information off of those regarding other murders and crimes. That leads to more arrests, plus, the Criminal Assets Bureau gets involved, and they end up seizing four or five houses, over thirty cars, a couple of commercial buildings, all thought to be proceeds of crime."

"So who does this point to?"

"Two idiots, brothers, Liam and Cullen Gibbs. Their father was one of the knackers arrested. The family home was taken by the Criminal Assets Bureau, and now they're taking orders from their mother and trying to build the business back, without much success."

"You know anything about them?"

"I know they're here, in Finglas, actually. I know they'd think it would be a right feather in their cap if they took out Rafferty. I know they're stupid enough to try something like that. Come on back to my desk. I've got copies of their files," Suel said and stood.

Dillon took a sip from his mug. The coffee turning lukewarm did nothing to improve the taste. "Let me get a fresh mug, and I'll join you." He hurried into the break room, poured his mug down the sink, refilled it, and went over to Suel's desk.

Suel pushed two files toward Dillon and said, "Here, commit all this to your memory and let me know your thoughts."

"You mind if I take these over to my desk?"

"Not a bother, just don't let them out of your sight. I signed them out, and they'll take their payment in blood if I lose those files."

"I'll try to remember that," Dillon said.

He'd been at his desk for over three hours reading through the files.

Suel stepped over to Dillon and said, "So what do you think?"

Dillon was so absorbed in the file that he jumped at the sound of Suel's voice. "What do I think? Well, they certainly are capable of attempting to do this. That said, they've been arrested so many times I can't see these two idiots pulling something like this off. Following Rafferty from Skerries to the M1 and actually shooting him from a moving vehicle? It strikes me as something completely out of their reach. Would these two fools even know where Skerries is located?"

"You got a better idea?"

"Yeah, let's grab a lunch after I check with Emily in the tech lab."

"Sounds like a plan," Suel said.

Dillon phoned Emily. She answered on the second ring. "Dillon, you calling about the facial recognition on the image you sent down?"

"Yeah, that and any link on the round that killed him. Of course, the fact that you're even asking me suggests that you've come up with a big, fat, nothing."

"Can you stop down, and we can go over it while I show you on the screen what we're dealing with," she said and then waited for Dillon's response.

"I'll be down in just a minute," he said.

TWENTY

illon headed down to the Tech Lab. He pushed the intercom button next to the door, and Emily answered a moment later.

"Yes."

"Hi Emily, Jack Dillon."

"Perfect timing, just started running it now. You want to come in?"

"Yeah, buzz me in, please."

"You're not stinky, are you?"

"So not funny."

The door buzzed, and Dillon stepped into the lab. There were three long counters with computers, sinks, and a host of gadgets. Emily stood at the back counter. She turned and waved at Dillon.

A computer screen was mounted on the wall. At the moment, it displayed the facial image of the guy renting the BMW at Enterprise. All sorts of numbers were flashing across the screen.

"You coming up with anything?" Dillon asked as he approached.

"Probably a headache and a feeling of absolute disappointment. I can tell you one thing. Whoever that person is, they were prepared for this process."

"What do you mean?" Dillon asked.

"A couple of things, those glasses with the heavy black frames, I'm willing to bet those are not prescription lenses in there."

"You mean they're just for reading?"

"Not exactly. I think they may be worn just to confuse the facial recognition process. The glasses, plus the bandage on the bridge of the nose and on the chin, are textbook examples of how to screw the program."

"That would seem to suggest someone who knew what they were doing and not some street punk."

"Exactly. My guess, and it's strictly a guess, but this could well be a highly paid professional. Those bandages are perfectly placed to eliminate key recognizable points in the recognition program. One other thing, I don't know if you could catch this on your laptop screen, but this individual is wearing a wig. See how the hair is combed forward? That wig had been arranged not only to disguise the actual color of the guy's hair, but it effectively covers any indication of what his actual hairline would be."

"Based on the eyebrows, I'd say he's dark-haired, brunette, or maybe dark brown."

"That's another thing. The eyebrows are tattooed."

"Tattooed?"

She gave Dillon a look that suggested he get up to date. "You can get them at any pharmacy for about five euros."

"A tattoo?"

"Very temporary, they're applied with water, and they'll last for three to six days. Or you can get the microblading eyebrow tattoo. Those are temporary, too, but they last maybe six to thirty-six months, depending."

"God, I'm really out of touch. Did you notice his ears are pierced?" Dillon asked.

She nodded. "Yes and two things, based on the piercing. The ears were pierced some time ago, years ago, many years ago. And although there are no earrings in this image, this person is usually wearing earrings. Based on the actual piercing, I would say small earrings, probably posts, maybe a diamond or something."

"I keep thinking this guy looks distantly familiar, but I can't come up with anyone."

"No surprise. Whoever this individual is, he's very clever, very experienced, and is doing everything short of wearing a balaclava to make sure no one recognizes him. This program will run for probably another hour, but I fear it's going to come up with no real result, sorry."

"Damn it. Unfortunately, that's turning out not to be surprising."

"Wish I had more for you, Dillon. But right now, that's it."

"Anything on the recovered round?"

"Not yet."

"Okay, thanks, Emily. Give me a call when this is finished," Dillon said and gave a final glance at the computer screen with all sorts of percentage numbers flashing around the face.

"Good luck," Emily called as Dillon walked out of the lab.

He went back up to Special Branch and grabbed Suel. They headed out of the building and into Phoenix Park. A pizza food truck was parked just next to the entrance to the parking lot. There was a line with eight people ahead of them.

"The Tech lab come up with anything?" Suel asked.

"Yeah, we're even more screwed than we thought. Emily is running the facial image from Enterprise through the recognition program. To quote her, 'Whoever the individual is, he's very clever, very experienced, and is doing everything short of wearing a balaclava to make sure no one recognizes him.'"

"What the hell does that mean?" Suel said as they moved forward a couple of feet in the line.

"It means that the bandages on the bridge of the guy's nose and his chin were put there to screw up any hopes of the facial recognition. Oh, and get this, the guy is wearing a wig. Okay, so I said he's probably got dark hair. I mean, look at his eyebrows. She tells me it doesn't matter because the guy's eyebrows are tattooed."

"What?"

"Apparently, you can get eyebrow tattoos that last for a couple of days or up to a year and a half."

"Who the hell gets their eyebrows tattooed?"

"Oh, great, you're just as out of touch as I am," Dillon said as they stepped forward to place their order.

"I'll have three slices with everything and extra cheese. Oh, and no anchovies," Suel said.

"Better give me the same," Dillon said.

The woman nodded, quickly placed three slices of pizza into a white cardboard container and handed it to Suel.

"I'll pay for both of them," Suel said.

She smiled, placed three slices into another container, and handed it to Dillon. Suel handed her a twenty and a ten.

"You mind if I ask you something?" Dillon said to her. "You ever hear of anyone getting their eyebrows tattooed?"

She smiled and said, "We all do that."

Dillon shook his head and said, "Keep the change."

TWENTY-ONE

Dillon spent the rest of the afternoon going through the files on Liam and Cullen Gibbs and then reviewed the notes he'd made regarding the cases Kevin Rafferty had been involved in over the past year. By the end of the afternoon, no one stood out as a potential killer of Kevin Rafferty. Dillon was tired, frustrated, and at another dead end.

His desk phone rang, and he picked it up on the second ring. "Dillon."

"Can I talk you into an early dinner?" Suel said.

Dillon glanced over at Suel sitting at his desk. "You think it would help?"

"It sure as hell can't hurt."

Rather than dine from one of the food trucks, they walked for ten minutes through Phoenix Park and exited the park at the gate next to The Hole in the Wall pub. There was indoor dining just to the left, inside the pub building. Dillon and Suel turned to the right, where the outside dining shack stood surrounded by picnic tables. They ordered chips, a sandwich, coffee, and settled in at a picnic table.

Dillon took a sip of his coffee and raised his eyebrows. It was good, very good, but then compared to the stuff from the break room, that shouldn't come as a surprise. They each took a bite from their sandwich before either one spoke.

"I talked with Emily before we came over. She hasn't gotten to the bullet analysis yet."

Suel shook his head. "Yet another dead end. What the hell?"

"When I spoke with her earlier, she was pretty adamant that whoever that was renting the car, they were very aware of how the facial recognition program works, and they successfully thwarted it."

Suel shook his head and took another bite of his sandwich.

"That leads me to the next thing," Dillon said. "After reading the files on Liam and Cullen Gibbs, they don't strike me as the type who would be up on technology."

Suel nodded. "Couldn't agree more. Their father, God bless him, is serving a life sentence. He worked for the past twenty-five years to make them the lords of Dublin. As far as I know, they never failed to disappoint. I know you have a thing about children of the wealthy, that they're spoiled, never have to work. These two could serve as the poster children for that. Everything delivered on a silver platter, and they somehow have the impression they've earned it."

Dillon shook his head. "You really think they killed Kevin Rafferty?"

"Theoretically, they'd have a motive, what with the Criminal Assets Bureau seizing the home and the business, a pub, by the way. Do I think they're capable of pulling this off on the M1? Probably not. What I do think they're capable of is getting in touch with someone who could do it and then paying them to do the job."

"You said their mother is directing them?"

"Not a happy woman, but then why would she be? Her privileged lifestyle was seized, her husband's serving a life sentence, and she's left with two sons who never miss an opportunity to screw things up."

"What do you want to do?"

"Maybe just have a nice little chat with the boys, see where that leads us."

"You want to bring them in?"

Suel shook his head. "Word has it, Liam spends his time at an adults-only club called The Mari Gold Club. Theoretically, he's running the place, but his mother has to be behind the scenes. He's simply incapable."

"And the other brother, Cullen?"

"Up until recently, he was at one of the gambling clubs. He's persona non grata until his debt is paid, so rumor has it he'll either be in your favorite place, The Cabra House, or passed out in his flat."

"They sound like two guys with a wonderful future to look forward to."

"They're pure shite, but then that shouldn't be any surprise."

"You up for checking them out today?" Dillon asked.

"If I can have five more minutes to finish my dinner."

Dillon took their empty plates back up to the counter, and thanked the couple working there. They walked back into Phoenix Park and headed toward the office. They checked phone messages at their desks and then headed out the door. Suel drove along the Liffey for a bit and then crossed over. They entered the Liberties section of Dublin, passed the Brazen Head pub, drove up the hill, and turned onto Francis Street. The Mari Gold Club was just across the street from the Drop Dead pub. Suel parked halfway up on the sidewalk, and they got out.

Oddly, the Mari Gold was on the second floor of the building, just above a dry cleaner. The door into the Mari Gold was painted black. The club name was painted on the door in gold letters but not in a way that made it stand out. It was the sort of entry you wouldn't pay any attention to. Dillon and Suel pushed the door open and climbed up the steep, narrow, dimly lit staircase.

There was no door at the top of the stairs. A simple entry led into a darkened room with a small stage attached to the far wall. The stage was at least three feet high and barely large enough to accommodate more than two people. It was edged by little white Christmas tree lights. The room was furnished with a number of small, empty tables. A bar, maybe five feet long, was on the opposite wall. There didn't appear to be a bartender.

Music was playing. At no surprise, Dillon couldn't recognize the tune. A woman in a leopard print thong moved from side to side somewhat in time to the music. Even though it was essentially the end of a workday, the place was empty, with the exception of a table where three men were seated. They were dressed casually, jeans and short sleeve shirts on two of the men. The third man had his back to Dillon and Suel and wore a light blue Dublin jersey. The table held close to a dozen empty pint glasses, and all three were laughing as Dillon and Suel stepped into the room.

"That's your man Liam Gibbs in the jersey," Suel said and headed toward the table. As they approached, the two men facing them stopped laughing and sat up with their hands placed out in front of them, palms down.

"What the…Oh, for God's sake. Now what's the problem?" Gibbs said as he turned and watched Dillon and Suel approach.

"Good evening, lads. How you's gettin' on?" Suel asked.

Gibbs looked over at the dancer on the stage and ran his right hand across his neck, signaling her to cut the music. She was staring off into the distance and kept dancing. "Monica, give it a rest," he shouted, and she came back to reality, grabbed a remote from a small shelf, and turned off the music.

"Thanks, love," Gibbs said then faced Dillon and Suel. "Now, why do I think you didn't stop in for a pint and a lap dance. On the house, of course, for the likes of gentlemen such as yourselves."

"Just like to have a word with you, Liam," Suel said.

"Ahh, you must be joking. Are you fixing to haul me down to the station again? I can tell you's right now. I haven't done a bleedin' thing. In case you haven't noticed, I'm trying to run an entertainment business here."

"Looks like you're doing about as well as we expected. Maybe just a moment of your time, and then you can get back to whatever your entertainment business is," Suel said and gave half a nod at the woman standing on stage with her hands on her hips.

"Monica, take a break back in the dressing room."

She climbed off the stage and walked past the table. As she passed, she flashed a smile at Suel.

"We should be going, Liam. Things to do," one of the men at the table said as they both stood.

"Good luck," the other said. He shot a look at Dillon and Suel and then the two of them hurried out of the room and down the stairs.

"Happy, lads? You just chased away all my evening business."

"Yeah, and they forgot to pay. Thanks for letting us join you," Suel said as he turned a chair around and sat down. He folded his arms over the back of the chair and leaned toward Gibbs. "So, Liam, we're dying to know how your business is going."

"We're still in the early stages. Just getting all the kinks out, and it's about to take off. I can feel it."

"Yeah, I'm sure you can. We thought it might be a good idea to stop by and pass on a message. Your friend Kevin Rafferty sends his regards," Suel said in a tone that was anything but friendly.

Gibbs shook his head. "I'm not sure who you're talking about. Kevin Rafferty? I don't know anyone named Kevin…oh, now, hold on just a minute. You're talking about that bollox what put the bastards onto me da, aren't you? Put the family out in the street, they did. Took the house. Me ma's car, her fur coats. I've to deal with her now, and she is not a happy bunny. Let me tell you."

"You spend much time out in Skerries?" Dillon asked.

"Skerries? Hate to burst your bubble, mate, but I've never, ever been there. Wouldn't know the first thing about finding my way to it. So what is it that I was supposed to have done out there? I suppose there's some bollox fingering me for a crime I didn't commit. Let me fill you's in, lads. I'm here all day, every day, seven days a week. You can check it out. Like I told you's before, I'm here getting all the kinks out and don't have any idea what the hell happened out in the back of nowhere, in someplace like fecking Skerries."

"If you were involved, Gibbs, my advice to you would be to get on the next flight out of the country because, if we find out you're lying, we're not going to arrest you." Suel leaned forward and lowered his voice, "We're going to come for you and settle up."

It was just dark enough in the room that Dillon wasn't sure if the color had drained from Gibbs' face. Either way, Suel had gotten his attention.

"Listen, lads, I've no idea what the hell you're talking about. Honest, I ain't lying to you's. Whatever it is, I didn't have nothin' to do with it. God's honest truth. I'm here seven days a week, and when I'm not here, I'm at home asleep. Swear to God," he said, holding his right hand up.

"I hope for your sake you're telling the truth, Liam. I really do," Suel said as he stood. "We'll let you get back to work. Pleasure chatting with you. Hope you have a big crowd tonight. You just watch yourself," Suel said, pointing his index finger about three inches from the end of Gibbs's nose.

Dillon nodded a goodbye, followed Suel out of the room and down the stairs.

"What do you think?" Dillon asked as he walked back to the car.

"My gut tells me there's a slim to zero chance he was involved in any way, shape, or form. He never gave a hint he had any idea Kevin was murdered. I think there's even less of a chance his brother Cullen knows anything, but as long as we're out and about, we should check him out."

"We should check the Cabra Club. That's probably our best shot," Dillon said.

TWENTY-TWO

At no surprise, the Cabra Club is located in Cabra. It's not the fanciest looking place. In fact, with the front painted a dingy, peeling black, the place looks like it might be closed and waiting for demolition. That said, it's a popular local with a certain level of society.

Suel parked across the street and down a half-block just to be sure no one in the club would be able to pick out his car. They walked back and stepped in the front door.

If The Mari Gold Club had been empty, the Cabra Club was jammed. Music blared, people shouted back and forth. The place was literally alive. Folks were two deep standing all along the bar. Two guys were busy pouring pints nonstop while three servers carried trays of drinks to tables. Dillon and Suel stepped a few feet in from the front door and scanned the crowd. More than one head turned and studied them in return.

It was loud enough that Dillon had to lean close to Suel's ear. "Back table off to the right. Does that look like your man Cullen?"

Suel turned his head and quickly nodded. They wound their way past three or four tables and settled into two chairs opposite Cullen Gibbs. He appeared to be the only person sitting alone. Four empty pint glasses rested on the table in front of him.

"Hey, Cullen, great to see you. What do you say to us buying you another pint?" Suel asked.

Gibbs slowly raised his head and seemed to blink himself awake. "You're buying?"

"You bet, and happy to get you served. We were just talking with your brother, Liam. He was telling us you're doing what you want."

"Did he tell you I'm finally enjoying life and not doing anything with the likes of him?"

"Well, no, he didn't say that exactly, but he…oh, ma'am, maybe a round of Guinness for your man here and both of us," Suel said, as a waitress set two pint-sized glasses on the table next to them.

"And you'll be paying? Because Cullen here is once again cut off until he pays his tab."

"Mmm, yeah, we'll pay. Dillon, you have any cash with you?"

Dillon reached into his pocket and came up with two twenty euro notes. "Three pints of Guinness, what's that going to—"

"This should cover it," the woman said. She snatched the cash from Dillon's hand and made her way to the bar.

"So tell me, what have you been up to lately?" Suel said.

Cullen raised his head, blinked a few times, and appeared to be coming awake again. "Doing whatever in the hell I want. Not a care in the world."

"Yeah, I can tell," Suel said, shaking his head as he looked over at Dillon. "Say, Kevin Rafferty told us to say hi to you and to tell you he's doing fine."

"Good for him," Gibbs said.

Dillon and Suel watched as Gibbs's head slowly drifted down until his chin rested on his chest, and he began breathing heavily.

"What the hell," Dillon said. "We're not going to get anything from him. I don't think he could remember his own name, let alone get in touch with someone who would want to do the deed for him."

Just as Suel nodded, the woman returned carrying a tray with three freshly poured pints of Guinness. She set the tray on the table and placed a pint glass in front of each of them. There was a ten euro note and another six euros in coins on the tray.

She was just about to reach for the change when Suel said, "Not a bother, keep the change, dear."

"Thank you," she said and hurried away.

"Suel, you plonker," Dillon said.

Suel smiled, took a hearty sip, and said, "What do you say we take our pints and drink outside? I can barely think with the music blaring, and your man Gibbs is turning out to be our most recent dead end in the case."

"Both of them, he and his brother, are dead ends, in more ways than one," Dillon said. He stood, grabbed his pint, and headed for the door.

They stood outside, leaning against the front of the pub, sipping and chatting. They weren't the only ones out there, although typical for a local, everyone kept their distance from them. They got the occasional quick glance, but that was the extent of any interaction. Once they finished their pints, they set their glasses next to two empties on a windowsill and headed down the street to the car.

Suel pulled into the headquarters parking lot ten minutes later. "Fancy another pint?" he asked.

"I'd love to, but I'd better not. I have to get home and let Lucifer out. Then I plan to sit back and try to figure out who in the hell did this to Rafferty. We're missing something, Paddy. Something big and I can't for the life of me figure out what in the hell it is."

"You're not alone in that, mate. But I have no idea what the hell it is either. I'll see you tomorrow. Don't stay up too late. Oh, and thanks for the pint," Suel said.

Dillon climbed out of the car and watched as Suel drove off. He headed up to Special Branch. His desk phone was flashing, signaling he had a message waiting. He debated checking it out and then figured he'd better. He punched in the three-digit code and listened.

The message was from Emily. "Yeah, Dillon, just beginning to run the Integrated Ballistics Identification System. Always a big 'if,' but *if* there is a match, I will have that information for you tomorrow morning. Thanks for your patience."

God forbid someone might finally come up with some information, Dillon thought. He locked his desk and took the elevator to the main floor. On a whim, he walked down the long hall to the Tech Lab and pushed the intercom button. He waited for thirty seconds and pushed it again. At no surprise, no one answered. Everyone had probably been home for a couple of hours, and Dillon figured that would be the best place for him to go.

He climbed in his car and drove home. He debated stopping at The Grape Vine, a local wine store, but then an image of Cullen Gibbs asleep at the table in the Cabra Club flashed in his mind, and he continued home. He pulled into his parking place, climbed out of the car, and closed the front gates. As soon as he opened the door, Lucifer bounded out the door, circled twice, and assumed the position next to the driver's door.

Dillon recalled his brief conversation the night before with the always unpleasant Deitora next door. He decided he'd leave things until tomorrow to clean up. He stepped inside the house, turned off the alarm, and then checked the back door. Everything appeared to be in order.

He unlocked the back door, picked up the jeans and shirt he'd tossed onto the patio the other day, and carried them over to the trash bin. Then stepped back inside and locked the door. He let Lucifer back in, tossed him a biscuit, and dished up a bowl of ice cream for himself. He settled in on the couch in front of the TV and woke up just after 11:00. He double-checked the doors, made his way upstairs, and crawled into bed next to Lucifer.

TWENTY-THREE

Lucifer woke Dillon the following morning by licking his face. It was the most action Dillon'd had in bed in at least a month. He let Lucifer out the front door then headed into the shower. He made a light breakfast consisting of two pieces of toast with close to a half-jar of blackberry jam and was at his desk before anyone else in Special Branch.

The first thing he did was leave a message for Emily. "Good morning, Emily, Dillon here. Call me as soon as you have results from the ballistic test. Keeping my fingers crossed."

He went back over Kevin Rafferty's file, specifically what Kevin had been involved in leading up to his murder. Once again, for the umpteenth time, absolutely nothing stood out. As a matter of fact, for the seventy-two hours prior to taking Dillon out to Skerries, Rafferty had been slogging through desk work and waiting to be called to testify in an ongoing trial. He never did get the call, and that was why he was available to take Suel's place on the Hickey case out in Skerries.

Dillon placed a call to Declan Reilly out in Skerries and ended up leaving a message. "Hi, Declan. Jack Dillon with Special Branch. Just checking to see if you've come up with anything else on the Hickey murder. We've contacted the American Embassy, and they're reaching out to the family. At this stage, nothing has proven notable as far as moving the case forward. Please give me a call at your convenience. Thank you."

He stepped outside the building and purchased a large coffee from the pizza truck. Three people were in the process of arranging the pizzas they'd be baking just before the noon hour. One was the woman with the tattooed eyebrows. She smiled as Dillon approached. "Good morning, how are you today?" she said.

Dillon guessed her accent as Spanish or possibly Italian. "Fine, thank you. I'd like a large coffee, black, please. No cream or sugar."

She nodded, filled a large paper cup, placed a plastic lid on top, and set it on the counter for Dillon.

"What do I owe you?"

"There is no charge for you. I've had so much fun telling my daughters and girlfriends that you asked if I knew about eyebrow tattoos. And you the Gardai. We laughed and laughed."

"Glad I was able to brighten your day. Thank you for the coffee," Dillon said and made his way back into the building. On a whim, he headed down the long hall to the tech lab.

Emily answered on the intercom just a few seconds after he pushed the button. "Yes."

"Hi Emily, Jack Dillon."

"Oh, I just hung up after leaving you a message. You have a moment?"

"I do," he said, and the door buzzed open.

Emily was sipping a coffee, or maybe it was a tea, at the back counter. "Good morning. Is this about the headlines?"

"The headlines?"

"You haven't seen this morning's Irish Independent or the Irish Times?"

"No, why? What have they got?"

"Here," she said and clicked a couple of keys on the keyboard. The front page of both papers suddenly appeared. In the lower right-hand corner of both papers was an article on Kevin Rafferty's murder. The respective headlines read, 'Special Branch officer murder on M1' and 'Dublin Gardai shot driving.'

"Oh great," Dillon said and shook his head. "They happen to say who did it?"

"Do they know?" Emily asked.

"Sorry, bad joke. What did you find out?"

Emily took a sip from her paper cup and said, "Hey, ignore my message when you get upstairs. I mentioned we got a big fat zero with facial recognition. Not that I don't think the individual isn't in one of the databases we ran, but with the glasses, the bandages, the wig, probably something else we aren't even aware of, we've got nothing to compare it to."

"And the bullet?"

"That's a little more interesting."

"Oh?"

"We ran the round from Kevin Rafferty and came up with nothing, other than the round is a .22 caliber, my guess would be a .22 LR suppressed semi-automatic, but there's no way to be sure of that without the actual weapon."

"That sounds more like a professional hit."

"That's what I suggested in my message but again, without the actual weapon...."

"Anything like a match to an earlier shooting?"

"That's where this becomes interesting. There was no match when we ran ballistics on the round from Kevin Rafferty, but—"

"Oh, God, I knew it. Another dead end."

"If you'd hold on and let me finish, please. No match when we ran ballistics on Kevin Rafferty. But, once we finished, the next round we ran was from Dennis Hickey, the American murdered in Skerries. Guess what?"

"Don't tell me they matched," Dillon said.

"Yep, the same weapon," Emily said as she ran her fingers on the keyboard and brought images of both rounds up on the screen. "What would that be, something like fifteen or sixteen hours apart? One shooting out in Skerries and the other on the M1."

Dillon nodded and said, "Rafferty was coming from Skerries. He was part of our initial investigation into that murder. He was only there for an hour, maybe two, until Suel joined us."

"There has to be a connection in some way. I'd love it if you could get the weapon."

"Yeah, me too. Are you sure about this?"

"I ran them three times, just to be absolutely sure, Dillon. There's no doubt. They were definitely fired from the same weapon."

"Umm, thanks, Emily. Finally, some progress. I gotta run," Dillon said.

"One more thing, we went through his phone and—"

"Please tell me you found something."

"Sorry to say, nothing really. He sent one text message just after landing. He signed it 'Dad' and sent it to a contact named Maggie. I'm guessing his daughter. The text just said he'd landed safely, and he'd be home in four days."

Dillon shook his head. "Humph, it figures. Okay, thanks," he said and hurried toward the door.

"Dillon, your coffee," Emily called, picking up his cup and meeting him halfway.

"Thanks," he said and hurried out of the lab.

He took the elevator up to Special Branch. Spilled coffee on his jeans as he punched in the code on the keypad next to the door and hurried toward his desk.

Two guys were standing at Suel's desk, all three of them laughing at something.

"Dillon, there's a loo on every floor," Suel said and nodded at the fresh coffee stain running down the leg of his jeans. The two other men laughed.

"Ballistics found a match on the round from Rafferty," Dillon said.

"Let's tell McCabe, now," Suel said and hurried out of his chair. They made a B-line to McCabe's office. Dillon knocked on the doorframe and they entered.

McCabe was just hanging up his desk phone and looked at them. "Problem? Is this about the newspaper articles?"

Dillon shook his head. "No, sir, nothing about the articles. But we may have the beginning of a break. Or at least something, finally. I was just down in tech. Turns out there's a match to the round that killed Kevin Rafferty—"

"A match?"

"Yes, sir, it matches the round recovered from Dennis Hickey. The American murdered in Skerries the night before."

"What? Rafferty and Hickey? That doesn't make sense. Are you sure?"

"Emily said she ran them three times just to be sure. She thinks a .22 LR suppressed semi-automatic was probably the weapon, but without the actual weapon, that's just an educated guess. But she was absolutely positive that the two rounds match."

"Dillon, I want you on the phone to any and all sources you have in the US. See what you can find on this Hickey gentleman. Suel, go through Rafferty's background. Did he ever travel to the US? Is there a connection between him and Hickey? Could they have simply run into one another in Skerries, or the airport, or somewhere?"

Dillon and Suel hurried out of McCabe's office. "What do you think?" Suel asked.

"It's sketchy, tenuous, and the only thing we've come up with so far," Dillon said.

Dillon phoned Eric Bergman at the US Embassy and left a message. "Eric, it's Jack Dillon. Would you please give me a call? We may have a possible connection between Dennis Hickey, the US citizen murdered in Skerries, and Kevin Rafferty, the Special Branch officer murdered the following day on the M1. Give me a call as soon as you can."

Dillon hung up and started going through his Rolodex, searching for Chicago contacts.

TWENTY-FOUR

Dillon made three calls to contacts in Chicago. One was retired and had moved to Florida three years ago. He apologized for not being able to help and offered to put Dillon up for a weekend if he wanted to fly down to Florida. Dillon thanked him for the invitation and got off the line. Another number had been disconnected, and no further information was available. The third call was to a pal in the Marshals' Service who'd been transferred from Chicago to Seattle four years earlier. He was aware of Hickey's murder but only because he'd caught a thirty-second blurb on a national news site. He didn't offer to connect Dillon with anyone back in Chicago, and Dillon was off the line in a couple of minutes.

He began to feel the dead ends returning to the case when his desk phone rang. "Jack Dillon," was how he answered.

"Hi, Jack, Eric Bergman, returning your call. Sorry it took a while. We're up to our proverbials. We've got two senators arriving tomorrow, so everything here is crazy. What's up?"

"Thanks for returning my call, Eric. I'm working two cases, Kevin Rafferty, the officer shot on the M1, and Dennis Hickey, the American shot in Skerries."

"Didn't you tell me Rafferty had been working with you that morning on Hickey's murder?"

"Yeah, that's correct."

"Are you aware of any connection between the two?" Bergman asked.

"Strange connection," Dillon said and went on to fill Bergman in on the matching rounds. "What I was hoping is you could give me some contact information or give mine to whatever individuals you may have spoken with back in the States. I'm thinking there has to be some connection between Hickey and Rafferty, but I'll be damned if we can find it."

"I'd be breaking policy if I gave out their information, but I'd be happy to pass yours on. I've mainly dealt with a daughter, Margaret. She goes by Maggie O'Hara now, lives in the Chicago area. Interestingly, her mother, Maureen, was actually an Irish citizen from Sligo. She married Dennis Hickey back in 1989 and moved to the US. She died of cancer a couple of months back, and the husband, Dennis, traveled over here to have her ashes buried out in the family plot in Sligo."

"How was she taking it, the daughter?"

"How do you think? Not well. She and her siblings are going to come over at some point and have both of them buried out in Sligo. At least that's the plan at this stage."

"She didn't happen to mention anything about Kevin Rafferty, did she?"

"No, and to be honest, I've had three conversations with her and never mentioned his murder. She's got more than enough to deal with right now. The mother dying on Valentine's day and now her father being murdered."

"Yeah, yeah, I know. I'm sorry, we just can't seem to get a leg to stand on in our investigation. Now this, both men shot with the same weapon. There has to be something there, but I'll be damned if we've found it yet."

"I wish I could help you out, Jack. But other than marrying the woman here thirty some years ago, Dennis Hickey hadn't returned to Ireland until just a few days ago."

"The wife didn't have family here?"

"None to speak of. Parents were killed in a car accident, and she went into an orphanage at the age of eight, stayed there for ten years, got out at age eighteen, and went to Dublin. She worked for Dublin parks for four years, met and married Hickey, and went to the States to live happily ever after."

"The daughter tell you what he did in the States?"

"Yeah, he worked for public broadcasting, behind the scenes, not a broadcaster or anything. They lived in a Chicago suburb up on the north side called Wilmette."

"I've been there a couple of times, nice area."

"The daughter Maggie and her family still live there. She seemed a very nice lady. I'll pass your name on. Is it all right if I give her your cellphone number?"

"Yeah, if you would, please, along with my email address. Just trying to figure out what in the hell the connection was between the two of them, Rafferty and Hickey. There has to be something, but I'll be damned if I can find it."

"I'll send your information off to her this morning. Let me know if I can do anything else. Sorry I can't pass on her phone number to you."

"Don't worry about it, Eric. I get it. You're just doing your job."

"Thanks, Jack. Hope you hear from her," Bergman said and disconnected.

Dillon began dialing another number. Someone stepped out of McCabe's office holding a stack of papers. He pulled a sheet from the top of the stack, nodded at Dillon as he placed it on the desk, and headed over to the next desk. Dillon hung up the phone and looked at the paper. The wake for Kevin Rafferty was scheduled for tonight in the Rafferty home. The funeral was tomorrow morning, 10:00, at St. Mary's Catholic Pro Cathedral.

Dillon immediately got a lump in his throat and glanced around the office. He wasn't the only one, and it was suddenly very quiet. His desk phone rang a few minutes later, "Jack Dillon."

"Hiya, Dillon. Declan Reilly, returning your call. Sorry I'm just getting back to you now. We've been running ever since the events of the other night."

"Not a problem, Declan. I completely understand. Have you learned anything?"

"Oh, if only. Unfortunately, no, nothing. I've talked to the staff at The Stoop, but they couldn't tell me anything. Your man was a pleasant customer during the hour he was in there. He paid with a credit card, added a tip. He dined alone. The only person he spoke to was the server, and that was just ordering dinner. Have you learned anything?"

Dillon gave him an update on the facial recognition that didn't work and then told him about the ballistics match.

"That has to be a mistake. Did you tell them to run it again?"

"They ran it three times, Declan. It came up a match every damn time. We've got everyone trying to find out what the connection is between the two, Hickey and Rafferty, and we're coming up empty. The last time Hickey was in Ireland was back in 1989 when he married an Irish woman. They lived in the US. Her folks had been killed in a car accident, and she didn't have any family here. The only reason he was here was to bury her ashes out in Sligo, some family cemetery or a plot."

"Was Rafferty maybe originally from Sligo?" Reilly asked.

"No, Dublin born and raised, Rathmines," Dillon said. "There has to be something, but I'll be damned if we've found it yet." They chatted for a few more minutes but never came up with anything.

Dillon reviewed Kevin Rafferty's file yet again. At this stage, he'd gone through it so many times he was repeating lines before he even read them.

"You going tonight?" Suel asked, pulling Dillon from his focus on the Rafferty file.

"What?"

"The Rafferty wake. Are you going tonight?"

Dillon nodded. "Yeah, I'll be there. I plan on heading home first, get cleaned up, change into something a little more presentable. Are you bringing anything?"

"Bringing anything?"

"Yeah, flowers, a bottle, maybe some food."

Suel shook his head. "No, she'll have it well in hand, and she's sisters to help her through. Not looking forward to it. God, I wish we had something on this."

"You and me both, I've been through Kevin's file so many times I've got it memorized."

"You call over to the States?"

"Yeah, no luck, no contacts in Chicago. Bergman at the Embassy is going to pass my contact information on to Hickey's daughter, but who knows if she'll call. I just feel like we're missing something, and whatever it is, is right out there in front of us."

"I'm about ready to subscribe to the theory that it was some knacker who wanted to see what it was like to kill someone, so he shot Hickey. He's watching the next day, sees you and Kevin, follows Kevin, and shoots him on the M1."

"Yeah, okay, except why rent a car wearing a disguise? Why rent a car at all? Clearly, he shot Hickey and was simply able to walk away."

"Maybe to make us think he's not from here?"

Dillon shook his head. "If he hadn't rented that car, we wouldn't have the little we know about the bastard, which is next to f'ing nothing. Rafferty in Skerries the following morning was a split-second decision based on you being unavailable and Rafferty not having to testify in that trial. He left shortly after you arrived, and someone followed him and killed him. Who? Why? God, I can't for the life of me figure it out."

"Unfortunately, you're not alone," Suel said.

TWENTY-FIVE

Dillon took a long, hot shower. He let the water run over him for a good twenty minutes. It didn't really help. He never came up with anything new. He dressed in a white shirt and a dark suit. He thought about having a small whiskey, just to fortify before leaving, and decided that might be one of the more stupid things he could do.

The Rafferty home was on the south side of Dublin in an area called Rathmines. The house was located on a street named Castlewood Park. It took Dillon twenty minutes to drive through the city center and make his way into Rathmines. He ended up parking two blocks away and walking toward the house. Cars were parked bumper to bumper on both sides of the street for blocks. It was growing dark, and not every house had address numbers on the front. Not that it mattered, Dillon spotted the Rafferty place from a block away. There were easily fifty or sixty people standing in the front garden.

As he approached, someone from across the street called and said, "A word, sir?"

Dillon glanced over at a man holding what looked like a recorder and a guy with a film camera standing just a few feet behind. He was tempted to shout something along the lines of 'A little God damned respect' but bit his tongue, shook his head, and kept walking.

The homes were all attached, two-story, red-brick structures with slate roofs. Dillon guessed they were probably built in the very early 1900s. Rafferty's unit looked about half the size of Dillon's, and instead of the three-foot wall Dillon had across his front, there was a black wrought iron fence, no doubt original to the place.

The front garden was covered in gravel with four flowerpots positioned up against the house, just below a large window. A pile of flower bouquets, cards, and lit candles were on the sidewalk, and Dillon could have kicked himself for not thinking ahead and getting some flowers.

There were quite a few uniformed individuals, and a number of heads turned as he approached. He got a nod from more than a few people he recognized, even though he couldn't recall their names. What appeared to be a line of people led out the front door and onto the side-walk. Dillon sidestepped the line and moved onto the gravel area. Three red trash bins were at the far side of the garden and next to them, a child's bicycle and a green tractor with push pedals. He reminded himself that Kate was the wife and James and Michael were the names of the Rafferty boys'.

"Dillon," a familiar voice called. He glanced over toward a group of five men. Suel gave a quick wave, and Dillon hurried over.

"I think you lads know the infamous Marshal Dillon," Suel said, and everyone nodded.

"You been here long?" Dillon asked.

"Only fifteen minutes. No room inside, God bless," Suel said.

"Kate's got her sisters around her. She seems to be holding up pretty well, all things considered," one of the men said.

They chatted for thirty or forty minutes. A couple of men left, only to be replaced by others. After maybe another hour, the line gradually shortened. Dillon excused himself, stepped into the house, and worked his way through the hallway and into the sitting room.

The coffin was closed and rested at the far end of the room. A woman he presumed was Kate was surrounded by three women, sisters he figured, based on the similar appearance. They were all standing in front of the fireplace. An older couple Dillon presumed were her parents stood off to the side. Another couple, maybe in their mid-sixties, sat in two chairs next to Kate's parents. The woman was shaking and constantly dabbing her eyes with a tissue. The man was holding her hand. *No doubt Kevin Rafferty's folks*, Dillon thought. He swallowed a few times in an effort to get rid of the lump in his throat, but it didn't work.

Eventually, Kate thanked the couple in front of Dillon for coming and turned to face him.

"Kate, my name is Jack Dillon. I worked with Kevin in Special Branch."

Her eyes seemed to brighten. "Oh, yes. You're the American. Kevin spoke of you often. He always seemed to have a funny story. You were with him that morning, weren't you?"

Dillon nodded. "Yes, last minute, he came along and…" Dillon suddenly teared up and squeaked out the words, "I'm so sorry, Kate."

Kate wrapped her arms around Dillon and hung on for a long moment then leaned back, gave him a kiss on the cheek, and looked at him. "Thank you for coming," she said. She turned to the couple behind Dillon. He nodded at the sisters and then the parents standing next to them. He stepped to the side and caught the eye of Kevin's father.

"You're the American?" the man asked, letting go of his wife's hand and standing.

"Yes, I'm Jack Dillon. I worked with—"

"I know. You worked with Kevin. You were at the airport three or four years back. We want you to find whoever did this and kill the bastard. I'm going to say a prayer for you every night until you get him, and I know you will." With that, he sat down, leaned over, and whispered into his wife's ear.

She looked up at Dillon, nodded, and made the sign of the cross.

Dillon wasn't sure what to do, so he simply nodded and made his way out of the house.

He caught Suel's eye as he stepped out into the front garden. Suel gave a nod but didn't call him over. Dillon gave a slight nod back, walked out of the front garden and back to his car.

TWENTY-SIX

Following a fitful night's sleep, Dillon was up an hour before the alarm went off. It was still dark outside. He let Lucifer sleep, slipped into sweatpants and a Dublin jersey, and headed downstairs. He got the coffee going and turned on his computer. He checked the YouTube Chanel for news updates and sipped coffee for forty-five minutes. Lucifer was still asleep when he stepped out of the shower. He climbed into his bathrobe, went back downstairs, and proceeded to make breakfast.

The sausages frying in the pan apparently were enough to wake Lucifer. Dillon let him outside and tossed him a biscuit. He ate his breakfast, cut up half a sausage, placed it in Lucifer's food dish, and let him back in the house. Lucifer entered the house, sniffed, and hurried into the kitchen.

Dillon closed and locked the front door, and in the three seconds it took to enter the kitchen, Lucifer had already finished the sausage. He gave a longing look at Dillon.

"Sorry, buddy, that's all that was left, and you were lucky to get that much."

He took his time dressing in the same shirt and suit he'd worn the night before. He let Lucifer out once more and then climbed in the car and drove to St. Mary's Catholic Pro Cathedral in the city center.

The Cathedral was on Marlborough Street, just a block off O'Connell Street. Dillon parked three blocks away in a parking ramp and walked toward the Cathedral. It was more than an hour before the service was scheduled, and groups of men and women in An Garda Síochána dress uniforms were on the streets headed toward the cathedral. The front of the Cathedral was surrounded by a seven or eight-foot high wrought-iron fence. A set of double gates were open, leading up four steps to the massive doors into the Cathedral. The uniformed officers would form an honor guard positioned on either side of Marlborough Street. They'd stand at attention and present arms as the hearse with Kevin Rafferty's body and the vehicles with his family passed by.

Suel and a number of Special Branch officers were all in uniform next to the wrought-iron gates leading into the main entrance. D.C.I. McCabe was there chatting. He glanced over as Dillon approached and smiled. "Dillon, good to see you. You'll stand with us to honor Rafferty when he arrives?"

"As you can see, I'm not in uniform, sir."

"And you don't need to be. I know it would mean a lot to the family and everyone out here if you were with us."

"All right, thank you. I'll join you."

"Do me the honor of standing next to me."

"Thank you, sir."

They formed up forty minutes before the funeral was to begin. Looking at the ranks on either side of the street, Dillon guessed there had to be at least six hundred uniformed officers. At exactly thirty minutes before, everyone was called to attention. Approximately five minutes later, a hearse, led by six uniformed officers on motorcycles, came around the corner.

"Present arms," D.C.I. McCabe shouted, and the ranks saluted as the cars slowly drove past, making their way down the street to the cathedral. The hearse stopped directly in front of the open gates. Two men in black suits and starched shirts hurried out of the hearse and opened the rear doors. The doors on the vehicle behind the hearse opened, and six men hurried out and lined up just to the rear of the hearse. The other vehicles came to a stop, and family members, including Kate with her two sons, her parents, and Kevin's parents, climbed out and made their way toward the hearse.

Once everyone was assembled, one of the men gave a nod, and the coffin was slowly pulled out of the back of the hearse. The pallbearers took hold of the handles and then, on command, hoisted the coffin up onto their shoulders. A bagpiper suddenly began to play as they slowly walked through the open gates, up the four steps, and into the Cathedral. A lump suddenly grew in Dillon's throat.

Once the family was in the church, D.C.I. McCabe shouted, "Order arms." Everyone lowered their salute and then turned toward the Cathedral. They marched in ranks into the cathedral. Dillon followed McCabe into the church. He took a seat next to McCabe and just behind the family.

The service, complete with a choir and including the bishop speaking from the pulpit, went on for the better part of ninety minutes. The pallbearers and family led the way out of the church, followed by the uniformed officers. Dillon dutifully followed McCabe, and everyone returned to their positions along both sides of the street. McCabe ordered "Present arms," as the hearse followed by family vehicles slowly drove back up the street and disappeared around the corner.

After giving the order arms command, McCabe turned to Dillon and said, "The burial is over in Glasnevin cemetery."

"Yes, I was planning to go," Dillon said. "Thank you for including me, sir. It was an honor. I'd better get my car. It's over in a parking ramp."

McCabe nodded and said, "I'll see you in Glasnevin."

Dillon hurried to his car and pulled out of the ramp. As it turned out, he really didn't need to hurry. There was a line of cars a block long slowly entering the cemetery. Rather than wait in the line, Dillon drove past, parked on the street like so many others were doing, and walked into the cemetery through a side gate. A crowd was visible on a distant rise. Dillon and others walked past countless graves and headed toward the crowd. No sooner had he arrived than a bagpiper began playing for a few minutes. Once he finished, the priests, there were three of them, began praying and sprinkling holy water on the coffin and gravesite. Dillon was far enough away that he was unable to hear what they were saying.

He watched as Kevin Rafferty's coffin was slowly lowered into the ground. Family members, including Rafferty's two little boys, stepped next to the gravesite and tossed a handful of dirt into the grave. Hugs and kisses were exchanged, and the bagpiper began playing as he walked away from the crowd toward a far corner of the cemetery. The crowd slowly began to disperse.

Over the course of the next twenty minutes, Dillon slowly worked his way up toward the actual gravesite, nodding, smiling, and saying "Hello" to a number of people along the way. He waited until there were just a couple of folks remaining, not staring at the grave but involved in casual conversations. Off to the side, a crew of three men with shovels waited for everyone to leave.

Dillon stepped over to the grave, shook his head, and said, "I give you my word. I will get whoever did this, Kevin." He silently said a short prayer, made the sign of the cross, and headed back toward the side gate. Along the way, he ran into the bagpiper.

"How you doing?" the piper asked.

"Good, under the circumstances," Dillon replied.

"You knew your man?"

"Yeah, in fact, we were together out in Skerries that morning."

"Mmm-mmm, yeah, heard about you. The American. My condolences. I didn't know your man, but from everything I've heard, he was a very nice lad."

"Yeah, he was. Very nice. Can I ask you something?"

"You mean like what do I wear under me kilt?"

Dillon smiled at that. "No, not that. But at the end, you walked away as you were playing. Why didn't you stay there? It was a big crowd. Everyone seemed to like your music."

"Oh, yeah, but the tradition is that I confuse the Devil, and he follows the music. Gives the deceased the chance to get to heaven and not have to deal with the Devil in his way."

Dillon smiled at that. "Hey, you got a card? I may need you at some point."

"Yeah, sure," he said, reaching into his sporran, the purse hanging from his waist. He pulled out a business card.

Dillon looked at the card. The name Daniel Sexton with a phone number and an email address. "Thanks, Dan. I'll give you a call sometime."

"Good, I'm sorry, I didn't catch your name."

"Dillon, Jack Dillon."

"Pleasure to meet you, Mr. Dillon. I'm parked on the far side next to the Gravediggers pub. I look forward to your call," he said and picked up his pace. Dillon exited through the side gate, drove home, changed, and headed to Special Branch.

TWENTY-SEVEN

Suel was seated at his desk, still wearing his dress uniform. At the moment, he was on the phone, as were a number of other people. Dillon gave a wave as he passed by. He gathered the plate and the tea mugs left on his desk, carried them into the break room, and set them in the sink.

He filled his coffee mug from the existing pot, shuddered after taking a sip, and went back to his desk. He phoned Emily, Eric Bergman, and Declan Reilly just to check in and hope that they may have uncovered something, anything. No such luck. No one could come up with any correlation between Hickey and Rafferty except for the fact that they had apparently been shot, murdered, with the same gun.

Dillon had just finished talking with Declan Reilly and hung up his desk phone when his cell phone rang. He pulled the phone from his pocket and checked the screen. 'Unknown Number,' with the number displayed below. Someone was calling from the US.

He thought for a moment and then answered, "Jack Dillon's office."

"Hi, I'm trying to reach Jack Dillon with the US Marshals."

"You got him."

"Oh, Marshal, my name is Maggie O'Hara. Dennis Hickey is my father. I got your name from an Eric Bergman in the American Embassy."

"Oh, yes, Maggie. Thank you for calling. My condolences on your father."

"Yeah, thanks, it's going to take a while, a long while."

There was a long pause, and Dillon finally said, "I'm hoping you might be able to provide information on your father that would help our investigation."

"Information? Like what?"

"We've been grasping at straws over here. Your father had just arrived. He had dinner in a little restaurant and ate alone. The only person he spoke to was a waitress, but that was just ordering the meal. Are you aware of anyone he may have been in contact with over here?"

"No. I can't think of anyone. Other than meeting our mom in Ireland almost forty years ago, he never had any contact with anyone over there. They never traveled back, if that's your question. My mom was raised in an orphanage. She was never abused or anything that I know, but with her folks dying in a car crash, she didn't have happy memories growing up. Her mom and dad were killed when she was seven or eight. As far as we know, there was never any involvement with relatives."

"Well, that matches up with the information we have. But yet she wanted to be buried over here?"

"Yes, next to her parents. She always spoke very fondly of them. They were from Sligo County and had a little grocery in a village called Geevagh. My mom was in hospice care. She died of cancer last February. She told my dad she wanted to be buried with her parents. That's why he had traveled over. He was going to have her buried in that graveyard. I mean, have her ashes buried."

"And did your mom ever have any connection with anyone there? Maybe phone calls, or letters, or something?"

"Not really, at least until her last year. I know they had talked about her being buried there, and my dad contacted someone at the church in the village. It turns out that when her parents were killed, they had three cemetery plots, two for my mom's parents and I guess one for her."

"And your dad dealt with someone there?"

"Yeah, but I don't know who. My dad worked for public broadcasting, and he was always lining up interviews for the news people, so it wouldn't have been unusual for him to make a couple of phone calls and get to the right person. I could send you the information, I think. It might take a while to find it, but I'm in the process of going through his papers and things."

"Yeah, anything you could send me would help. I spoke to someone at the Embassy, and he said you were thinking of coming over here."

"Yes, along with my brother and sister. Actually, we've been thinking it would be nice if our parents were buried together. That said, we're still in the throes of dealing with all sorts of stuff, the house, insurance, medical bills. We haven't been able to make any plans yet."

"I understand. If you could send me the name of whoever your father dealt with at the church, that would help."

"Happy to do it. I'll just have to find it first."

"I understand. Feel free to call me anytime, Maggie. If I can help you in any way, please let me know. Oh, I should mention, we have your mother's ashes. They are safe and in the wooden cremation urn with her name."

"Oh, thank you, that was going to be my next question. If you wouldn't mind keeping us up to date on your investigation, that would be much appreciated."

"Well, I can tell you that, thus far, we don't have much. It appears at this stage to be a random incident. But this isn't like the States. A random shooting is pretty much unheard of over here."

"I just hope you find whoever is responsible for this and arrest them."

"I'm working on it. Believe me, we all are."

"Let me see if I can find the name of whoever Dad dealt with at the church, and I'll send it to you."

"That would be great, Maggie. Thank you for the phone call. Don't hesitate to call me at any time. You're in Chicago, right?"

"Yes."

"We're six hours ahead of you, time-wise, so if you call and I don't answer, it may just be the time difference."

"Yeah, not a problem."

"Thanks again, Maggie. God bless your parents. I hope to meet you in person someday."

"Me too, thank you," she said and disconnected.

Dillon added her name and number to the contacts on his phone. He went online and looked up the village of Geevagh out in the west of Ireland in Sligo county. It was a small rural area in the southeast corner of the county. The name Geevagh meant 'windy place'. *In the back of beyond*, Dillon thought, using an Irish phrase.

TWENTY-EIGHT

Dillon worked at his desk going over the same files for the umpteenth time and still didn't come up with anything new.

"I'm thinking about stopping for a pint with a few of the team. You up for joining us?" Suel asked.

Dillon glanced up with a surprised look on his face. "Oh, sorry, I didn't hear you coming over. Umm, a pint? You know, if you don't mind, I think I'll take a pass. I've got some things to take care of at home, and I'd better stay focused on them," Dillon lied.

"You could always bring her along," Suel said.

"No, really, there's no woman involved, unfortunately," Dillon said. "I've just got a lot to take care of on the home front."

"Okay, well, enjoy yourself. You change your mind, we'll be at the Nancy Hands. I'll see you in the morning," Suel said and headed out the door.

For a long minute Dillon reconsidered going before deciding against it. He knew he simply wasn't in the mood. He'd sit and nurse one pint for the entire night, not saying a word and basically turning into a wet blanket. In short order, he'd place a damper over everyone's evening. No, it was just a better idea to head home.

He turned off his computer, locked up his desk, and peeked into D.C.I. McCabe's office.

"Excuse me, sir," Dillon said.

"Yes, Dillon. Everything all right?"

"Yes, sir, just wanted to thank you for involving me in things this morning. Very much appreciated."

"Don't kid yourself, Dillon. You earned it, and it was an honor to have you there. You've no idea what that meant to the Rafferty family."

"Thank you, sir, again much appreciated."

"My pleasure, Dillon. Thank you for being there. Now, may I suggest you go home and attempt to relax. It's been a crazy week thus far, with no end in sight. I'll see you back here bright and early tomorrow morning."

"Yes, sir," Dillon replied and headed out the door. He climbed in his car and drove home. Tonight, he decided, he would stop at The Grape Vine, his local wine store. He was able to park almost right in front and hurried out of his car and into the store.

It took a couple of minutes, reading the labels and various two or three-sentence reviews taped on the wine rack above each bottle. Just like always, he decided on a Pinot Noir and a Sauvignon Blanc. From the wine store, he drove up to the EuroSpar just two blocks from his house. He entered the store and made a b-line for the meat counter.

Fortunately, the guy ahead of Dillon was handed his package just as Dillon stepped behind him.

"Can I help you, sir?" the butcher asked. He was dressed in a knee-length white coat and a white hat. The name Patrick was embroidered over his left breast.

"Yeah, I just need a bone for my dog. You have any back there?"

"Hold on just a moment. I believe we do," he said and hurried toward the chopping blocks in the rear of the section. He was back a moment later with three bones.

"These beef rib bones will be just the thing for him," he said. He pulled a length of white paper from the rack, wrapped the bones, and handed them to Dillon.

"What do I owe you?" Dillon asked.

"Nothing, glad you can use them."

"Thank you. That's really kind of you, Patrick. I'll mention your name to my dog," Dillon said. "He'll be your friend for life."

"God knows I can use it," Patrick replied. "Enjoy your evening, sir."

"I intend to." Dillon gave a wave, and headed back to his car.

He pulled into his parking place just in front of the stoop leading to the front door. His neighbor Deitora was out in her front garden, cutting two yellow roses from a plant. He climbed out, grabbing the bag with the bottles of wine and the package of rib bones. He pressed the fob to lock the car and closed the double gates behind the car. He hoped to make it into the house without having to speak with Deitora. Luck was not with him on that front.

"Oh, Dillon, good evening. I must say, it's a much more pleasant evening after your friend stopped by to pick up."

"Friend?"

"Yes, she wanted to surprise you. I wasn't sure what she was up to, and after she was parked in front for fifteen minutes studying your house, I decided to ask what, exactly, she was up to. That's when she told me she had stopped by to pick up after your little friend. She did a wonderful job and so quick about it."

Dillon looked around. Sure enough, all the piles Lucifer had left were gone. There had been at least a week's worth. Even the area where whoever had stepped in a pile the other night had been cleaned up. "Did she happen to tell you her name? I mentioned it to a pair of sisters, and I just want to make sure I thank the right one," Dillon lied.

"No, unfortunately, she didn't tell me her name. She bustled about with a white trash bag and a little shovel. It couldn't have taken more than five minutes at the most. You might want to keep that in mind or, even better, simply clean up after your dog when he makes a deposit. It's part of being a responsible adult and dog owner."

"I'll be sure to remember that. Can you describe her? What did she look like?"

Deitora shook her head. "One would think you'd be able to remember after asking them to clean up after your dog. I knew I should have had a talk with her and set her straight. I'm sure she has better things to do with her time than pick up after your dog. Let me simply say she had a lovely figure, short blonde hair, and obviously quite a bit of patience."

'None of your attributes,' Dillon thought. "You have a nice evening, Deitora," he said and hurried into the house. Lucifer met him at the door and was about to hurry outside when he apparently smelled the rib bones wrapped in the butcher's paper.

"Go on outside," Dillon said and gave him a little push. He leapt off the stoop, circled twice next to the driver's door, and squatted.

"Oh, no, not again," Deitora said. Dillon quickly closed the front door and went into the kitchen.

TWENTY-NINE

Dillon set the bottles of wine on the kitchen counter and unwrapped the package of rib bones. He set a bone in Lucifer's food dish, rewrapped the package, and placed it in the refrigerator. He debated opening one of the wine bottles and decided to place them both in the cabinet.

He opened the front door and glanced over at Deitora's. She was nowhere to be seen. "Lucifer, come on, boy. Come on in, Lucifer," Dillon called.

Lucifer wandered back into the house, and Dillon gave him a good head scratch. "Good job, boy, good job. I should put you in charge of dealing with mean old Deitora from now on."

Lucifer followed him into the kitchen and then hurried over to his food dish. He snatched the rib bone from the food dish and dashed out of the kitchen so he wouldn't have to share it with Dillon.

Dillon set about making dinner. A fried pork chop, boiled potato, and some red peppers fried in a small dose of olive oil. While he stood at the stove, he thought about Deitora's description of the woman with the short blonde hair. Try as he might, he couldn't come up with anyone who matched that description. From there, he jumped to the image of the guy renting the car from Enterprise, but he was a guy, so that didn't count.

There was one woman he knew who maybe fit the description. He turned on his phone and got her name on his contact list. There it was, Anne Mulroney. He debated calling her. She'd seemed pretty adamant two years ago when she told him in no uncertain terms that she didn't wish to see him and to please not contact her. As much as it pained him, he needed a better description from Deitora. That sounded like the world's most unpleasant task, asking Deitora for assistance.

In the end, he decided it might be better to simply have a glass of wine. He reached into the cabinet, and since he was going to have pork for dinner, he took out the bottle of Pinot Noir and poured a glass.

He let the wine sit on the kitchen counter while the pork and peppers finished cooking. He dished everything onto his plate, added a slice of butter on the potatoes, and settled in at the table. After the first sip of wine, he knew he'd made the right choice. After the second glass, he knew there was absolutely no point in talking to Deitora.

Lucifer was focused on the rib bone as Dillon settled onto the couch with his third glass of wine. He poured the remnants of the bottle into his glass halfway through the movie and then woke up, never knowing how the movie had ended. He let Lucifer out, and once he was back in, he checked the locks on the front and back door, set the alarm, and headed upstairs to bed.

Despite having a bottle of wine, he was up twice in the middle of the night looking out the front and back windows. He never saw anything that suggested someone was watching the house, let alone attempting to break in.

The alarm on his clock radio woke him at six the following morning. He shuffled into the bathroom, spent a good twenty minutes in the shower, then dressed and went down to the kitchen. Two cups of coffee and toast with blackberry jam served as breakfast.

After he let Lucifer out the front, he stepped into the back garden and looked around. There was nothing to suggest anyone had been in there last night. He went back in the house, locked the door, and then pulled the shade halfway down the double doors so that, in the odd event someone did enter the back garden, all they'd see in the house was the floor beneath the dining room table.

He let Lucifer in the house, set the alarm, and drove to work. Against his better judgment, he poured a mug of coffee from the break room and settled in at his desk. He opened his email account, and there was an email from Dennis Hickey's daughter, Maggie O'Hara. The email was short, just two sentences, thanking Dillon for his time on the phone and giving him the name and phone number of James Hart, the man her father had spoken to regarding the burial of Maureen Hickey's ashes.

Dillon glanced at the time. It wasn't even 8:00, and too early to phone Hart in Sligo. Suel arrived a half-hour later and regaled Dillon with a five-minute tale of the previous evening. Dillon smiled at the story and was glad he'd spent the night at home.

Just before 9:00, he placed a call to James Hart and left a message.

Hart returned the call not two minutes later.

Dillon answered his phone, "Jack Dillon."

"Yes, this is Jimmy Hart, returning the call you left for me."

"Oh, thanks for the quick response," Dillon said and then explained why he'd called, mentioning Hart's phone contact with Dennis Hickey and ending with the fact that Hickey had been killed.

"Oh, God bless. I was afraid of that. I heard an American with the name Dennis Hickey had been shot, and I was afraid it might be your man, but I didn't know who to call. His was the only phone number I had."

"Did he happen to mention anyone he knew in Ireland? Or any distant family?"

"No, nothing of that sort. His wife, Maureen Gowan was her maiden name. Her parents had three plots, actually. They were killed in a car accident back in the late seventies, and your man Hickey wanted to bury her next to the parents. Now, he also purchased a plot next to where the wife was going to be buried."

"Wait a minute, Dennis Hickey has a plot there in the cemetery?"

"He does, purchased it maybe two-and-a-half months ago. Have you been out here before?"

"I've been to Sligo Town but never up to Geevagh."

"Well, we're a small village, and the cemetery is actually located on the back property of the church, St. Joseph's Church."

"When you spoke to Hickey, did he mention anyone he had contact with in Ireland?"

"No, in fact, he made a point of saying that he didn't know anyone out this way."

"You aware of anyone the wife may have been related to?" Dillon asked.

"Maureen Gowan? That's a somewhat common surname in these parts. But I'm not aware of anyone. I can tell you there's never been a flower placed on that gravesite in all the years I've been here, and that's shaping up to be close to forty."

"Okay, well, I appreciate the update. Would you mind if I gave you the email address of Hickey's daughter? Her name is Maggie O'Hara. I spoke with her earlier, and she mentioned she and her two siblings were thinking of burying the parents together. If you could give her the official word that her father purchased that additional plot, it would help with what is obviously a stressful situation."

"Yeah, I'd be happy to do that. I might have to get the wife to help me. I'm not one for the computers. You can send your woman's address to my wife." He gave

Dillon the wife's email address. They chatted a moment or two longer and disconnected.

Dillon sent Maggie O'Hara's address to Jimmy Hart's wife with a brief explanation of his earlier phone call with Jimmy. He sent an email to Maggie O'Hara, telling her she would hear from Jimmy via his wife and that her father, Dennis Hickey, had purchased a plot next to Maureen's plot at St. Joseph's cemetery in the village of Geevagh, just in case she was unaware.

THIRTY

Dillon spent most of the afternoon reviewing files yet again, making phone calls, and still coming up empty-handed in both the Hickey and Rafferty cases. It was close to the end of the day when his desk phone rang.

"Jack Dillon."

"Dillon, it's Emily. Do you have a minute to come down here?"

"Is everything all right?"

"Yeah, it's just that I never liked that image of your man renting the car out at the airport."

"Enterprise Car Rental, the gray BMW?"

"Yeah, that's the one. Anyway, I've made some ad-justments, and some things have come up. Kind of strange. Would you mind coming down and taking a look?"

"I'd love to. This will be the first positive thing I've been involved in all day."

"You might be getting ahead of yourself with the word positive. But if you could come down, I'll—"

"On my way. See you in a minute or two," Dillon said. He turned off his computer and locked his desk drawers. Suel was just hanging up his phone and shaking his head as Dillon walked past. "Everything, okay?" Dillon asked.

"Yeah, I guess. I'm just off the line with Declan Reilly. Skerries is coming up empty-handed. Nothing on who might have pulled the trigger on Hickey and, by extension, Kevin Rafferty. There has to be something out there, somewhere. I just can't believe it."

Dillon nodded and said, "I just got a call from Emily down in Tech. She made some sort of adjustment on the image of your man renting the car out at the airport. She said something's come up."

"Don't tell me she's got a match," Suel said.

"Okay, I won't, because she doesn't. At least she didn't say she did. Come on down with me. Two heads are better than one."

"Mmm-mmm, I don't know about my head today. I haven't come up with a bleedin' thing all day. And it ain't for lack of trying."

"Same with me, just more dead ends. Not so much as the hint of a decent clue. Come on, it will probably take two or three minutes before we realize we're wasting our time, and we can get back to being disappointed up here."

"Not too far from the truth," Suel said and followed Dillon out of the office. They rode the elevator down to the ground floor and made their way to the Tech Lab. Dillon pressed the intercom button on the door, and Emily's voice answered a moment later. "Dillon?"

"Yeah, against my better judgment, I brought D.I. Suel with me."

The door buzzed open, and they stepped into the lab. Emily was at the back counter and gave a wave.

"So, what do you have?" Dillon asked as they approached.

"Hi, lads, thanks for coming down. Okay," she said and ran her fingers across the keyboard. "So, I just had some problems with the image you got from the car rental out at the airport."

"The guy with the blonde wig," Dillon said.

"Yes, the wig was part of it, but my bigger problem was the bandages on his nose and chin and one other thing. Let me deal with the bandages first. Dillon, I mentioned to you that I thought they were placed to hamper the facial recognition program," she said and clicked some more keys.

"Yeah, that's what you told me."

"So, this is what I did. First, I removed the bandage across the bridge of his nose," she said and clicked a final key. A new image came up with the bandage over the bridge of the nose removed. "Next, I removed the glasses," she said and brought up a new image without the heavy black glasses.

Dillon stared at the image for a long moment. Something was attempting to click in the back of his mind.

Emily watched Dillon for a second and said, "I removed the bandage on the chin." A new image appeared.

Dillon slowly nodded. "It looks like someone I know or knew, but she's a woman and not that heavy. Maybe a brother?"

"Maybe, but probably not. Check this out," Emily said and brought up another image of a thinner face with makeup and auburn hair.

Dillon took in a deep breath. "Amelia Maher," he said, staring at the image on the screen.

"Actually, yes and no. That image is identified by the Facial Recognition program as a woman named Sinead Lynch. She was serving a life sentence for the murder of Mickey Coonan back in 2014. She escaped from the Dochas Centre, the female prison in Mountjoy, back in 2016. After I removed the bandages, I thinned the cheeks, and her image came up immediately. I'm thinking she probably had padding stuffed in the sides of her mouth to make her look heavier and more like a guy."

"I know her as Amelia Maher," Dillon said. "She's wanted for the murder of the American couple mistaken for Punchy Sheehan down in Desertserges, County Cork, along with Keegan Donnelly, Tommy Thompson, Brennan O'Rourke, and Cullen Fink." He continued to stare at the screen.

"Busy lady," Suel said.

"Sinead Lynch is the name Facial Recognition landed on. That's an image taken when she went into the Dochas Centre in 2014. It came up as a ninety-four percent match. The fact that it isn't a hundred percent is probably due to my removing the bandages and filling in her nose and chin."

"Damn it," Dillon said. "Okay, can you forward that file to D.C.I. McCabe? I'd better get up there and give him an update."

"Yes, I'll send the information out to airport security and Dublin Ferry Port as well. Unfortunately, we're almost seventy-two hours behind. Any idea what her connection is to Dennis Hickey?" Emily asked.

"Yeah, virtually nothing. I think he was just at the wrong place at the wrong time. Jesus Christ," Dillon said and shook his head.

"What are you thinking?" Suel asked. They were on the elevator heading back up to Special Branch.

"What am I thinking? All of a sudden, I've gone from absolutely nothing to being flooded with all sorts of possibilities."

As they stepped off the elevator, a man moved to the side to let them pass. "How's it going, lads?" he asked, then watched as they didn't respond and made their way toward Special Branch. "Enjoy your day, ya gobshites," he said under his breath as he stepped onto the elevator.

Suel entered the security code on the keypad at the door to Special Branch. When the door buzzed, he held it open for Dillon.

Dillon stepped in and shook his head. "I'm going to go see McCabe and bring him up to date. You don't have to come. In fact, it might be a good idea if you let me take the heat on this one. God, I can't believe it. Amelia or Sinead Lynch, or whatever in the hell her name is. Christ, if there was ever a time I should have kept it in my pants, this is it. I am so screwed."

Suel chuckled and said, "No, Dillon, you were screwed, royally by the looks of it. But that's ancient history. I'm going in with you. I wouldn't want to miss this."

"Thanks, Paddy, I mean it. Shit," Dillon half-shouted. A couple of people at their desks turned and looked for a brief moment. Dillon made his way up to the front of the office. He took a deep breath and knocked on the doorframe of D.C.I. McCabe's office.

"Oh, Dillon, Suel, come in. Please tell me you finally have something positive."

"I'm not sure the word 'positive' is the term I'd use, sir. But we do have something."

"Has there been another shooting?" McCabe asked.

"No, sir. We've just come from the Tech Lab," Dillon said. "Emily has come up with a facial recognition of the man renting the BMW out at the airport."

"Oh, well, that sounds positive. So what's the problem?"

"It's a bit complicated," Dillon said as they sat down opposite McCabe. "Emily just emailed the Facial Recognition file to you. It turns out that the individual renting the car wasn't a man."

"What?" McCabe said.

"It gets much worse, sir."

THIRTY-ONE

illon filled McCabe in on what they'd learned. How the name Amelia Maher was apparently an alias for an Irish woman by the name of Sinead Lynch. "She is suspected in the murder of the American couple, Dennis and Maureen Sheehan, down in Desertserges, County Cork a few months back. Plus, the murders of Keegan Donnelly, Brennan O'Rourke, and Tommy Thompson up here in Dublin. Add to all that, the murder of Cullen Fink, who worked for the Linnehans, managing the strip club known as The Fantasy House."

"And she was involved with you, wasn't she?" McCabe asked.

Dillon exhaled, "Yes, sir, she was. That was me acting—"

"Stop," McCabe said, holding up his hand. "I want you off this case immediately. Not that I think you can't, or won't, do a good job. That's not the point here. On the contrary, I'm more worried about your safety, and I think the less you are involved in this investigation, the better it will be for all of us, including you. Therefore, you are off the case immediately."

"With all due respect, sir. I would like to continue working on this and—"

"Let me give you a simple answer, Dillon, and I appreciate your dedication, but no. You're too close to this individual, based on past history, and I think that you—"

"Hold on a minute," Dillon said.

Suel shot a quick look at Dillon.

"Excuse me," McCabe said and grew red-faced.

"Sorry, sir. I didn't mean to sound like I was arguing with you, but what you said just popped a thought into my head."

"Go on," McCabe said, in a tone that suggested Dillon should tread carefully.

"Kevin Rafferty's murder, out in Skerries. We're there viewing the scene of the crime. Dennis Hickey's body is on the way to the Dublin morgue. It's misting and threatening to rain. I'm wearing a raincoat and Rafferty is with me because D.I. Suel had an emergency dental appointment."

McCabe nodded slowly.

"Because of parking difficulties, Rafferty and I are driven to the Harbor Hotel by Declan Reilly, the officer in charge on the Skerries force. The rain begins to pick up. D.I. Suel arrives, and Rafferty departs because he has a physical exam that he's missed and has rescheduled twice already. As a matter of fact, you made a point of telling him he had better appear on time for the exam."

"Yes, and he's murdered on the M1 by some idiot."

"Here's my thought, sir. Because Reilly gave us a ride to the Harbor Hotel and then returned to the An Garda headquarters in Skerries, Rafferty had to walk back to the car. The rain had increased, and he borrowed my raincoat, a tan raincoat, and my hat. What if Sinead Lynch is waiting for me because I'm the only person who has had physical interaction with her and can link her to the six murders? What if she's back in Ireland to kill me? Rafferty steps out of the Harbor Hotel when it's raining. He's wearing my coat and hat. He's approximately my size. He hurries to the car, climbs in, and drives out of Skerries. We have a, what did Emily say, a ninety percent match on the Facial Recognition tape?"

"Actually a ninety-four percent match," Suel added.

"Yeah, okay, ninety-four percent match that she was the individual posing as a man to rent the vehicle that followed Rafferty onto the M1. She'd already killed six people and apparently gotten away with it. What's one more?"

"You think she killed Rafferty?"

"I do, sir, thinking Rafferty was actually me."

"But then why the American, Mr. Hickey?"

"Just a long shot, but what if the intent in killing Hickey was to get me out to Skerries to aid in the investigation. In the rare instance there's a major crime in Skerries, Dublin An Garda is involved. Certainly, a murder would automatically involve Special Branch."

"That's quite the long shot, Dillon."

"Yes, I agree, but if that was her intent, it worked. Plus, two more things. The other night, my dog growling in the middle of the night woke me. I glanced out the window, and the security light had flashed on in my back garden. I looked out the front window and saw a pair of taillights pulling around the corner. It was 3:00 in the morning. I stepped outside to investigate, and the gate to my back garden had been opened. It can only be opened from the inside. When I went out the next morning, someone had stepped in a pile left by my dog. All this sounds coincidental, except that my neighbor mentioned to me that a blonde woman was sitting in her car watching my house yesterday. The neighbor is nosey and goes outside to confront the woman. The woman told her that she was there to clean up after my dog, which she then proceeded to do."

"How very nice of her," McCabe said.

"Absolutely," Dillon replied. "The thing is, I never had a conversation with anyone about cleaning up my front garden, and I certainly don't know a woman who would do that without contacting me. In fact, I don't know a woman who would even think of doing that, ever."

McCabe nodded and said, "I would have to agree with you there. This seems so far-fetched, Dillon, and yet…. I don't know. I do know this, for the time being, I want you off this case until we get this aspect straightened out, for everyone's safety, not just yours."

"But, sir, this might be the perfect opportunity to lure this individual into a situation where we could catch her."

"Well, if that's the case, why don't we just set you up under a spotlight out in the middle of Phoenix Park? I'm sure that would allow us to get all manner of ne'er-do-wells off the Dublin streets. No, Dillon, thank you for the information. I intend to act sensibly. As of this moment, you are off the case. I would appreciate it if you'd write up a report before you leave for the evening, and we will take it from there. I believe you had been dabbling in the McGinn case prior to the Rafferty situation, is that correct?"

"Yes, sir, Sophie McGinn. The Trinity student assaulted in Temple Bar. I believe she is still in a coma."

"Focus on that, and we'll deal with this situation. Anything else?"

"Only that I think the department might be better served if I remained on—"

"Read my lips, Dillon, and listen carefully. No," McCabe said, drawing out the last word for three or four seconds.

Dillon and Suel left McCabe's office. "For the love of God," Suel said once they were at Dillon's desk. "Is there anything else you've decided to keep to yourself that the rest of us just might be interested in?"

"Will you calm down? It's not like I was keeping this a big secret. It only started to come together when Emily brought up the image of Amelia, or I guess now

it's Sinead's face, that it suddenly clicked. I kept thinking I was missing something, but I was never able to put
it together. Once I saw the face, all of a sudden, there it
was."

"You're going to write that report for McCabe?"

"Yeah, before I go home."

"Let me know when you're finished, and I'll follow
you home."

"You don't have to do—"

"You're right. I don't. But I'm going to, and you
don't have anything to say about it. It happens to be what
friends do for friends."

Dillon nodded, took a deep breath, and said, "Okay,
Paddy, and thanks, much appreciated."

"God, I can't believe it. I finally get to give you directions. This will be so much fun," Suel said.

THIRTY-TWO

Dillon spent the next two-and-a-half hours writing up his report on Amelia Maher/Sinead Lynch for D.C.I. McCabe. He reviewed the report in McCabe's office, along with Suel and three other officers over the better part of an hour. Once they were finished, Dillon returned to his desk, opened the file on the Sophie McGinn assault, and began to work his way through that, again.

Sometime later, Suel stepped out of McCabe's office and approached Dillon's desk. He cleared his throat and said, "Are you about ready to call it a day?"

"I want to finish going over this McGinn file. Maybe another hour or so. Are you heading out?"

"Well, I'd like to, but I've just been officially assigned to follow you home and make sure you don't do anything stupid along the way."

"Oh, will you relax, Paddy? You don't have to go crazy and—"

"Hey, I'm just following orders from on high. Think about it, Dillon. Kevin Rafferty was murdered driving on the M1. If what you said is true, that he was mistaken for you, that means the killer is still out there, and they're likely to try to get a second chance. So, I've been detailed to follow you to and from Special Branch for the time being. Lucky you."

"What's your schedule? When do you want me to leave?"

Suel glanced around and then said, "Oh, maybe an hour ago."

"Okay, give me ten minutes to shut everything down and lock up. And Paddy, thanks. I really do appreciate it. Sorry to be a pain in the ass."

Suel grinned and said, "One of the many things you're good at."

Ten minutes later, they walked out of the office. Suel followed Dillon home. He pulled partway over the sidewalk as Dillon pulled into his front garden and turned off his car. As he climbed out and closed the wrought iron gates behind his car, a pair of headlights suddenly appeared around the corner at the top of the lane. The car slowly headed down the lane toward Dillon and Suel.

Dillon saw the driver's window on Suel's car go down as Suel pulled a pistol from his shoulder holster. Dillon pulled his Beretta from the holster tucked in his belt and stepped back alongside his car. As the vehicle approached, it slowed slightly, and the older woman behind the wheel honked, waved, and kept going. Dillon recognized her as Michelle, one of his neighbors. He relaxed, took a deep breath, and watched as she drove around the corner and disappeared.

Suel lowered the window on the passenger side and said, "Now, would you please get your dumb ass in the house. Text me tomorrow when you're going to leave for work, and I'll be here to escort the likes of you. I mean it, Jack. You're not to go in without an escort, understand?"

"Yeah, I get it, Paddy. I'm not happy about it, but I get it. See you in the morning. Stay safe and thank you."

"You do the same, you gobshite," Suel said. He laughed, pulled back into the lane, and disappeared around the corner.

Dillon watched him go and then unlocked the front door and stepped inside.

At the sound of the door opening, Lucifer bounded down the stairs and met Dillon in the entryway. "Well, good evening, pal," Dillon said as he turned off the alarm. He bent over, gave Lucifer a good scratch behind the ears, and headed into the kitchen. He checked the backdoor just to make sure it was still locked. He took a biscuit from the jar on the counter and led Lucifer to the front door. He tossed the biscuit out the door. Lucifer leaped off the stoop and caught the biscuit on the second bounce. Dillon glanced up and down the lane, then closed and locked the door. He headed upstairs to change into some comfortable clothes. He glanced in the refrigerator, debated finishing the chicken breast from the other day, and decided a walk might be the better idea.

He pulled on a windbreaker to cover the pistol in his belt. He grabbed Lucifer's leash, glanced out the window, and once more looked up and down the lane. No one was around, and he hurried out the door. He clipped the leash onto Lucifer's collar, and they hurried around the corner. It wasn't the most direct route to Albert Park, which was next to DCU, Dublin City University, but it was the less traveled. Dillon lost count of how many times along the way he looked back over his shoulder. Fortunately, he never saw anyone. They quickly made their way through the EuroSpar parking lot, hurried across the four lanes of traffic on Ballymun Road, and entered Albert Park.

The park was a walking park with a tennis club, a children's playground, and three very large sports fields. The important thing to Dillon was there were no roads in the park. Everyone in the park was either on foot or occasionally riding a bicycle, although technically, bicycles weren't allowed. The path circling the outer edges of the park was 1.2 miles long.

At this hour, most people would be settled in at the dinner table. Over the course of the first lap, Dillon and Lucifer passed three different couples and a woman with an ancient collie on a leash. They did a second lap and then a third.

As they finished the third lap, the number of walkers had begun to increase. Dillon took that as a sign that they should head home, and they retraced their earlier route back to the house. Once again, he glanced continually over his shoulder but never saw anyone. As they turned the corner and crossed the lane, the house was about a hundred feet away. At exactly the same moment, a pair of headlights suddenly appeared at the top of the lane.

Dillon slowed at his neighbor's gate, pushed it open, and prepared to jump behind the brick wall if necessary. The headlights turned out to be on a delivery truck that drove past and continued on its way and around the corner. Their entry into the front garden and the house was uneventful. Dillon hung the leash up on the hook, put a frozen pizza in the oven, and tossed a biscuit to Lucifer.

They settled in front of the television, watched a movie Dillon had seen before, and headed up to bed at 11:00. Dillon placed the Beretta on the nightstand and settled into a decent night's sleep. He woke to the sound of his alarm clock the following morning. Lucifer glanced up, then drifted back to sleep as Dillon climbed out of bed. He went downstairs, turned on the coffee, and made his way back upstairs and into the shower.

He eventually let Lucifer out into the front garden and sent a text message to Suel that said he was ready to head to the office. Suel arrived twenty minutes later and followed Dillon on an uneventful drive to the Headquarters building.

Dillon spent the day at his desk, studying Sophie McGinn's file. He made phone calls to three individuals, all girlfriends of Sophie, who had provided statements regarding the apparent violent breakup she had had with a former boyfriend.

The boyfriend, Niall Gilmartin, was a twenty-three-year-old truck driver. He had been interviewed and provided an alibi for his location on the night of Sophie McGinn's assault. He'd been all the way over on the western side of the island, in the city of Sligo Town, where both he and Sophie McGinn were originally from. Just in case there was any doubt, a video from the security camera in the Shoot The Magpies pub pictured Gilmartin with four other individuals in the pub the night of the assault. The videotape was even dated in the lower righthand corner. 'Fri. 24/7/21'

Throughout the morning, Dillon had the feeling he was getting looks and whispers behind his back from other members in Special Branch. Nothing necessarily against him, but the word had clearly spread that Kevin Rafferty's murder may well have been due to Rafferty borrowing Dillon's raincoat and hat.

In case he had any doubts, D.C.I. McCabe gathered everyone in front of his office just before noon. He explained his suspicions concerning Rafferty's murder and the mistaken identity of Dillon. He then mentioned that, until further notice, Dillon would be assigned desk duty and was, under no circumstances, to leave the office other than to be escorted to his home.

Just after 3:00 that afternoon, Dillon received a phone call from the Mater Hospital. Sophie McGinn had passed away earlier in the day. She'd never regained consciousness. Her parents had been at the hospital the entire time. Dillon decided they had more than enough on their plates, and this was not the time to talk to them.

THIRTY-THREE

t exactly 5:00, Suel stepped over to Dillon's desk and said, "What do you say? Ready to call it a day?"

"Yeah, I gotta tell you, I'm about to go stir crazy sitting at this desk all day."

"Well, the alternative is even less attractive."

"I did get some bad news. Sophie McGinn, the Sligo girl who was assaulted in Temple Bar and ended up in a coma, passed away."

"Were you ever able to interview her?"

"No, she never regained consciousness."

"Was she raped?" Suel asked.

"No. But whoever attacked her must have beaten the hell out of her…God, I just don't get it."

"Yeah, well, if you ever figure it out, you can enlighten the rest of us. You ready to take off?"

Dillon nodded and said, "Yeah, give me a couple of minutes to lock up, and we can go."

Suel followed Dillon home and pulled up onto the sidewalk as Dillon pulled into his parking place. He climbed out of his car, glanced up and down the street, and then chatted with Dillon for a couple of minutes.

Suel pulled away once Dillon stepped into the house and locked the door.

After scratching Lucifer on the head, the first thing Dillon did was check the back door and garden. There was no sign of anyone having climbed over the wall and breaking into the house. For a half-second Dillon was almost disappointed. At least it would have served as some excitement in his life, not that he really wanted that kind of excitement.

He ate the leftover pizza from the night before for dinner while watching the evening news. Something in the back of his mind was bothering him, and he eventually got up off the couch and went into the kitchen. He pulled the calendar from the side of the wall and turned the pages back to July. He recalled the video of Niall Gilmartin with his four friends drinking a pint in the Shoot The Magpies pub in Sligo Town. The date in the corner of the image had been 'Fri. 24/7/21.' Dillon glanced at the calendar. July twenty-fourth was the night Sophie McGinn was assaulted. Dillon's calendar listed it as a Saturday, not Friday.

He debated checking the tape in the morning, but he didn't want to wait. It would only take a couple of minutes, drive over and bring the tape up on his computer. If his assumption that the date was wrong turned out to be correct, it meant that someone had altered the date on the tape. That would seem to indicate that Sophie McGinn's former boyfriend, Niall Gilmartin, needed the date altered to provide cover for where he had actually been that night, which, in turn, meant that there was an awfully good chance he was the figure on the CCTV tapes following her and the person who ultimately assaulted Sophie McGinn.

Dillon checked the clock. It was almost 8 PM. Traffic would be light. He could be in and out and back home in maybe thirty minutes. Calling Suel, even if he did agree to go, would probably double the time involved. He shoved the Beretta in his waistband, watched out the window for a couple of minutes, and hurried out the door. He opened the wrought iron gates, got behind the wheel, and drove up the lane.

He pulled into the parking lot at the Headquarters building ten minutes later. There were just a few cars in the lot. Dillon pulled into an empty handicapped parking place, one of five and the one closest to the door. He was up in Special Branch three minutes later. The lights were on in the office, but no one was in there. The door to D.C.I. McCabe's office was closed, and the lights were off.

Dillon hurried to his desk. He turned on his computer, logged in a minute later, and brought up the security tape from the Shoot The Magpies pub. He focused in on the date and time stamp in the lower righthand corner. Definitely' Fri. 24/7/21.' He paged through the calendar on his desk to the month of July just to triple-check. July twenty-fourth was definitely on Saturday, not Friday. Dillon shook his head and smiled.

He shut down his computer, gave a quick look around, and headed out the door. He studied the empty parking lot through the glass doors for a minute or two. There was absolutely no activity, and he hurried out to his car. Sixty seconds later, he was pulling onto the street and heading home.

He took a left off Ballymun and onto St. Pappin's Road. He drove past his lane and took the next left, checking in his rearview mirror to see if anyone was following. His car was the only one on the street. He took the next right, drove around the small plot of land known as St. Canice's Park, turned back onto St. Pappin's Road, and headed for his lane just a half-block away. There wasn't a car or a person in sight, and he relaxed as he took a right and drove down the lane headed toward his house. He pulled into his parking place in the front garden. He double-checked for any traffic, quickly climbed out of his car, and closed the gates behind him.

The lane was quiet. Everyone appeared to be settled in for the evening. Dillon carefully stepped around three separate piles left by Lucifer and unlocked the front door.

The first round slammed into one of two glass door panels before he even heard the shot. He dove onto the entryway floor just as a second round burst a hole through the door above and to the right of the doorknob. He kicked the door closed, reached up to lock it, pulled out his phone, and dialed 999.

"Emergency services. How may I direct your call?" a male answered using a calm voice.

"Shots fired. Request support," Dillon shouted into the phone.

"Please state your name."

"Dillon, I'm with Special Branch. Get someone out here now."

"What is your location?"

Dillon gave his address as he reached up and turned off the light in the entryway.

"Please remain on the line," the voice calmly replied. A moment later, he was back. "Garda have been alerted. Estimated time of arrival is three minutes. I'll remain on the line with you. Are you injured?"

"No, thank God. Someone fired two shots. I don't know where the shooter is. Whoever it was, they fired two shots and missed me by about an inch." Dillon rose to his feet. He stayed away from the front door and the window on the landing leading up to the second floor. Three minutes. He figured they were either coming from the Ballymun or the Glencloy Road station.

"May I have your name, please. You said you were with Special Branch?"

"Yeah, my name is Jack Dillon. I'm a US Marshal assigned to Special Branch, here in Dublin."

Dillon heard the sound of a distant siren gradually growing closer. He figured they'd be out front in another minute at most. He decided the wise decision would be to wait until after they pulled up and cleared the area. "I can hear a siren now. They're almost here," he said just as the noise suddenly increased and he caught illumination caused by a set of flashing lights out on the street.

"Is it all right if I get off the line and talk to the officers?"

"Stay where you are. Do not go outside until the area has been secured."

"Yeah, okay. I'll do that. Thanks for your help," he said. As he disconnected, he heard two car doors slam. He waited a while longer just to be on the safe side. Off in the distance, another siren could be heard approaching.

Dillon waited until the second squad car arrived, and he heard the car doors slamming closed. He could hear voices outside but couldn't make out what was being said. After a few more minutes, he opened the front door.

"Please remain inside and don't step out, sir," an officer said. From the sound of his voice, he couldn't have been more than five feet away. Dillon pushed the door almost closed but didn't close it firmly, just in case the officer needed some protective cover in a hurry.

It was at least ten minutes before there was a knock on the door. Dillon reached over and opened the door but didn't stand in the doorway. He kept the entryway light off.

"Hi, Eamon Russell," the officer said, stepping inside the entry. "You're Dillon with Special Branch?"

"Yeah, thanks for the fast response. Much appreciated. You find anything?"

The officer shook his head and said, "Not yet, but we're just getting started. Where was the shooter?"

Dillon shook his head. "I have absolutely no idea. The moment that glass panel exploded with the first shot, I dove into the entry and slammed the door closed."

"That's probably what saved you. If you don't mind, I think it would be a good idea to pull all the shades and close your shutters. Do it throughout the house. No lights on in any room until you've done that." The officer turned and glanced at the open front door behind him.

"Two shots. Any more than that?"

"No, just the two. More than enough for my taste," Dillon said.

Officer Russell smiled at that. "No doubt. Any idea who or why?"

Dillon nodded. "I suspect it might be tied into the murder out in Skerries and the murder of the officer on the M1."

Russell shook his head. "We ever find who's responsible for that, it will be a big surprise if they even make it to trial."

Dillon nodded, and after this latest incident, he couldn't agree more. If he ever got his hands on Amelia Maher, Sinead Lynch, or whatever the hell her name was, he would give her no quarter after tonight.

THIRTY-FOUR

Suel asked, "And you didn't see her? No car? She didn't call your name? Call you a dumb feck?" He was leaning against Dillon's kitchen counter. He took another sip from his bottle of Stella Artois.

"No, and she didn't wave or laugh out loud. Nothing. All of a sudden, the glass panel shattered, and I dropped to the ground. No sooner did I do that, than another shot was fired and left that hole just above the doorknob where I'd been standing a half-second earlier."

"What the hell were you doing outside anyway?"

"Paddy, I already told you. I just went out to get Lucifer back inside. There were no cars on the lane. No one was outside."

"Yeah, well, you were obviously wrong on that count. Jesus. And you've no idea where the shots came from?"

"You kidding? Once that glass shattered, all I could think of was getting my ass the hell out of the way as fast as possible."

"And you left Lucifer out there?"

"Yeah, I mean, no. He, umm, jumped over me, ran into the kitchen, and hid under the dining room table," Dillon lied.

Suel gave Dillon a look over his beer bottle. He gulped down what was left in the bottle and set it on the counter next to the earlier beer he'd had. "I think you'd better practice and get your story straight before tomorrow morning. McCabe is going to want some answers."

"What do you mean, get it straight? Sorry if I'm a little mixed up, but it all happened so damn fast. One moment I'm about to step inside, and the next, I'm on the floor, and there are two bullet holes in my front door that were meant for me."

"Yeah, whatever," Suel said and opened the refrigerator door. He glanced around at the contents and said, "I don't know, Dillon. Like I said, you better get your damn act together. You'd better get some more beer, too. You're out."

They adjourned to the sitting room. Dillon gave a verbal report to two uniformed officers from the Ballymun station. Two additional officers from Special Branch had arrived. They seemed to listen intently and took the occasional note. A team from forensics was in the process of removing two rounds from the wall opposite the front door. After an hour or so, everyone but Suel had left.

"I don't know what to say, Jack. You want to spend the night at my place?"

"Thanks, Paddy. But I'd just as soon stay here." Dillon leaned forward on the couch and glanced into the entryway. The shattered glass panel was now covered by a length of brown cardboard taped to the doorframe. The bullet hole above the doorknob had a square of masking tape over it.

"Well, any more excitement tonight, feel free to call someone else," Suel said as he stood. "You sure you're okay?"

"Yeah, I'm fine. Now relax and stop worrying. I'll be okay," Dillon said. He patted Suel on the shoulder as they headed toward the front door. Dillon opened the door and glanced outside. His front garden was taped off with blue and white tape that read in English and Irish, 'AN GARDA SIOCHANA DO NOT CROSS.' The entrance into his front garden was blocked by a squad car. Two officers wearing protective vests were leaning against the squad car. The word GARDA was centered on the back of their neon-green high-visibility vests. They were laughing at something and unaware that Suel had stepped outside.

"Thanks again for coming over, Paddy," Dillon said.

"I'm just glad whoever did this was a lousy shot," Suel said.

"Mmm, not so sure they were lousy. Missed by maybe an inch, and I was moving. All the same, they were close enough to get my attention," Dillon said. "I'll give you a call tomorrow to follow me in. Probably around seven-thirty or so."

"Yeah, whenever. I'll be up. You just get your ass back into that house. The lads are going to be standing guard all night. You'll owe the likes of them more than a couple of pints."

"You're telling me, " Dillon said.

Suel walked out to his car. He stopped and said something to the two officers out front and then turned toward Dillon and said, "For Christ's sake, would you ever close the damn door."

Dillon did just that, then walked through the house, not for the first time, making sure all the shutters were closed and the shades were drawn. He settled in on the couch in front of the TV and proceeded to wonder about Amelia/Sinead and exactly what the hell she was thinking. He wandered up to the bedroom a little after 1:00. He climbed in, slept fitfully, and turned off his alarm an hour before it was set to go off. Lucifer never even opened an eye.

He was downstairs, dressed and ready to go, and it was only 5:30 AM. He left the lights off in the sitting room and cautiously peeked out as he adjusted a shutter. It was still dark outside, and he couldn't see anything other than one of the uniformed officers leaning against the squad car parked in front of his house. He presumed the partner was probably asleep in the back seat of the vehicle.

Dillon walked into the kitchen. He made sure all the shades were pulled over the windows and the double doors leading out to the back garden before he turned on a light. He made eight cups of coffee, figuring both officers out front would want some.

He opened the front door at 6:00 and called to the officer leaning against the squad car. "Can I interest you in a coffee or a tea?"

The officer half-jumped, either waking up or simply surprised at the sound of a voice behind him. He turned and looked at Dillon. "That sounds wonderful, but I'll come and get it. No need for you to step out of the house."

"How do you take it?"

"Black coffee for me. Partner is still resting up, so he might be a while," he said and shook his head.

"Be right back," Dillon said. He filled a mug with coffee and hurried back to the front door. The officer was standing on the stoop and in the process of stretching.

"Oh, thanks, much appreciated," he said as Dillon handed the steaming mug to him.

"Any activity last night?" Dillon asked.

"No, just the way I like it, nice and quiet. You got an idea who might have done it?"

"We have a pretty good idea. Just difficult to find the individual, as you might imagine."

"They're all nuts. They ought to be locked up in the looney bin, and we throw away the key. Absolutely crazy."

"How long do they have you stationed here?" Dillon asked.

"Well, we're supposed to be relieved at seven," he said and glanced at his watch. "Theoretically, we'll be leaving in thirty-five minutes, but you know how that can go."

"Unfortunately, I do." They both glanced over at the squad car as the officer asleep in the back suddenly sat up, rubbed his eyes, and looked around. "I'll get a mug for your partner. How does he take it?"

"Black would do him just fine. Thank you. I'd better let him out before he pisses the car."

Dillon chuckled and said, "Don't let me hold you up. I'll get that coffee." He walked back into the kitchen. He poured another mug for himself then poured a fresh mug and grabbed the coffee pot, just in case the officer he'd been talking with wanted a top-up. Dillon handed the mug to the officer on the stoop in the process of blinking his eyes awake. His partner held out his empty mug, and Dillon filled it.

"Sorry you had to be out here last night," Dillon said once he'd refilled the mug.

"I'm just glad they didn't hit you. You're one lucky soldier," the officer getting the refill said.

"You're out of Ballymun station?" Dillon asked.

Both men nodded and took a sip. "You're the American with Special Branch, aren't you?"

Dillon nodded and said, "Can I get you something for breakfast. I don't have all that much, but I could scramble some eggs or do up some toast. Sorry, I don't have any sausage. I've got some strawberry ice cream if that would appeal to you."

Both men shook their heads. "Coffee will do just fine. Hope we get this guy. This is a bunch of bullshit, waiting to shoot you when you step out the door."

"Couldn't agree more," Dillon said. "I'm going to be leaving in an hour and heading to Headquarters over in Phoenix Park. Either one of you have to use the loo?"

They glanced at one another and shook their heads *no*, which meant they'd relieved themselves somewhere. Dillon could only hope it was in Deitora's garden. If only he'd thought to tell them to use it last night.

"Just ring the doorbell if you need something," Dillon said. He topped up their coffee mugs and closed the door. He set his mug on the kitchen counter and then placed a call to Suel.

"So, you made it through the night?" was how Suel answered.

"Yeah, not the most comfortable night's sleep, but I'm still here to tell the story. Just finished chatting with the two officers standing watch. Luckily, they had a boring night."

"You thinking of going into Special Branch?" Suel asked.

"Yeah, I'm ready whenever you are."

"Give me a few minutes to finish breakfast, and I'll be over. No point in pressing your luck, so stay indoors until I knock on your door."

Dillon was tempted to respond but then thought better of it. Suel probably didn't need any wise-ass comments just now.

THIRTY-FIVE

Suel pulled in front about forty minutes later. Dillon just happened to glance through the shutters in the sitting room and watched as he parked and climbed out of the car. He headed toward the two officers standing next to their squad car. Dillon noticed that they were a different pair than the two he'd given coffee. He closed the shutter and hurried into the kitchen. He let Lucifer out into the back garden, thinking his barking might discourage anyone who thought about climbing over the garden wall.

He hurried back into the front entryway and stood by the door, waiting for Suel to ring the doorbell. He needn't have hurried. He actually lost count of how often he checked the time on his cellphone. Finally, the doorbell rang, and Dillon opened the door a half-second later.

"Don't tell me you were standing there inside, waiting for me to ring your doorbell."

"No, I just happened to be passing by. Come on, let's go. I can't wait to get the third degree from D.C.I. McCabe this morning."

"Did he contact you?"

"No, thankfully. But I'm sure he'll have all sorts of questions." He nodded at the two uniformed officers standing next to their squad car. "Thanks for being here, lads. Very much appreciated."

"Be sure to put in a good word for us with the bigwigs at Headquarters," one of them said, and they both laughed.

Suel walked around to the passenger side and opened the door for Dillon.

"What the hell?" Dillon said.

"Eternally at your service," Suel replied and finished up with a gracious bow. "Now get your ass in the car."

They chatted back and forth all the way to the Headquarters building, going over the previous night's activity. "Here's the problem as I see it, Dillon," Suel said as he pulled into the parking lot. "Until we get this slapper, you're not safe in your own home. I suppose we could lock you up in a security cell in The Joy. But then what? I can see McCabe putting you on an extended leave immediately. You think you might consider heading back to the States for a bit?"

"I don't want to head back to the States. I don't want to be locked up in a security cell in Mountjoy Prison. And, I absolutely do not want to be stuck doing desk work until the end of time."

Once at the Headquarters building Suel parked next to the front door and said, "Well, let's find out what the boss decides you're going to do. Now, wait here for a moment while I check things out."

"I think I'm perfectly capable of getting out—"

"I said stay in the damn car for a moment, Dillon. Let's play it safe, for God's sake," Suel said as he opened the driver's door and stepped out of the car. He glanced around and then studied the two people chatting at one of the fast-food trucks just outside the parking lot. After a bit, he leaned in and said, "Let's go inside."

They both hurried inside. Once the door closed behind them, Dillon said, "Do you really think that was necessary?"

"Let me ask you, do you really think your woman will miss the next time she has you in her sights?"

Dillon nodded and said, "Sorry, Paddy. You're right. Thanks for doing that."

They took the elevator up to Special Branch. Dillon punched in the code on the keypad, and they entered the office. As Dillon walked in, a couple of people at the back desks began to clap. Someone else gave a loud whistle, and suddenly, everyone was clapping as Dillon and Suel made their way to their respective desks.

Just as things settled down, D.C.I. McCabe stepped from his office and said, "Dillon, Suel, grab a tea or coffee and join me."

"That was fast," Dillon said as Suel walked over to his desk and they headed into the break room. Suel made tea. Dillon filled his coffee mug and took a sip. It was just as bad as always. Once Suel's tea was ready, they both took a deep breath and headed into McCabe's office.

"Gentlemen, please have a seat," McCabe said as he hung up his phone. "Sounds as though you had a rather interesting evening, Dillon. Please, fill me in."

Dillon glanced at Suel and then proceeded to tell McCabe about the evening. He left out the part about driving back to Special Branch and double-checking the time and date on the security tape from the Shoot The Magpies pub in Sligo Town. He pretty much told McCabe the same version he'd told Suel the previous evening. That he was bringing Lucifer into the house, and suddenly two shots were fired, narrowly missing him.

"And you never saw the shooter?" McCabe asked.

"No, sir. I immediately dropped to the floor. Closed and locked the door and dialed 999."

McCabe nodded and said, "I've listened to the tape. Good job on the part of the officer answering the phone."

"Absolutely," Dillon said. "I'm unaware of a vehicle speeding away. I had checked the lane for any cars moving, never saw one. Never saw anyone on the lane, for that matter. My guess is someone had positioned themselves across the street and behind a front wall so they wouldn't be spotted. I opened the door. I can't recall if my dog barked, but all of a sudden, one of the glass panels in my front door shattered, and a second later, a round tore through the door just above the doorknob."

"And then they disappeared into thin air," McCabe said.

"From the time I called 999 until the first squad car arrived, it may have been three or four minutes. That's an exceedingly fast response time. Yet still enough time for an individual to walk around the corner, climb into their vehicle, and casually drive away."

McCabe seemed to think about that and nodded. "So, what do you think we should do. Your safety is what's most important, and at the moment, I don't believe you're safe remaining in your home."

"After failing in last night's attempt, I really can't see whoever fired those shots returning."

"Well, there's part of the problem, Marshal. You see, since we don't know who fired the shots, virtually everyone is a suspect. They may have failed last night, but will that be the case when you're at the market buying food, driving here to Special Branch, or simply cutting your lawn?"

"I'm aware we can't have someone standing guard over me twenty-four hours a day, seven days a week."

"What other option do we currently have? Do you want to return to the States?" McCabe asked.

"No, sir. But I do have another idea."

"I do not intend to set you out somewhere as a target in the hopes we'll get to the shooter before they get to you. So if that's your idea, forget it."

"What about this," Dillon said. "I've been looking into an unsolved case. The murder of a college student by the name of Sophie McGinn. She's from Sligo Town but attending Trinity here in Dublin."

McCabe seemed to think for a moment then said, "Is this the young woman assaulted in Temple Bar some weeks back? She's been in a coma ever since."

"That's been her situation up until recently. But yesterday, I received a phone call from the Mater hospital. She was slowly beginning to come out of that coma and suddenly passed. At this point, the news of her death has only been released to her family."

"And so what are you thinking?"

"Actually, in reviewing the file, there was a question concerning a former boyfriend. Their breakup was listed as being violent by three of Miss McGinn's friends. I viewed the security tape from a pub in Sligo Town. Niall Gilmartin, he was the boyfriend, is also from Sligo Town. I just happened to check the date on the security tape that's serving as his alibi. It shows him drinking with friends in a pub. But when I checked the date on the tape with the day mentioned, they don't match up."

"Help me out here, Dillon. I'm not quite following."

"The McGinn woman was assaulted on Saturday, July twenty-fourth of this year."

"Yes."

"The date on the security tape from the pub in Sligo Town where Niall Gilmartin is drinking with his friends lists July twenty-fourth as a Friday. I checked the calendar. It was a Saturday. I think someone adjusted the date on the tape to read the twenty-fourth but never changed the day on the tape from Friday to Saturday."

"Meaning the security tape is essentially false," McCabe said.

"Exactly, which would seem to point an extremely strong finger toward the former boyfriend, Niall Gilmartin. What I would suggest is, if I'm to disappear, might it not make sense to send me out to Sligo Town where I can pursue the McGinn case?"

McCabe thought for a moment and slowly began to nod. "Yes, I think that is an excellent idea. Let me suggest two things. First, return home and pack a bag. D.I. Suel, you'll follow Dillon home and—"

"Actually, sir. D.I. Suel drove me in this morning."

"Even better. Suel will drive you home. Pack a bag and return here, leaving your vehicle in front of your home. You'll be loaned a vehicle from our department and drive yourself out to Sligo Town. Questions?"

"No, sir, I'll just tidy up at my desk and be off in an hour or so."

"I'll phone Sligo Town and establish a point of contact. D.I. Suel, you'll serve as Dillon's point of contact with Special Branch. Dillon, I'll expect a brief phone call morning, noon, and night to Suel."

"Yes, sir."

"Anything else," McCabe asked.

Both Dillon and Suel shook their heads.

"Very well then, check in with me when you are back in the office. Now off with you."

THIRTY-SIX

Dillon and Suel hurried out to their respective desks. Dillon pulled out his cellphone and called Tara, his neighbor across the street. He ended up leaving a message. "Hi, Tara, Jack Dillon calling. Hoping you might be able to help me out. Time now is 9:15. Call me if you get this in the next forty-five minutes. Thanks."

He disconnected and began assembling the Sophie McGinn files. His cellphone rang just a minute later. Tara returning his call.

"Hi, Tara. Thanks for getting back to me so quickly."

"Sorry, I was on the line with family and couldn't get off fast enough."

"Is everything okay?"

"Oh, yeah, just talking to my aunt. She's been retired for nearly five years and apparently has all morning to tell me how busy she is. What can I do for you?"

"Well, first off, feel free to tell me no. Here's the deal. I've been called out of town to work a case out in the west. Not sure how long I'll be gone. It could be a day or maybe a week, or even longer. I just don't know, and—"

"And you want me to keep an eye on Lucifer?"

"Yeah, I mean, if you can. Like I said before, if you have something going on or—"

"Relax. I'd love to watch him. By the way, what's with the two Garda out in front of your place and your front garden taped off? Did someone try to break in?"

"Yeah, something like that," he said in an effort to not get into last night's attempt on his life. "I'm going to head back home in a minute. You going to be around for an hour?"

"Yeah, sure."

"I'll stop over with charming Lucifer in just a bit."

"Oh, so all of a sudden, he's charming, now. When did that happen?"

"Yeah, well, he probably takes after me. I'll see you in a bit and thank you."

"Not a bother, see you," she said and disconnected. Dillon cleared off the top of his desk, locked the drawers, and carried the McGinn files over to Suel's desk.

"You all set to go?" Suel asked.

"Yeah, let's get started," Dillon said. As they headed out of Special Branch, Dillon got nods from a number of officers, and one gave him a thumbs-up. Down in the lobby, Suel told Dillon to wait, and Dillon decided the best action would be to follow directions, so he just nodded.

Suel hurried out to his car and gazed around the parking lot for a long moment before he climbed in behind the wheel. He reversed the car and made a quick drive through the lot. He pulled to a stop just in front of the double doors. Dillon hurried out of the building and was in the car in about three seconds.

"You see anything interesting?" Dillon asked as he buckled up and Suel pulled out of the lot.

"Just a couple making love in their front seat, but I've seen them a number of times before."

Dillon shot a quick glance at Suel and said, "Turn around. I want to see."

Fortunately, the drive to Dillon's was uneventful. Suel pulled up over the sidewalk and parked in front of the squad car blocking Dillon's car in the front garden. "Let me just check for a moment," Suel said as Dillon unbuckled his seat belt. Suel stepped out of the car and glanced over at the two officers.

"Anything of interest?"

"Wonderfully boring," one of the officers said.

Suel gave another quick look around and then leaned in the driver's door and said, "Okay, good to go."

Dillon hurried out the passenger side, half-shouted a quick, "Thanks, lads," and headed to the front door. Suel remained with the two uniformed officers, all three of them looking up and down the street and into the front gardens of the nearby homes.

Dillon called to Suel, "The door's open for you, Paddy. Ask the lads if they'd like a tea."

Dillon walked into the kitchen and cautiously raised a shutter. Everything seemed to look okay. He carefully pulled the shade up over the double doors leading to the back garden, waited a moment, then unlocked the door and called, "Lucifer. Lucifer, treat."

Lucifer appeared a moment later and hurried into the kitchen. Dillon quickly locked the door and pulled the shade down. He grabbed a biscuit from the jar on the counter and tossed it to Lucifer, who hurried out into the sitting room. Suel stepped into the entry just as Lucifer ran past.

"Dillon, two teas for the lads," Suel called.

Dillon filled the kettle and placed it on the stove. He took two mugs from the cupboard, tossed a tea bag in each, and stepped out of the kitchen.

"Kettle's on. Mugs are on the counter. I'm going upstairs to pack a suitcase, and I'll be right down. I've got to take Lucifer across the street to a neighbor who'll watch him while I'm gone."

"Might be better if one of the lads or I take him over."

"She's just across the street. I can hurry over and—"

"We've two lads stationed out front twenty-four hours a day. We're sneaking you out of town to the back of beyond. And your plan is to stroll across the street with your dog? I don't think so."

"Yeah, okay. Serve up the teas, and I'll be down in a minute," Dillon said and hurried up the stairs.

He grabbed a suitcase compact enough to fit in the overhead luggage bin of an airplane, although he'd be driving out to Sligo Town. He tossed in the McGinn files, five t-shirts, boxers, and pairs of socks, along with three long-sleeve shirts and another pair of jeans. He packed his razor and shaving cream, zipped the suitcase shut, and was coming down the stairs just as Suel headed out the door with two tea mugs.

Dillon set the suitcase next to the front entry and carried the pillow that served as Lucifer's bed from the sitting room and set it next to his suitcase. He grabbed Lucifer's food and water dishes, along with the bag of dog food, and placed them on the pillow. Suel stepped back into the entryway.

"Okay, here's Lucifer's bed, dishes, and food," Dillon said.

"You got a grocery bag? I'll stuff all this in the bag along with that jar of biscuits. Oh, and grab the leash, wherever that is."

"Good idea," Dillon said.

Suel stuffed everything but the pillow and the leash in the grocery bag. Dillon clicked the leash onto Lucifer's collar, gave him a scratch behind the ears, and then pointed the house out to Suel.

"Her name is Tara, and she's expecting you," Dillon called as Lucifer and Suel headed out of the front garden.

While Suel was gone, Dillon went into the sitting room and opened his liquor cabinet. He pulled out an unopened bottle of Jameson, placed it in a pouch on the front of his suitcase, and waited for Suel to return. He waited some more, checking the time on his phone at three-minute intervals.

Suel returned after sixteen minutes. "All set?" Suel asked as he stepped back into the house.

"What the hell? You were just dropping Lucifer off. Did she give you a tour of her place?"

"She can't help herself. She meets someone like me, and she wants my card. You know how it is. I just gave her my phone number, told her I'd look forward to her call, and she got all happy."

"Let's just go," Dillon said. He followed Suel out and locked the door behind them. He placed his suitcase in the back seat and climbed into the passenger seat as Suel and the two officers scanned up and down the lane.

"All set?" Suel said as he climbed in behind the wheel.

"As ready as I'll ever be," Dillon replied.

THIRTY-SEVEN

Back at the Headquarters building Suel pulled into the same handicap parking place, quickly climbed out, and scanned the parking lot. "All clear," he said.

Dillon hurried out of the passenger seat, and opened the rear door. He pulled the bottle of Jameson from his suitcase and placed it on the floor of the back seat.

"Come on, get your ass inside," Suel said and grinned.

They were up in Special Branch a few minutes later. They headed straight for McCabe's office. Dillon left his suitcase next to his desk, and they stopped at McCabe's door. McCabe was on the phone, but he waved them in and pointed to the two chairs in front of his desk. He talked legal terms to someone on the other end of the line for another minute or two and then hung up.

"Everything go okay?"

Dillon nodded. "All packed and ready to go."

"Excellent. I made a call to Sligo Town. D.I. Emmett Roberts will be your point of contact. I've also reserved a room for you at the Glasshouse Hotel in Sligo Town. Similar to your recent activity here, you are to mind yourself. No point in entering a pub, socializing with people in the hotel, or chatting up respectable ladies. Anything you do regarding the McGinn case will be run past D.I. Roberts before you take any action. Clear?"

Dillon nodded.

"I'm sorry, I didn't hear your response," McCabe said.

"Yes, sir, very clear," Dillon said.

McCabe smiled. "There's a vehicle waiting for you downstairs in the motor pool. Again, follow department procedure, record mileage, and hold on to your receipts for fuel purchases. Any questions?"

"No sir, thank you," Dillon said as he stood.

McCabe smiled and held out his hand, "Let me remind you to touch base with D.I. Suel morning, noon, and night. That's three times a day, every day. Now, mind yourself, Dillon. Whoever this is, they're still out there."

"Will do, sir. Thank you."

McCabe nodded, and they headed out the door.

"Give me a call when you make it to Sligo Town. Maybe check into the Glasshouse before you link up with Roberts," Suel said.

"You know him?"

Suel nodded and said, "He's good. I've dealt with him a couple of times. Straight shooter with a bit of a sense of humor. You'll like him. Now, you take care of yourself, stay safe," Suel said and held out his hand.

Dillon went to shake his hand, and Suel suddenly wrapped his arms around Dillon. "I mean it. You stay safe, Jack."

"I left a little something for you in the back seat of your car, Paddy. I appreciate all you've done for me."

"I hope it's nothing Lucifer left behind," Suel said.

"Oh, God, if only I'd thought of that."

Dillon dragged his suitcase and his computer bag down to the motor pool and stopped in front of the office. It was barely large enough for two desks, and they had somehow crammed three into the place. One of the desks was next to a small window that opened onto the exit gate from the motor pool. A gray-haired man sat at the desk. At the moment, he was the only person in the office.

The room looked too small to accommodate Dillon and his suitcase, so he left it with the computer bag next to the door and stepped inside. As he stepped in, the gray-haired man looked over and studied him for a moment. "You the one from Special Branch?"

"Yeah, Dillon, Jack Dillon."

The man nodded then quickly sifted through a stack of papers. He handed Dillon three sheets stapled together. "Read through this, initial where it tells you to, sign and date the back sheet."

Dillon set the sheets on the empty desk next to him, leaned over, and began to read through. He initialed four areas, signed his name, wrote the date at the bottom of the third page, then looked up at the man.

"All right. You've a full tank. There's a road map in the pocket of the driver's door and GPS on the dash. Your vehicle is in parking place number nineteen. Before you leave, walk around, and inspect the body of the vehicle. If you see any damage, let me know immediately, and you won't be charged. If we find a problem when you return the vehicle, you're going to be charged for repairs, so bear that in mind. Any questions?"

Dillon shook his head and said, "No, sir," as he handed the three-page form back to the man.

"All right, safe travels," he said and handed a set of keys to Dillon.

Dillon nodded, said, "Thank you," and stepped out of the office. He walked through the parking lot with his luggage until he came to the parking space numbered nineteen. He stopped and stared then double-checked the number on the wall in front of the car. It was definitely numbered nineteen. He stared at the rear of the shiny white vehicle, a Mercedes Benz C-Class. Based on the license plate, it was a 2021 model. No doubt confiscated from some criminal and now in the Dublin motor pool.

Dillon clicked the fob twice on the vehicle. The lights flashed, and the trunk rose. He stared for a moment and then placed his suitcase and the computer bag in the trunk. He opened the driver's door, slid in, and adjusted the seat. He was about to press the ignition button when he remembered the warning about examining the exterior. He climbed out, did a quick check, and then climbed back in.

Three minutes later, he was out of the parking lot and headed toward the M50. He remained on the M50 through Blanchardstown and Castleknock then turned onto the N4 and headed west. Just after Mullingar, the four lanes changed to two. Luckily, there wasn't much traffic, and he kept a steady pace just a little above the speed limit. He remained on the N4 heading northwest. He drove through Carrick On Shannon and Garraroe before finally reaching the outskirts of Sligo Town.

Once in the city, he drove for a few miles, and the GPS directed him to turn right on the R292. The Glasshouse Hotel appeared off to the left in the center of the city. He made a left turn onto Lower New Street and pulled into the underground parking lot. He was able to park close to the entrance to the elevators, and after pulling his suitcase and computer bag from the trunk of the Mercedes, he was standing in front of the receptionist desk a few minutes later.

"Good afternoon. How may I help you?" the receptionist said. She had black hair below her shoulders, dark brown eyes, and an accent Dillon guessed might be Indian.

"Hi, I have a reservation. Jack Dillon," Dillon said and handed her a credit card.

"Thank you. Let me just bring that up," she said and ran her fingers across the keyboard. A moment later, she got a funny look on her face as she ran her fingers across the keyboard again.

"I'm sorry, sir. But there doesn't appear to be a reservation in your name. Might it be in someone else's name or perhaps a company's name?"

Dillon nodded and said, "Maybe try An Garda Síochána, Dublin, or, if that doesn't work, Sligo Town."

She typed again and suddenly smiled, "Oh, yes. Here we are. Much better. She typed again then pulled out two key cards and handed them to Dillon. You are in room four-twelve. The room is on the Garda account. The elevator is directly behind you. Did you drive?"

"Yes, I parked in the garage below."

"That's just fine. Use your room key for access to privileged parking. Breakfast is complimentary until 10:00 every morning, and dinner is served until nine every evening. Is there anything else I can help you with?"

"No, I think that will do it. Thank you."

She flashed a quick smile, handed his credit card back, and said, "Enjoy your stay, sir."

Dillon took hold of his computer bag and rolled his suitcase over to the elevator. Riding the elevator up to the fourth floor, he stepped out and took a left, following the direction of the arrow pointing down the hall. His room, 412, was the third door on the left. The keycard worked, and he stepped into a nicely appointed room with two twin beds, a desk, and floor-to-ceiling windows that looked down on the Hyde Bridge that ran across the Garavogue River.

The river appeared calm on the far side of the bridge but was churning white caps as it flowed beneath. Clearly, there was a strong current. Dillon set his suitcase on the bed closest to the door, pulled his phone out, and called Suel.

"Everything okay?" was how Suel answered.

"Yeah, everything is fine. Just checked into the Glasshouse. I'll give Roberts a call once we're off the line. Anything on Sinead Lynch?"

"No, unfortunately. I'm trying to think back a few months. Last time we were dealing with her, did we ever determine where she stayed?"

"All we came up with was she had been with the men we found dead. I can't prove it, but my guess would be that she killed them, spent the night in their dump, and then moved on to the next one. She ended up in the mansion listed to Cullen Fink."

"Not a bad way to go," Suel said.

"She probably killed them before any 'benefits' were taken. Anyway, everything's good here. If you call the hotel to talk with me, I'm in room four-twelve. Probably easier to get me on my cell. I'll give you a call tomorrow morning. I don't expect much to happen this afternoon other than giving an update to Roberts. He may not even know Sophie McGinn has passed away."

"Chat tomorrow," Suel said and disconnected. Dillon looked out the window for a moment and then phoned D.I. Roberts.

THIRTY-EIGHT

After three rings a recording played. "You've reached Detective Inspector Emmett Roberts. I'm unable to take your call at the moment. Please leave a message, and I'll get back to you just as soon as possible."

"Hi, D.I. Roberts. This is Jack Dillon. I'm with An Garda Síochána, Special Branch in Dublin. I'm staying at the Glasshouse Hotel. If you could call me at your convenience, I have some updates on the Sophie McGinn assault that occurred in Dublin. I look forward to talking with you," Dillon said, left his cellphone number, and disconnected.

He looked down at the river and decided to give Roberts thirty minutes to return his call before heading over to the Sligo Town police department. He grabbed his computer bag and stepped out of the room. He took the elevator down to the main floor, headed outside, then walked across the Hyde Bridge. The Garavogue River was churning beneath the bridge.

With the exception of the contemporary Glasshouse Hotel, based on the age and style of the buildings, Dillon was definitely in the city center and the older part of town. He walked past the W.B Yeats memorial, up two blocks, then crossed the street and headed back toward the hotel. He still had almost fifteen minutes to go before he hit his thirty-minute mark, and so he stepped into a coffee shop called WB's Coffee House. The building was a three-story structure painted blue with white trim. Dillon ordered a medium-sized coffee, and just as the woman pulled the cup from the stack, his cellphone rang. The screen read 'Unknown Number.'

"Jack Dillon," he amswered.

"Hi Dillon, Emmett Roberts. Sorry I missed your call. I was in a briefing, and we're required to turn our phones off."

"Not a problem. Hang on for a second. Can I get that coffee to go?" Dillon asked.

The woman nodded.

"Hey, I'm hoping we can meet. I'm out here for a couple of days, looking into the assault on Sophie McGinn. She was a student at Trinity, assaulted in Dublin a couple of weeks ago."

"I'm somewhat familiar with it. Meaning, I'm aware she was assaulted. Have you been able to interview her yet?"

"No, but I have some additional information I'd like to review with you," Dillon said, not wanting to mention her death over the phone.

"As it looks now, I should be in the office for the next couple of hours. Do you know where we're located?"

"Not exactly, but I've got GPS in the car."

"We're not too far from your hotel. We're just across the street from Louis J. Doherty and Sons."

"Is that a pub?"

Roberts chuckled. "I only wish. No, actually, it's a furniture store, a three-story white structure with blue shutters. We're located on the corner of Pearse Road, and Abbeyquarter North. There's usually a squad car or two parked in front."

"I'll find it. See you shortly," Dillon said and disconnected. He paid for his coffee and thanked the woman. He walked back to the Glasshouse Hotel and down to the lower-level garage entrance. He climbed in the car, placed the coffee in the console, turned on the GPS, and typed in Sligo Town Garda station. A map immediately appeared, and he pulled out of the underground garage. Following the audible directions, he drove across Hyde Bridge, took an immediate left, and drove along the river for twenty seconds before taking a right on Connaughton Road. He took the next right, which was Bridge Street. He drove across the river, where again, in typical Irish fashion, Bridge Street suddenly changed its name to Thomas Street. From there, it was just two long blocks, and suddenly, there was the Garda station off to the left, just as Roberts had described. In case he had any doubt, there were two squad cars parked in front of the building.

Dillon pulled ahead of the squad cars and parked. He took a few more sips of coffee and returned the cup to the console holder. He grabbed his computer bag and walked back to the station. The stone front on the three-story building was lined with flowers on both sides of the entrance.

There was a U-shaped counter just inside the door with two uniformed officers seated behind it. A muscular officer with black hair and piercing blue eyes studied Dillon as he approached. He did not strike Dillon as the sort of man you would give a 'wise-guy' answer to." Can I help you?"

"Hi, I'm Marshal Jack Dillon, attached to An Garda Síochána Special Branch in Dublin. I'm here to see D.I. Emmett Roberts. I spoke with him on the phone not ten minutes ago. He's expecting me."

The officer nodded and said, "Let me give him a call. May I see your I.D., please?"

Dillon pulled his ID from his pocket and handed it to the officer. The man actually studied it for a brief moment, looking up from the I.D. to Dillon's face and then back down again.

Finally, he picked up the phone and hit three buttons. A moment later, he said, "Yes, D.I. Roberts, I have a Marshal Dillon down here in the lobby. He'd like to speak with you. All right, I'll tell him," the officer said, nodding at Dillon.

"He's on his way down. If you want to grab a seat, shouldn't be more than a minute or two," he said as he handed back Dillon's I.D.

"Thank you," Dillon said. He stepped over to a long wooden bench and sat down. Thirty seconds later, a dark-haired man with a neatly trimmed mustache suddenly appeared.

Since Dillon was the only person waiting in the lobby, Roberts approached and asked, "Dillon?"

"Nice to meet you, D.I. Roberts," Dillon said as he stood.

"I'd prefer if you refer to me as Detective Inspector Roberts," the man said and waited for a second or two before he burst out laughing. "I'm sorry. Your friend, D.I. Suel called earlier and told me to do that. We'll have to come up with a way to get back at him."

"I have to admit, you had me going there," Dillon said.

"Good, it worked. Let's go upstairs. Can I get you a coffee or something?"

"Thanks, but I'm fine," Dillon said and followed. They climbed four flights of stairs to get to the third floor. Roberts led the way, answering Dillon's questions about the makeup of the Sligo Town force.

Roberts opened a door labeled 'Homicide,' and they stepped into a room similar to Special Branch, only without as many desks. It wasn't lost on Dillon that there wasn't a keypad to input a code before you gained entrance.

They headed toward a desk in the corner. As they approached, Roberts pointed to one of two chairs in front of the desk, and Dillon settled in.

Once Roberts was seated, he said, "So, Miss McGinn."

"Well, to start, I have some unfortunate news. I received a call that she never recovered from her coma and passed away early yesterday."

Roberts shook his head. "Damn it. I thought as much when we spoke on the phone. You sounded a bit off mentioning her."

"Did you know her or the family?"

Roberts shook his head.

THIRTY-NINE

Dillon told him about the phone call he'd received from the Mater.

"So now you're dealing with a murder investigation. The little I know suggested you had nothing resembling any clues. Wasn't there a series of CCTV tapes of some guy following her? She was assaulted in Temple Bar, wasn't she?"

"Yes, on both counts," Dillon said as he opened his computer bag and pulled out his laptop. "Let me show you what we have." He brought up the tape from various sites along the route she walked.

"The guy behind Sophie McGinn is walking in the same direction. He appears briefly on another security tape outside a pub. He continues in the same direction, apparently not in a hurry, and although Sophie glanced back and was aware of him, she never appeared concerned. She turns onto Curved Street, and he follows, but that isn't necessarily unusual. Then eleven minutes later, he exits and disappears into a crowd on a busy street, and she's found unconscious back on Curved Street. I walked the street the other day. It took me less than a minute."

"Eleven minutes, that's a long time. Anything could have happened."

Dillon nodded and said, "She wasn't raped. We don't know if they met someone they both knew or if he even assaulted her. We've no idea. Unfortunately, there are no security cameras on Curved Street."

"So it could be the perfect place to attack someone and get away with it," Roberts said.

"Yes, absolutely. Now, we had information on a former boyfriend named Niall Gilmartin. Are you aware of him?"

Roberts shook his head. "It's not ringing a bell."

"We received three statements from girlfriends who said the couple had a violent falling out. Violent as in shouting and some name-calling. Again, Sophie McGinn was not physically assaulted, according to these girls. But here's where it gets interesting," Dillon said as he clicked on the link and brought up the short security tape from the pub. "Take a look at this."

"That looks like the Shoot the Magpies," Roberts said almost immediately.

"You're right. It is. This is dated the same evening as the assault on Sophie McGinn. Niall Gilmartin was in the pub having a pint with friends."

"So he's not a suspect. If he was in the pub at that hour, even if he flew a plane, he couldn't get to Dublin by the time she was assaulted."

"That's what we thought. But I was going over this for the umpteenth time, and I just happened to check on the date and timestamp. They're good, and you're right. There is no way he could have made it to Dublin. Here's the problem. The date displayed is the twenty-fourth of July. But it's also listed on the tape as Friday. I checked my calendar. The twenty-fourth was actually on a Saturday."

"What?"

"I think someone went in and changed the date. I'm willing to bet Niall Gilmartin was in there on Friday night. Someone adjusted the date on the tape to cover Gilmartin's ass but never changed the day."

"I'm in there, off and on. It's a nice place. He doesn't look familiar. Does he work there?"

"My information is he's a truck driver. Do you know the owners of the pub?"

"I know them to say hi, but don't really know them personally." Roberts seemed to think for a moment and said, "Why don't we stop over there and check things out. I can't believe they're involved in this. They're running a successful business. It's one of the places where all the visitors coming to town want to stop. All us locals know them for serving a good pint. Bring your computer and let's go pay them a visit," Roberts said.

Dillon stuffed the laptop back in his computer bag and stood.

"It's more or less around the corner. It will be faster if we just walk," Roberts said. He led them along a hall, down a set of backstairs, and out a side door into a parking lot. They cut across the parking lot and out onto the street. Roberts checked for traffic, they hurried across the street, walked a half-block, and around the corner. Shoot The Magpies was a tiny-looking pub a block up and across the street. They waited for a car to pass then crossed the street. A narrow alley ran along the side of the pub. Dillon could see the Garavogue river at the far end.

They stepped into a narrow, cozy room that looked about a hundred and fifty years old. Two booths were on the right with the bar just beyond. Two people were sitting at the bar, an archway at the back led into a small space.

Roberts stepped over and spoke briefly with the bartender. He nodded, made a quick phone call, hung up, and said, "Go on back, Emmett. Conor will see ya's. Pint waiting for you's when you're finished if you want it."

"Thanks, Kevin, we'll see," Roberts said and headed toward the archway. Dillon followed. "Conor McRann is who we're going to see. He's good. Does a lot for the town."

They stepped through a small hall with a fireplace. The front of the fireplace had a large, carved stone tree on either side, meeting in the middle. Dillon made a mental note to come back some night and check the place out. Roberts stopped at the door marked private. He knocked, and they stepped inside.

A bald man wearing a black sports shirt embroidered with 'Shoot the Magpies' nodded as he rose from his desk.

"Thanks for making the time, Conor," Roberts said as they shook hands. "This is Jack Dillon. He's working a case in Dublin and wanted to run something by you."

"Nice to meet you, Conor," Dillon said, and they shook hands.

"American?" McRann asked.

"Yeah, but don't hold it against me."

They all laughed at that, and McRann said, "Oh, we're blessed to have Americans in here every night. Please, take a seat. Sit down, lads. How can I help you?"

Dillon explained the situation to some extent. He did not mention the fact that Sophie McGinn had died. Instead, he played the video on his laptop for McRann and pointed out the date discrepancy.

McRann shook his head and said, "Hang on, let me check it out. I'm not aware of any problem we've had." He turned in his chair and typed a few keys using both index fingers. A moment later, the screen came to life. He typed some more, and the security cameras suddenly appeared. A half-dozen different black and white images filled the screen.

"Let me see your picture again," he said to Dillon.

Dillon turned his laptop toward McRann.

"Yeah, they're in the snook. Hmm," he said, typing in the date and time as it appeared on Dillon's laptop. He didn't add the day. The screen flickered for a few seconds and then brought up the exact same area, but not the same image. Instead of Niall Gilmartin and four other men, the image had two couples, maybe mid-fifties. The women were drinking half-pint glasses, and the men had full pints. The date in the right-hand corner read 'Sat 24/7/21.'

"Can you bring up the day before, same time, but on the twenty-third?"

McRann typed in the new date, and the image appeared. There it was, Niall Gilmartin and four other men. Dillon looked at the image on his screen. With the exception of the date, it was exactly the same.

"Someone altered the tape they sent to us, probably made a copy," Dillon said.

"Bloody hell," McRann said, not looking very happy. "Just a minute, let me check." He typed some more, striking the keys much harder. He made a mistake three different times and had to erase and retype. Each time that happened, his face grew a little more red. Eventually, a list came up with names, addresses, and phone numbers.

"Here we go. It's about damn time. Let me just call Eoin here. He deals with the tapes. In fact, he's the lad in the tape with the glass raised to his lips." McRann reached for his phone and brought the receiver up to his ear. "Been with us for the better part of two years. I'll find out what the hell happened and—"

"Maybe hold off on the phone call, Conor," Roberts said.

McRann looked at Roberts and said, "I can have Eoin's ass in here in fifteen bleeding minutes. We'll get to the bottom of this, and then I'm going to fire that bollox."

"I think it would be better if we paid him a visit. For one thing, he won't have the opportunity to warn Gilmartin. We'll take him down to the station and have a little chat. Based on his response, he may or may not spend the night."

"You can tell him from me, he's no longer employed. Not here at Shoot the Magpies."

"We'll leave that bit up to you, Conor. If you can give us that address, we'll get out of your hair."

McRann grabbed a notepad and a pencil and copied down the address. He added the phone number, finishing up with a period, slamming the pencil into the pad of paper so hard that the tip broke off. "Oh, Mother of God," he half-shouted and tossed the pencil into the far wall.

"Sorry, lads, but we've worked our asses off for the past twenty years building a relationship with the town and our customers, and now this bollox just pissed on everything we've done. You's better lock him up because, if I get a hold of him, there's no telling what I'll do."

"I think we can keep it quiet, and we'll be listing you as being a most helpful asset in solving the case," Dillon said.

McRann nodded, whispered, "Bloody hell," and shook his head.

FORTY

Dillon and Roberts left McRann's office, promising to stay in touch and closing the door behind them. "Oh my God. I don't envy Eoin Lally when he has to deal with McRann," Dillon said.

Roberts shook his head. "Young and dumb. You have to ask yourself what in the hell did he think was going to happen? You got a good job, you're probably getting paid fairly well, and you pull a stunt like this. His name is going to be on the 'Do not hire' list in Sligo Town for the rest of his life."

"You know him?" Dillon asked.

Roberts shook his head again. "No, and I still feel sorry for him. It's a stupid move with long-term consequences. It's a real shame."

They stepped into the front barroom. Kevin, the bartender, asked, "What do you say, lads? Can I talk ya's into a pint of Guinness?"

"Not that we wouldn't love to, Kevin, but we've places to be. Afraid we'll have to take a raincheck. Thanks, all the same," Roberts said.

They made their way back around the corner and across the street to the Garda station. "You think we might head over to Lally's place right now?" Dillon said.

"I can't think of a better time. Given the look on McRann's face when we left, I've a feeling the word will be all over the street by the end of the night."

"You know where Lally lives?" Dillon asked.

"I recognize the address, a series of new buildings out on the edge of town. Nice enough and priced to be affordable under the building license agreements for another ten years."

"I'll drive," Dillon said.

"Oh, you drove all the way over here from bloody Dublin. I can drive."

"Actually, it wasn't that bad a trip. Took just a little over two hours to get here. I'm parked just ahead of the squad cars," Dillon said. He indicated the white Mercedes with a nod of his head and clicked on the fob, unlocking the doors and flashing the lights.

"That's what you're driving? A bleeding Mercedes?" Roberts said. "Jaysus, Dublin Special Branch. What the feck? Looks like you're on the Gold Coast, Dillon."

"Yeah, well, I've a pretty good feeling it was confiscated from some lowlife living the dream until it turned into a nightmare. Still, it was a nice ride driving out here. Come on, I'll drive, and you can give me the directions."

"Oh, I should take a picture," Roberts said as he opened the passenger door and climbed in.

Dillon slipped in behind the wheel and started the Mercedes.

"Drive up to the roundabout and take the second exit," Roberts said.

It was a fifteen-minute drive. Along the way, Roberts studied the back seat, opened the glove compartment, and the area on the back of the console. "Just checking for a roll of cash," he told Dillon. "If I find any, I'll split it with you."

They pulled into an area with six large, five-story structures forming a 'U' around parking lots and a path with recently planted trees. Large parking lots were in front of each building, and a series of parking lanes for buses were spread out across the rear of the parking lots. Two large playgrounds with swing sets, climbing bars, and slides were at either end of the 'U.'

The structures themselves appeared identical. Each building was made of buff-colored brick with black slate roofs. A large picture window and a small, frosted glass window for a bathroom identified every apartment. Each unit had a small porch with a door leading out to it next to the picture window. Based on the quick glance Dillon made, there would only be room for one individual on the porch, if even that. Certainly, the porches weren't large enough for a chair, and he decided their purpose was merely as decoration and to present a more ostentatious appearance.

"That middle building is Lally's. Pull into the parking lot. There are visitor spaces up at the front of the building, next to the entrance doors," Roberts said.

"You come here often?" Dillon asked.

"Often enough. Sixty years ago, they would have built twenty-story towers. These look a lot nicer, but we've still got the same people living in them. Council house living wasn't designed for multiple generations, but unfortunately, that's the way it's become."

Dillon drove up to the front of the building and pulled into a visitor's space. He decided it wouldn't be the best idea to leave his An Garda Síochána card on the dashboard. They climbed out of the Mercedes and headed into the building.

The security lobby was relatively small. A solid steel door was centered on the far wall. Next to that was a keypad and a telephone attached to the wall.

"Used to be a glass door leading in, but after being broken on a weekly basis, this is what you end up with," Roberts said and hit the pound sign on the telephone keypad. Directions appeared on the phone; *Enter the first three letters of the tenant's surname and press 0'*. Roberts put in LAL for Lally, and a code appeared, 707#. He punched in the four-digit code, held the receiver to his ear, and waited. He nodded at Dillon when he heard the phone ringing.

"Good afternoon, Eoin. Sorry to bother you. This is D.I. Emmett Roberts. If you would buzz me in, please. No, sorry, I have to discuss this in person. What? No, I wouldn't worry about heading to work. We spoke with Conor McRann earlier this afternoon, and he suggested we get in touch with you. Now, please let us in before this goes bad for you. No, like I said, we need to discuss this in person."

The door suddenly buzzed. Dillon pushed the steel door open.

"Thank you, Eoin. What's your unit number? See you shortly," Roberts said and hung up.

"After you," Dillon said, holding the door.

"He's in three-oh-three," Roberts said as he pulled out his phone. He placed a call requesting a backup unit and had them wait at the front door of the building. Then they headed for the elevators.

There were two elevators standing side by side. One of them had an 'Out of Service' sign taped to it. Dillon pressed the 'up' button, and a moment later, the doors opened on the other elevator. They stepped inside, and Roberts pushed '3.'

There was an odor in the elevator that suggested someone had recently relieved themselves. Dillon checked the floor to make sure he wasn't standing in a puddle. Graffiti on the elevator wall written with a black marker described a woman named Dara in colorful terms. The doors opened on the third floor, and Dillon and Roberts hurried out.

"Oh, God, but that was dreadful," Roberts said.

"I'm thinking we'll take the stairs down on the way out," Dillon said.

They headed down the hall, walking past trash bags outside a number of doors. The bags added an unpleasant odor to the hall. Unit 303, Lally's apartment, had two trash bags next to the door. Roberts shook his head, draped a lanyard with his I.D. around his neck, and knocked on the door.

Eoin Lally opened the door a moment later. He looked the same as the young man on the security tape. Slightly overweight, heading toward pudgy. His brown hair was uncombed, and his sparse beard needed shaving. He was wearing what looked like pajama bottoms and a t-shirt from the 'Bad Ass Pub.' "You're with the Gardai?"

"D.I. Roberts," Roberts replied and held up his I.D.

Lally studied the I.D. for a moment. Maybe wondering which stupid thing he'd done that brought them to his door. After a moment, he stepped back and held the door open.

The apartment was compact. A two-burner stove with a small oven was inset in the counter on the wall off to the right. A small sink was next to the burners, and a refrigerator was inset beneath the counter next to a sink filled with dishes. The room featured a worn gray couch with three dirty plates and two mugs on the floor. A pile of dirty laundry was on the floor in front of an upside-down wastebasket with a small flatscreen resting on top. Just now, the flatscreen was paused on a Spiderman movie.

Dillon was tempted to pull on the pair of latex gloves in his pocket.

"How can I help you's?" Lally asked in a tone that suggested he knew exactly what the problem might be.

"Charming place you've got here, Eoin. I'm guessing there's not a lady present."

"She dumped me a few months back, but I didn't take that money from her. I don't care what she told you's."

"Actually, she didn't tell us anything. But a question has come up on a security tape. It shows you and three others having a pint with a lad by the name of Niall Gilmartin at the Shoot The Magpies pub."

"Yeah, I work there. Was there a problem?"

"What do you think?" Roberts said.

Lally seemed to think for a moment and then shook his head. "Oh, Jaysus, I knew I shouldn't have done it. Look, I'm sorry. I don't know what I was thinking. Niall asked me to do him a favor, and I wanted to get on his good side, ya know? I'll go back and fix it. I can change it back, and no one needs to know. Okay?"

"A little late for that, I'm afraid. I think your man Conor McRann might have something to say about it."

The color seemed to drain from Lally's face. "McRann knows about it?"

"He does. In fact, he's the one who gave us your phone number and address."

"Oh, feck," Lally said just under his breath. "Damn it. I knew it wouldn't work. Am I gonna go to jail?"

Roberts seemed to think about that and said, "What do you think?"

"Look, I'll do anything you's want. Please don't put me in jail. Christ, the old man will skin me alive."

"Really?" Roberts said. "Then jail might be the safest place for you."

Lally seemed to consider that for a moment.

"Here's the problem, Eoin. The young woman your pal Niall Gilmartin broke up with, guess what? She's dead."

"What?"

"Yeah, right now, you've got a lot more to worry about than the old man." Roberts pulled out a card and began to read, "You are not obliged to say anything unless you wish to do so, but whatever you say will be taken down in writing and may be given in evidence."

"No, oh no. Please, I didn't mean to do it. Niall just asked. I can change it back. No one has to know. It'll just take a minute, please, please."

FORTY-ONE

They led Eoin Lally down three flights of stairs. All the while, he kept saying, "Please, please." Once outside, two officers stepped out of a squad car and placed Eoin in the back seat.

Roberts talked to the officers for a moment and then walked over to Dillon. "They'll take him to the station and place him in an interview room. You interested in grabbing something to eat?"

Dillon shook his head. "I'm not really hungry. This kid just screwed up his life. There's a young woman dead. A college girl, no less. I'd like to find Niall Gilmartin if it's all the same to you."

"A man after my own heart. We can line up someone to take Lally's statement. Let me make a call," Roberts said and pulled out his phone.

As the squad car drove past, Dillon glanced over and saw a tear-stained Eoin Lally staring at him. Dillon watched until the squad car turned out of the parking lot and disappeared from sight.

They were almost back to the Sligo Town Station when Roberts' phone rang. "Yeah, Moira, what did you find out? Oh, really. Over by the University? No, we'll head there now. On our way, thank you."

"Change of plans?" Dillon asked.

"Niall Gilmartin has an address just out past the University."

"Let's see what happens," Dillon said. Roberts directed him over to O'Connell Street. He made a righthand turn and drove past the Glasshouse Hotel, crossed the river, and took a left, then a right, then another left, and maybe a mile later, they drove past the Sligo University Hospital. He took a right at the next corner and passed the Brewery Bar. After another quarter mile, Roberts said, "Yeah, we're near. Pull over here. I think that's Gilmartin's place three doors up."

Dillon pulled over to the curb and up over a portion of the sidewalk. The units were all similar, side by side, two-story, red-brick duplexes with white trim. Dillon's first thought was that the area looked awfully nice for a young guy driving a truck to be living in.

"How do you want to handle this?" Dillon asked.

"We'll pull up and block the driveway. Hopefully, he's home. Ask him to come with us to the station. If he refuses, we call for backup. We've got the dead girl and corroboration from McRann and Lally. We're not going to need a warrant."

"Is he living with his folks? This looks like a fairly nice area. Too pricey for some young guy driving trucks."

"Yeah, except that the unit he lives in has apparently been turned into multiple rentals. He's listed as being in apartment four," Roberts said.

Dillon pulled ahead and parked across the driveway blocking any exit from the two cars parked in the drive. Gilmartin's unit was on the left-hand side of the duplex. All the shades were drawn, but lights were clearly on in the front rooms on the first and second floors.

They headed for the door on the left side of the duplex, went up two steps, and onto the front stoop. There were four black mailboxes lined up just to the left of the front door, one on top of the other with number one at the top and number four at the bottom. The front door had a large, beveled glass panel with a curtain. The curtain was only partially closed, and they could see a hallway and a staircase leading up to the second floor.

The right-hand side of the doorframe had four doorbells, numbered in the same sequence as the mailboxes. Dillon reached down to the mailbox labeled four. A handwritten piece of paper with the name 'Gilmartin' was taped to the top of the mailbox. Dillon opened the mailbox and removed three circulars addressed to 'Occupant.' "At least the mailbox confirms he's in number four. Mind if I ring the doorbell?"

"Be my guest," Roberts said.

Dillon pressed the doorbell labeled '4.' After a minute, he pressed it again and held his finger in place just in case that was required. Still no answer.

Roberts reached over and pressed the doorbell labeled one. A moment later, a door in the hallway opened, and a man in his early thirties, stepped into the hall and walked toward the front door. Roberts glanced at the mailbox labeled one, but there was no name on it.

The man opened the front door. He had dark hair, blue eyes, and a slight paunch. He was chewing something, but he stopped and swallowed just before he opened the door. "Yeah?"

"Sorry to bother you. We're trying to see Niall Gilmartin. Would you happen to know if he's home?"

The guy shook his head and said, "I got no idea."

"Would you happen to know if he works evenings?"

"No. Anything else?"

"Does he live here?"

"You got me."

Roberts held up his lanyard with the card. "I'm going to ask you again, nicely. Does Niall Gilmartin live here?"

The guy focused on Roberts' I.D for a second, nodded, and said, "Yeah, I think he's in number four. I don't know him. Don't know where he works. Seems like he's gone for days at a time. Always parks out on the sidewalk. He drives a black car, but I don't know the make of the thing. It's an older model, and it's not here now," he said, looking over Dillon's shoulder toward the street.

"All right. Well, can't thank you enough for the time. If you happen to see him, maybe don't mention we were asking for him."

"Yes, sir,"

They stepped off the stoop and headed back to the Mercedes. The man waited a long moment before he closed the door, not quite slamming it but definitely using some force.

"Looks like we might be here a while," Dillon said.

"Apparently."

"You want to wait across the street, and I'll go get us some coffee. Where's the nearest place?" Dillon asked.

"You might want to go back to that pub called The Brewery. I've eaten there, food's good. How about I call in an order, sandwiches and coffees? We may be here a good while. You can pick them up when they're ready."

Dillon nodded and said, "That sounds like a pretty good idea. I'll have whatever you're getting."

As they climbed into the Mercedes, Roberts pulled out his phone. He ordered two cheeseburgers with bacon, two orders of sweet potato fries, two coffees to go and gave them a credit card number.

"They'll be ready in fifteen minutes," Roberts said once he disconnected.

Dillon drove to The Brewery bar and hurried inside. The food was in a paper bag, and the coffees were in a tray next to the cash register when Dillon walked inside.

"Good evening. Table for one?" the woman behind the cash register asked.

"No. Actually, I think that might be my order," Dillon said as he pointed toward the bag and the tray with the coffees.

The woman checked the receipt stapled to the bag, smiled, and said, "Mr. Roberts?"

Dillon nodded, and she handed the bag and tray to him. He hurried back into the Mercedes and drove back. Roberts was standing on a street corner.

Dillon pulled over and Roberts climbed into the passenger seat, carefully working his feet around the bag and the coffee tray. "Didn't want to attract any more attention than necessary," Roberts said as he placed his coffee in the cup holder on the console.

Dillon pulled back to where they had initially parked, three doors down from Gilmartin's unit. Roberts handed him a burger and was just about to hand him a coffee when Dillon's phone rang. He set the burger on his lap and pulled out his phone.

"Hey, Paddy, sorry I forgot to phone you. Everything all right on your end?" Dillon said.

"You plonker, you're not even gone one day, and you've already screwed up, at no surprise. Everything is fine here. How are things going on your end?"

"We're making a little bit of progress. We've got the guy who changed the date on the security tape. He's only twenty and at the very least is probably going to lose his job. Right now, we're waiting for the former boyfriend to come home. Anything on Sinead Lynch?"

"Not a sign. You think she might have left the country? Flown back to Spain or wherever in the hell she's living?"

"You think we could be that lucky?" Dillon replied.

"Yeah, point well taken. Hope you have a quiet evening. Now don't forget to check in tomorrow morning. And not too early, I need my beauty sleep."

"You think that will help?" Dillon asked.

"One can always hope," Suel said and disconnected.

FORTY-TWO

It was close to midnight. They'd been sitting in the Mercedes for nearly six hours, parked three doors from the duplex where Gilmartin lived. It seemed like six days since they'd been sitting in the car waiting for him to show up.

Dillon glanced up and down the street, checking for any foot traffic or headlights. There weren't any at this hour and hadn't been any for quite some time. "I'll be back in a minute," he said to Roberts.

"Be sure to wash your hands," Roberts said as Dillon stepped out of the car and hurried past the duplex. By now, all the lights, including the front porch light, were turned off. Apparently, anyone with any sense was already tucked in bed.

Dillon made his way to an evergreen hedge along the front garden of a duplex just two lots past Gilmartin's place. He gave a quick look around. Still no foot traffic and no headlights in either direction. He took a half-step closer to the evergreen hedge, looked once more, and unzipped his jeans. *'Oh, thank God'* was his immediate thought as he felt himself relax.

His shadow suddenly appeared against the hedge as a car pulled out of the alley behind him. He automatically took a half-step into the hedge and quickly detected a warm splashing on his hand as the car passed and pulled up onto the sidewalk in front of Gilmartin's place. Thankfully, whoever was driving turned off the headlights that illuminated the white Mercedes.

Dillon quickly zipped his fly and turned toward the vehicle. It appeared to be black, and based on the portion of the license plate he could read, it was a 2005 model. The driver's door opened, and a man stepped out. He was lean with dark hair.

Dillon was pretty sure it was Gilmartin. He waited for a moment until the figure moved away from the car.

If Roberts saw Gilmartin, he wasn't reacting yet, which was a good thing.

Gilmartin stretched and reached into the back seat. He pulled what looked like a nylon bag with handles from the back seat. He stretched again and closed the driver's door. He had just stepped in front of his car, headed for the duplex when Roberts opened the passenger door on the Mercedes. Unfortunately, the interior light flashed on as he stepped out of the car.

Gilmartin glanced over, stared for a second before he turned and headed back toward his driver's door. Dillon was suddenly on the run, and so was Roberts.

"Hold up, Naill, we want to talk. Naill, stop, don't run. Naill," Roberts called as he ran toward Gilmartin.

Gilmartin pulled the driver's door open and tossed the nylon bag at Roberts, who simply batted it away. He left the car door open and took three or four steps to the rear of the vehicle before Dillon charged into him with a solid shoulder to the solar plexus. Gilmartin's scream was cut short when he bounced off the rear of his car and landed face down on the sidewalk. He was momentarily stunned, which was just long enough for Dillon to plant a knee in the small of his back. Dillon pulled Gilmartin's left arm behind his back and slapped a handcuff onto the wrist.

"Uff, ahh," was all Gilmartin could say as Dillon slapped the cuffs onto his right wrist. Dillon rested for a moment with his knee in the small of Gilmartin's back. Then he stood, took hold of Gilmartin's arm, and half-pulled, half-helped him to his feet.

Roberts stepped over and spun Gilmartin around, leaned him against the rear of the car, and proceeded to pat him down. "You carrying anything sharp or danger-ous, a knife or a gun?" he asked, running his hands along Gilmartin's belt.

"No, no, I got nothing. Honest," Gilmartin said and began to cry. "I'm sorry. I'm sorry. I didn't mean to do it. It just happened so fast, and it was an accident. Hon-est. I didn't mean to hurt Sophie. I didn't," he said and continued to sob.

Roberts pulled out his card and began to read, "You are not obliged to say anything unless you wish to do so, but whatever you say will be taken down in writing and may be given in evidence...." When he'd finished, he looked at Dillon and said, "Watch him for a moment. I'll call for backup."

Dillon placed his hands on the cuffs behind Gilmartin's back and gently pushed him forward against the back of his car, a Hyundai. "You just stay right there."

Gilmartin continued to sob, occasionally uttering the phrase, "I'm so sorry."

Two squad cars quickly arrived, no more than a minute apart. Gilmartin was ushered into the back of one of the squad cars and driven down to the Sligo Town station.

Dillon gathered up the nylon bag Gilmartin had tossed at Roberts and set it in the back seat of the Mercedes. As they climbed into the Mercedes, Dillon glanced around. With the exception of two porch lights further down the road, all the houses were dark. No one was aware of the arrest that had just occurred in front of their home.

As Dillon pulled onto the street, Roberts said, "Not a bad shoulder you gave your man. You play rugby as a lad?"

"No, hockey, although I think in my old age, I'm probably going to feel that for a couple of days."

"Yeah, amazing how the recovery time has been extended for us," Roberts said and chuckled.

They had filled out the initial paperwork and were seated in an interview room with Niall Gilmartin just after 3 A.M. He continued to sob occasionally. His eyes were red and puffy. Just now, he was handcuffed to a steel ring in the center of a metal table. The chair he was seated in was bolted to the floor. The interview was being filmed.

"And so you drove to Dublin to see Sophie?" Dillon said.

Gilmartin nodded, "She agreed to meet me at a place in Temple Bar. It's called Gallaghers Boxty House."

"And did you meet her?"

Gilmartin nodded. "Yeah, I was there a half-hour early, just in case. She eventually showed up. I just wanted us to get back together. I told her I'd do anything. All she did was shake her head. We'd ordered some food, but she wanted to leave before it was even served. I had to pay, and I waited a minute or two. She just walked out, and I left forty euros on the table and tried to catch up. She told me to leave her alone a couple of times, but I thought, if I could just talk to her, let her know I didn't want the breakup. Well then…"

"So you followed her through Temple Bar?"

"Yeah, up through a couple of streets. I called her name a couple of times, but she just told me to go away. I thought if I just stayed there, you know, followed her at a distance like, she'd see that I loved her."

"But then you followed her on Curved Street, and you left there by yourself. What happened?"

"Oh God," Gilmartin said and began sobbing again.

Roberts passed some more tissues to him.

He blew his nose and said, "I just, I just wanted to talk to her. To get her to understand that what she was doing didn't make any sense. We were on that little lane, it was darker than hell, and she turned and told me it was over, and she didn't want to see me again, ever. Then I shouted something at her. I forget what. She shouted something back, and I just reacted."

"You hit her?"

Gilmartin looked up. Tears were running down his cheeks. "Oh no, no, I'd never do that. I only pushed her. That was all. I just pushed her a little, and she fell back. Oh, Jesus, her head bounced off of the stone windowsill on this old building."

"The Button Factory," Dillon said.

"Is that what it is? I'd never been there, so I don't know. She was on the ground, and she sort of twitched for a moment and then was just lying there, all still like. She wasn't dead. I could see she was breathing. I called her name a bunch of times, but she never opened her eyes. I...I just panicked, and after a bit, I saw a couple walk into the lane and I, I left. I didn't want to run because I thought it would draw attention, so I just walked away. I left her there and...and..." He broke down in tears again.

Dillon glanced over at Roberts, who gave a slight nod, then stood and walked over to the door.

"Mr. Gilmartin, it's late. We're all exhausted. This concludes our interview at this time," Dillon said, glancing at the clock on the wall and stating the time.

"I didn't mean to hurt her. Honest, I didn't. I wish it was me that had fallen. I...I..." He began sobbing all over again.

A moment later, two uniformed officers stepped into the interview room. Roberts said something to them. They nodded and led a sobbing Gilmartin away.

Once they were gone, Roberts said, "Long day. I told them to put him on suicide watch. I don't want to show up tomorrow and find out he took his own life."

"Probably a good idea. At least he's here, and we can keep an eye on him. No telling what he'd do left to his own devices."

FORTY-THREE

Dillon left the station a half-hour later and drove to the Glasshouse Hotel. He parked in the underground parking lot, took the elevator up to the lobby, stepped off, and took another elevator up to the fourth floor. He walked down the hall to his room.

He inserted his keycard and stepped into the room. He placed the keycard in the slot on the wall, and the lights in the room came on. He locked the door and flipped the bolt over so the door couldn't be opened. He phoned the front desk, and after a half-dozen rings, a man with a scratchy voice answered.

"Front, ahem, front desk."

"Yes, this is room four-twelve. I'd like to get a wake-up call at 9:00 tomorrow morning."

"All right, sir. I have you down for that, a 9:00 wake-up call."

"Thank you," Dillon said and hung up.

He sat on the edge of the bed and took a deep breath. It had been a very long day with a successful arrest at the end, and nobody got hurt. He actually felt a little sorry for Niall Gilmartin but felt even worse for Sophie McGinn and her family. God, the things people do. He crawled onto the bed, still dressed, and fell asleep almost immediately. The phone ringing at 9:00 the following morning woke him. He answered the phone. "Hello?"

The recording said, "Good Morning. It's 9:00."

He took a long, hot shower then hurried down to the breakfast dining room. They stopped serving at 10:00, but that still gave Dillon twelve minutes to load up a plate from the buffet counter. He actually loaded up two plates, scrambled eggs, hash brown potatoes, and bacon rashers on one, pancakes, and lots of maple syrup on the other. He settled in at a window overlooking the river. He'd just taken a mouthful of his scrambled eggs when his cellphone rang. D.I. Suel.

"Hey, Paddy. Late night. Didn't get back to the hotel until almost 4:00 this morning. Good news is we got your man, Niall Gilmartin. Sorry, I haven't called. I'm literally just ten minutes out of the shower."

"So much for keeping a low profile, Dillon."

"What are you talking about?"

"I just heard it on the news. That's the reason for my call. You're listed as one of the arresting officers of a suspect in the murder of Sophie McGinn. Interestingly, they didn't bother to mention the name of the knacker you arrested."

"What? Are you sure they mentioned me?"

"Let me think. Are you a United States Marshal assigned to Dublin's An Garda Síochána Special Branch, and were you involved in a shoot-out at Dublin Airport Terminal Two a few years ago?"

"Jesus Christ."

"Jesus Christ has got feck all to do with this, Dillon."

"I don't know how they would have gotten that information. We didn't—"

"Obviously, it was leaked somehow. We're in the process of scheduling a press conference where you'll be speaking late this afternoon."

"So you want me to head back to Dublin?"

"Absolutely not. In fact, that's the last thing you should do. We want you to stay in Sligo Town. We'll put the word out you're not at the press conference because you've returned to the United States, and hopefully, that will get Miss Sinead Lynch's hot little bum out of the country or, God forbid, under arrest. Either way, you are to keep a low profile. Maybe try staying under the bed in your hotel room."

Dillon thought for a moment and said, "So what you're thinking is, if Sinead Lynch were to see that news report, she might show up over here in Sligo Town?"

"Let's just say the news report defeats the purpose of getting your dumb ass the hell out of Dublin. I don't mean to cast a shadow on the arrest of your man, Gilmartin, which by the way, McCabe and the rest of us are applauding."

"But hang on a minute, Paddy. If she showed up, why wouldn't we be ready to arrest her or even take her out if she left no other option?"

"In other words, you're suggesting we use you as bait?"

"That's a little crude, but yeah, something along those lines."

"I'm not sure the powers that be would go for something like that," Suel said.

"Maybe I'll give D.C.I. McCabe a call and get his opinion."

"Good luck with that," Suel said and disconnected.

Dillon thought some more as he finished up his breakfast. A server stepped up to the table just as he placed the last bit of syrup-soaked pancake in his mouth. She nodded at his two empty plates, and Dillon nodded back. She placed his silverware on the pancake plate, put that on top of the egg plate, and quickly carried everything away.

Dillon finished his coffee and got up from the table. He walked past the buffet counter on his way out and grabbed an icing-covered cinnamon roll. He had devoured the roll by the time he got to the Mercedes in the underground parking. He drove to the Sligo Town Garda Station and parked on the street.

"Marshal Dillon. Good morning, sir. Excellent job last night. Congratulations. D.I. Roberts is upstairs at his desk. Do you know the way?" the sergeant at the front desk asked a half-second after Dillon stepped into the lobby.

"I think I can find my way. Thank you."

The sergeant and the other officer at the desk gave Dillon a thumbs-up.

Dillon headed down the hall and ended up next to the back stairs and the door leading out to the parking lot. He headed up the stairs to the third floor, took the long hallway back toward what he hoped was the front of the building, and eventually found the right door. Thankfully, there wasn't a keypad requiring a code number. Dillon opened the door, stepped in, and immediately spotted Roberts at his desk talking to two people.

"Well, it's about time. I've already been here for fifteen minutes," Roberts said as Dillon approached. "Let me introduce D.I. Mick O'Toole and D.I. Ann Walsh. I was just bringing them up to date on last night."

"Nice to meet you," O'Toole and Walsh said.

O'Toole had dark hair, thinning slightly, pale blue eyes, and a heavy build. He was big but not what you'd call fat. Maybe he was a former sports player in school. Walsh was an attractive blonde with her hair trimmed just above her shoulders, blue eyes, and a nice figure.

"Very nice to meet you," Dillon replied. "Mick O'Toole? Would you happen to be related to Lisa O'Toole in Special Branch up in Dublin? She just had knee surgery a couple of weeks ago."

He nodded and said, "Yeah, she's a cousin. My da is from Dublin. He grew up on the north side, where the real Dubs live."

"That's where I'm living."

"What? They let you in?"

"Oh, I had to ask permission," Dillon said.

"Good on ya's," O'Toole said, and everyone laughed.

"I heard there was a news report this morning on our arrest last night," Dillon said.

Roberts shook his head. "We were just talking about it. There's obviously a leak somewhere."

"The leak's been there for a while, but damned if anyone can seem to find it," Ann Walsh said.

"Did you hear the report?" Roberts asked.

"No, I got a call from my partner in Dublin. He mentioned it. That's got to be coming from inside somewhere. Has to be a pretty small group. Gilmartin wasn't even in here until sometime after midnight, and it was already broadcast this morning in Dublin."

"The leak has been a problem, but like Ann said, damned if we can figure out where in the hell it's coming from."

Dillon and Roberts settled in to write follow-up reports to the ones they submitted eight hours earlier. They were both on desk duty pending the standard review of last night's events. They walked out of the office and around the corner to the Shoot the Magpies pub for lunch.

Kevin was bartending again, but they waved off his offer for a free pint because they were on duty, even though it was just desk duty. Halfway through their lunch, Conor McRann came over to their table and sat down.

"Just wanted to congratulate the both of you's on your arrests last night. Glad you were able to arrest the murderer, and I can only hope you's keep idiot Eoin Lally behind bars for life."

"We've all done stupid things when we were young," Roberts said.

"Yeah, but none of that was faked reports to the Gardai. For the life of me," McRann said, shaking his head. "He was a good employee. On the one hand, I'm sorry to lose him. On the other, I've someone going over our records to see if he bolloxed up anything else. Anyway, another job well done. Lunch is on the house for the both of you's, and don't even try to tell me otherwise. Stay safe." With that, McRann got up and left.

"Never enough of that," Dillon said.

"Typical, he had to let the lad go, he feels bad about it, and he stops by to tell us lunch is on the house. One of the many reasons I like this place," Roberts said.

FORTY-FOUR

Back at the Sligo Town Garda station, Dillon excused himself and placed a call to D.C.I. McCabe in Dublin.

"McCabe," was how he answered.

"Good afternoon, sir. Jack Dillon calling from Sligo Town."

"Yes, Dillon, congratulations and well done on the arrest. Any problems?"

"No sir, other than the usual, a number of lives affected, and in the end, nothing for the better."

"Pretty much the standard. You spoke with D.I. Suel?"

"I did, sir. He mentioned there is a press conference scheduled for later this afternoon."

"Oh, that. Yes, well, hopefully, the word will go out that you've traveled back to the States, and we either find this woman, or she flees the country."

"Might I suggest an alternative, sir?"

"An alternative? Dillon, if you're thinking of returning and seeking her out, we've people on that task at present, and everyone is coming up empty-handed. With all respect, I don't believe your presence would make a noticeable difference and may, in fact, have a negative effect."

"I agree, sir, but what if you put the word out that I was involved in last night's arrest and that I'm remaining in Sligo Town to tie up some loose ends? Maybe she'd hurry down here, and we could be waiting."

"You're thinking she may head to Sligo Town?"

"I'm thinking there's at least a chance, sir, and we could be waiting."

"Interesting. Let me touch base with some people, and we'll see. Nice chatting," McCabe said and hung up.

Dillon and Roberts had been finalizing the arrest and interview reports for almost an hour when Mick O'Toole called across the room to Roberts. "Emmett, you and Dillon are wanted in the principal's office, again. When are you going to learn?" he said and chuckled.

"Oh, shit. Now what? Come on," Roberts said as he stepped from his desk.

Dillon followed him down a short hall to a corner office with two glass walls. Blinds were pulled on the glass walls. A plaque next to the door read LT Noah Madden. Roberts knocked on the office door.

A gruff voice replied, "Enter."

From the sound of the voice, Dillon's first thought was, *'He should have said enter at your own risk.'*

Roberts opened the door and stepped inside. Dillon followed him. Madden was partially hidden behind two stacks of files as he sat at his desk. He was a stocky-looking man with a crew cut, a neatly trimmed mustache, and a nose that had clearly been broken more than once. He wore a white shirt with the top two buttons undone and the sleeves rolled up to his elbows, exposing muscular forearms.

"Oh, grand, the both of ya's. Grab a seat, and I'll be with you in a second."

They settled into the worn leather chairs in front of Madden's desk. As Dillon settled into the chair, it creaked and rocked from side to side. He made a mental note not to shift his weight in the thing too quickly.

"All right then," Madden said as he closed a file and placed it on top of the shorter of the two stacks. "You must be Dillon, the American from Dublin Special Branch," Madden said as he reached across the stack of files to shake Dillon's hand.

"Pleasure to meet you, sir. I've enjoyed working with D.I. Roberts."

"Don't we all," Madden said and flashed a one-second smile. "From the reports I've read, it appears no one was injured in your arrests yesterday. You apprehended two individuals, and during your interview early this morning with Mr. Gilmartin, he willfully admitted to the murder of the McGinn girl. Am I missing anything?"

"No, sir. That pretty much sums it up. Conor McRann gave us the lead on Eoin Lally, the man responsible for adjusting the date on the security tape from Shoot the Magpie's pub," Roberts said.

"Yes, the now-former employee. I had a call from McRann earlier this morning. He spoke well of both of you. Paperwork on Gilmartin will be on its way to the solicitor's office later today. Well done."

"Yes, sir," Roberts said. "Umm, I believe Marshal Dillon has a thought he would like to run past you, sir."

Dillon looked at Robert's for a moment and then said, "Actually, sir, I received a phone call from my partner in Dublin Special Branch. He told me about a news broadcast that played in Dublin this morning regarding our arrests last night. My name happened to be mentioned in the newscast."

"And they were planning to hold a press conference this afternoon where they would mention that you had returned to the States. Correct?"

"Yeah, exactly," Dillon said, unable to hide his surprise that Madden knew of the plan.

"I had a nice chat with D.C.I. McCabe just a half-hour ago. We've known one another for quite a few years. He's concerned about your safety. That murder on the M1 and the murder of an American in that village out on the coast seemed to be related. He mentioned the officer murdered on the M1 was mistaken for you. Is that correct?"

"It would appear that the facts, such as we have them, would point to that. They sent me out here to follow up on a lead in the McGinn murder and slip quietly out of Dublin. Unfortunately, this morning's news report sunk that ship."

"McCabe mentioned you may have come up with a way to use this for our benefit," Madden said.

"As a matter of fact, I have, sir. Rather than hide me somewhere, what if we use this opportunity to lure the killer here and either arrest or eliminate them?"

"And the killer is believed to be a woman?"

"Yes, sir. A woman by the name of Sinead Lynch. I knew her first as Amelia Maher. We believe she has close ties with the Linnehan family, currently located in Costa del Sol."

"Cormac Linnehan," Madden said and shook his head. "He's been the root cause of a lot of the problems we've been dealing with over the last twenty years. His group of ne'er-do-wells, and that group of Muppets out of Limerick, the Doyles, have caused a lot of trouble. So how would you see this working in our favor?"

"Something low-key. Dublin could have their press conference where they congratulate your department for an arrest in the murder of Sophie McGinn. At the same time, we hold a press conference here with D.I. Roberts and me taking questions from reporters regarding the McGinn murder. We say something like we're continuing to look into additional aspects of the case. I might even mention I'm staying at the Glasshouse, or better yet, maybe we hold the press conference at the Glasshouse. Then we just sit and wait. If it's going to happen, I would think an attempt to kill me might occur within seventy-two hours."

"You're okay with this?"

"I want it over and done with, and the best way I can think of to get to that point is to get Sinead Lynch in custody."

"Do you know, does she work alone? Or does she have contacts, and we'd have all sorts of knackers winding up here. Is there a price on your head?"

Dillon seemed to think for a moment. "I believe the intent to kill me rests solely with Sinead Lynch. She's taken a personal interest as opposed to the organization feeling threatened by me."

"What makes you say that?"

Dillon went on to explain the murders of the American couple mistaken for the criminal, Dennis Punchy Sheehan down in Desertserges County Cork some months back, along with the murder of four men up in Dublin.

"You think she committed these murders by herself?"

"The shooter of the American couple was under her direction. We're sure of it. That said, we believe she acted alone and committed the murders of four men, one of whom actually killed the American couple in Cork. She's a true professional. As I mentioned earlier, we believe she's responsible for the murder of Dennis Hickey in Skerries. We believe she murdered Hickey in the hopes I would be sent to Skerries, along with my partner, to aid in the investigation. That was indeed the case. The officer briefly filling in for my partner, Kevin Rafferty, was murdered on the M1. A case of mistaken identity since he was wearing my hat and raincoat at the time."

"Did you have any personal interaction with this woman?"

Dillon wondered just how much Madden had learned from McCabe. "I interviewed her in relation to the killing of the individual who murdered the American couple in Cork. She led me to believe she had had a personal relationship with him at one time. That briefly developed into some personal interaction, a dinner, a lunch, and she suddenly became a prime suspect after a failed attempt at Weston airport."

Madden nodded, seemed to think for a moment, and then said, "Let me check with the powers that be. This is out of my pay grade. Anything else?"

"Only that I'll do whatever it takes to arrest this individual," Dillon said.

"We'll see about that. Thank you, gentlemen," Madden said and pulled the next file from the taller stack.

"Thank you, sir," Dillon and Roberts said in unison and exited the office.

"That was modestly pain-free, at least for me," Roberts said as they walked back to the Homicide room. "What did you think?"

"I think we've got at least a fighting chance they may try to encourage Sinead Lynch to come over here and attempt to take me out. Then I'll be able to deal with the problem."

Roberts looked at Dillon but didn't say anything.

FORTY-FIVE

Dillon and Roberts got the word later that afternoon that a news conference was scheduled for 5:00, at which they were both required to be present. The McGinn family would also be there, along with the upper echelon of the Sligo Town Gardai and their public relations staff.

At 4:00, Dillon and Roberts reported to the Public Relations office. They met with a woman named Fiona Horgan, a heavy-set, dark-haired woman who tried her best to make Dillon look a little more presentable.

"First off, sir, you are not going to appear wearing that t-shirt. Please follow me," she said and led Dillon and Roberts into a room off of her office. What looked like a barber's chair was positioned in the corner, just in front of a series of mirrors. Trays of makeup rested on the counter in front of the mirrors. She opened the doors on a white wardrobe positioned against a wall and slid her hands across a series of shirts on hangers.

"What's your size, medium or large?"

"Large, I guess," Dillon said.

"Mmm, that will be this one, this other, oh and maybe this one as well. Try these on," she said, handing three shirts on hangers to Dillon. He set the shirts on the barber's chair and pulled the first one, a light blue shirt, off the hanger. He had it halfway on when she said, "Stop. That won't do. Give me that." She held out her hand, and Dillon gave her the shirt.

"Looks like a tea stain," she said, holding up the shirt so Dillon could see the light brown stain running down the left side.

"Maybe Guinness," Roberts said and started to laugh. Her glare cut him off. "Oh, sorry," he said, which seemed to bring a smile to her face.

Dillon pulled on the next shirt.

She nodded and said, "Button it up. Yes, right, that will do. Now, they're going to discuss the arrest you've made, and they will allow just a few questions. The McGinn family will be meeting you privately, following the conference."

"They're not going to say anything at the conference?" Dillon asked.

"Do you think they should?" Horgan said.

"No, absolutely not. If they appear at the conference, even though the suspect has admitted his guilt, I would be afraid they might say something that the defense could use in court. If they want to make a statement, they can do it on their own time."

Horgan smiled and said, "Exactly. That's why they are meeting with the two of you privately. Any questions?"

"Are you going to put makeup on us?" Roberts asked.

"I don't think it would help," Horgan replied.

FORTY-SIX

At ten minutes before 5:00, Dillon and Roberts were led into the media room. Two-thirds of the room was filled with rows of chairs, all of which were occupied by reporters and media types. More people were lined up along the walls. Four large cameras on tripods were set up on a raised platform in the back of the room. A dark blue curtain ran across the front of the room. Dillon and Roberts were led behind the curtain where they joined a group of five uniformed officers.

Lieutenant Madden was one of the officers. He was now in his formal uniform and carried his hat in his right hand. He waved Dillon and Roberts over and began to introduce them to the other officers, the higher-ups in Sligo Town's An Garda Síochána. Everyone smiled and shook hands.

Fiona Horgan stepped in through the curtain and gave a nod to the Chief Superintendent. He stepped over toward the curtain, and everyone proceeded to line up behind him. Horgan stepped to the end of the line and directed Roberts and Dillon to line up behind her. She adjusted Dillon's shirt collar and brushed his shoulders twice. A moment later, a head peeked around the curtain and gave a nod.

"Alright forward," Horgan said, and the line began to move out into the main room. They took one step up onto a small stage and walked to the far end.

When Horgan was about to step out and onto the stage, she turned to Dillon and said, "You two follow me." As they stepped out from behind the curtain, they passed two burly uniformed officers apparently positioned to stop any reporters from going behind the curtain. Horgan proceeded to walk in front of everyone lined up on the stage and then stopped just before the lectern. Once she stopped, the Chief stepped over to the lectern.

"Good evening, ladies and gentlemen of the press, the citizens of Sligo Town, and the Republic of Ireland," the Chief said. There was a sudden flurry of flashes and camera clicks. "We're blessed tonight to announce an arrest in relation to the tragic death of one Sophie McGinn. A resident of Sligo Town and a student at Trinity College, Dublin." He went on for the next two minutes repeating a no doubt memorized text from previous press briefings describing the efforts of the department and then introducing the various individuals on stage.

Based on the reaction of the crowd that Dillon saw, they'd heard it all before. Two other people basically repeated a version of what the Chief had said, and then suddenly Horgan stepped to the lectern. She glanced over at Dillon and Roberts and said, "We will now hear from Detective Inspector Emmett Roberts."

Roberts stepped to the lectern and said, "Thank you. We were fortunate that our investigatory efforts paid off, and we were able to make two arrests without incident. I would like to give special thanks to Conor McRann, proprietor of Shoot the Magpies, for his assistance in breaking this case."

A number of hands were raised, and voices called out, "D.I. Roberts. D.I. Roberts."

Roberts nodded at one of the reporters in the second row and said, "Yes, Emma."

"Why the delay? This incident in Dublin happened two weeks ago."

"Thank you. Yes, it did occur over two weeks ago, but we were hoping for the recovery of Miss McGinn, the victim of this tragic incident. Unfortunately, she never woke from the coma she was in and passed a few days ago. That placed the case on an entirely different level."

"D.I. Roberts, D.I. Roberts." more hands waved, and voices called his name.

"Yes, Desmond," Roberts said.

"Don't take it personally, but is there a chance we might hear from the other officer? Rumor has it things have gotten so bad we need an American here to straighten things out."

Laughter enveloped the room for a few seconds. Roberts looked to Horgan, who stepped forward and nodded at Dillon.

Dillon took a deep breath and walked to the lectern. "Good evening, my name is Marshal Jack Dillon. I'm assigned to An Garda Síochána Special Branch in Dublin. I was fortunate enough to be able to get the assistance of D.I. Roberts and Sligo Town Gardai in this case."

"So you did something our lot was incapable of doing?" the man named Desmond shouted.

Dillon gave him a cold look for a moment, then leaned into the microphone. "On the contrary, quite the opposite. We had a question about the evidence we had received. D.I. Roberts, with the assistance of Mr. McRann at Shoot the Magpies, was able to point us in the right direction. D.I. Roberts and I were able to make an arrest. An arrest without incident, I might add. Although the crime was committed in Dublin, the suspect was here in Sligo Town. That said, I would like to remind everyone here that a local family has lost a daughter. A loss they will never get over and indeed a loss that will remain with the family for generations. The efforts of D.I. Roberts and the Sligo Town Gardai would not have been necessary had this tragedy not occurred in the first place. Thank you," Dillon said and stepped away from the microphone.

Horgan got a nod from the Chief and stepped up to the microphone. "Thank you for your time. You have my contact information should you have any other questions. Good evening," she said and then walked toward Dillon and Roberts, giving a nod toward the curtain as she did so.

Dillon turned and headed off stage. Roberts and everyone else followed as the media shouted questions. Once they were all offstage, the voices in the crowd quickly dwindled down to a conversational murmur.

Horgan walked over to Dillon and said, "Nice job."

"I'm sorry, I didn't mean to shut things down. I thought your man was going—"

"Dillon, relax. I meant what I said. Nice job. The focus should be on the family and their loss. And don't worry about that plonker, Desmond Farmer. He'd like nothing better than to trip you up, and suddenly, that's tomorrow's headline. No. Less is more. There's been an arrest. No one was injured. Think of the McGinn family and their daughter. Perfect. Speaking of which, they're in an adjoining room and want to meet the both of you's."

"If I could have everyone's attention for a moment," Horgan said. "We have a meeting in room two with the McGinn family. Parents, grandparents, and siblings of Sophie McGinn. Give your condolences, and then they're going to want to chat with D.I. Roberts and Marshal Dillon. You know the drill, so let's get started," Horgan nodded, walked to a back door in the room, and headed down a hall.

They entered a smaller room next door. The room was furnished with two couches and a number of chairs.

A table with teapots and a box of pastries with frosting was off in a corner. A large flatscreen was mounted on the wall behind the table. The sound appeared to be turned off, but you could still see the live image of a few people in the room where the press conference had been. Just now, they were standing and talking in a few small groups. Everyone else had already left.

The Chief and senior officers were shaking hands and hugging family members. The couple Dillon guessed was Sophie McGinn's parents were talking with the Chief. Their eyes were red and puffy, and at no surprise, they looked like they hadn't slept for days. They weren't the only ones who had been crying. Three older people, two women and a man, stood just behind the McGinn's. Dillon figured they were probably Sophie's grandparents and appeared to be in their early to mid-seventies. A number of younger people, siblings, maybe cousins or friends, were on the outer edges of the group. Dillon could see a physical resemblance to Sophie's photo in a number of them.

One by one, the officials left the room, and suddenly it was Dillon, Roberts, and Horgan left. Sophie's parents thanked them both, and her mother gave both of them a long hug. Dillon could feel her sobbing against his chest, and he pulled her closer, wishing he could do more.

They chatted for ten or fifteen minutes. The parents and grandparents cursed Naill Gilmartin and another round of hugs, thank you's, and God bless ensued before the family slowly headed out the door. They'd have the funeral in three days and then the rest of their lives to miss their daughter and wish they might give her a final hug and a kiss that was never going to happen.

FORTY-SEVEN

U p in the Homicide office, things were quiet. Roberts glanced at his watch. It was a little after 6:00. "I don't know about you, but I could use something a little stronger than tea. You interested in walking over to Shoot the Magpies? I suspect we're not going to be paying tonight."

"That sounds like an excellent idea," Dillon replied. Roberts turned off his computer, locked his desk, and they headed out the door. Just like before, they took the back stairs, went out across the parking lot, and then around the corner.

When they stepped into the pub, they made it maybe five feet inside before Roberts was stopped by two men shaking his hand and congratulating both him and Dillon. It took ten minutes, but they eventually made it to the bar where Kevin, the bartender, had two pints of Guinness waiting for them.

As he pushed the pints across the bar, one of the men they'd met on the way in stood on a barstool and said, "I'd like us all to raise a glass to Emmett Roberts and Jack Dillon. God bless, lads."

"Here, here," the room responded, and everyone took a sip.

Dillon raised his glass and said, "God watch over Sophie McGinn and bless the McGinn family."

"Here, here," the crowd repeated again, and everyone took another healthy sip.

"Well, the word is out," Roberts said to Dillon. "You're here in Sligo Town. I don't know if you caught it, but one of those cameras in the back of the room was RTE. That conference, at least part of it, will be broadcast all over the country tonight. Very low profile for you over the next few days. An image of Sinead Lynch will be sent to everyone's department email as of midnight tonight. Best to drink up. With the news conference being broadcast, you'll be locked in your room until further notice starting tomorrow. They're putting the word out that you've been assigned desk duty here in Sligo Town. We'll have people posted inside and outside hoping to grab her."

"Sounds like a plan," Dillon said and thought, *'They have no idea, who or what, they're dealing with.'*

He had a second pint and then begged off, pleading he was tired. Roberts promised to meet him for breakfast at 8:30 the following morning. Dillon stepped out of the pub, looked up and down the street, and then hurried around the corner and across to his car. Once in the Mercedes, he locked the doors, placed his Beretta on the passenger seat just in case, and pulled out. Traffic was relatively light, and he was pulling into the underground parking at the Glasshouse Hotel not ten minutes later. He pulled into an empty parking spot and then waited in the car for five minutes, checking for any movement.

He placed the Beretta in his belt, pulled his shirttail out over it, and climbed out of the Mercedes. He studied the parking area for a long moment and didn't detect any movement. He took the elevator up to the main floor. When the door opened, he glanced left and right before stepping out and hurrying over to the front desk.

"Good evening. How may I help you?" the young woman behind the front desk asked. She was very attractive, with shoulder-length black hair and dark brown eyes. She had a slight accent, and Dillon wondered if it might be Spanish or possibly Italian.

"Hello, I'm in room four-twelve. I'm going to be working in my room tomorrow, and I'd like to cancel the housekeeping service. They don't have to make up the room."

She smiled and quickly ran her hands across the keyboard. "Room four-twelve, and your name, sir?"

"Dillon, Jack Dillon. The room may be registered to An Garda Síochána Dublin."

She nodded and smiled. "Yes, all right, I've made a note. Is there anything else I can do for you?"

"No, thank you for your help."

"But of course. Enjoy the rest of your evening."

"Will do," Dillon said. He debated stopping in the bar for a Jameson but decided it would be better to head up to his room. He took the elevator up to the fourth floor. Once again, glancing left and right before stepping out of the elevator and hurrying to his room.

As he approached the door, he heard the phone ringing in his room. He quickly slipped his keycard into the slot. He was halfway to the phone when it stopped ringing. He picked up the receiver, but all he heard was a dial tone. He pressed the button for the front desk.

A moment later, a woman answered. "Front desk. How may I help you?" Based on the slight accent, Dillon thought it was probably the attractive woman he'd dealt with just minutes ago.

"Hi, sorry to bother you. This is Jack Dillon in four-twelve. I just missed a call. Would it have happened to be you calling?"

"No, sir, I didn't call."

"Oh, okay, well, umm, sorry to have bothered you. Thank you," he said and hung up.

He double-checked the locks on the door, undressed and headed into the shower. He took a long hot shower and seemed to relax a bit. He turned on the TV, went through a half-dozen channels, and turned it off. His cell-phone suddenly rang, and he stepped over to his jeans hanging on the chair and pulled the phone out of a front pocket. 'Unknown Number' it said on the screen.

"Jack Dillon."

"Hello, Marshal. This is Maggie O'Hara. Dennis Hickey's daughter."

"Oh, yes, Maggie."

"I hope I'm not calling too late."

"Too late? No. It's just a little after 8:00 here."

"Mmm. Six-hour difference, good to know."

"How are you doing, Maggie?"

"Oh, you know, none of us have quite come to grips with the whole thing yet. But I was able to get in touch with Jimmy Hart at St. Joseph's cemetery in Geevagh."

"Was he able to help?"

"Actually, that's why I'm calling. We have a funeral arranged for both my parents. We'll be heading over tomorrow, and the funeral will be next Tuesday in Geevagh. Hopefully, we'll be adjusted to the time change by then."

"Oh, that's good news. Is there anything I can do to help?"

"Mmm, no, not really. I was just hoping we might be able to meet you. You know, while we were in Dublin."

"I'm not sure about Dublin. I'm actually working a case out in Sligo, as a matter of fact. I could possibly meet you in the village of Geevagh. I'm only forty minutes away from there now. Are you staying in a hotel there?"

"No," she chuckled. "Apparently, there isn't one. But we're all in a B&B right in the village, three of us. We'd really like to meet you."

"Count on me being there. Can I reach you at this number?" Dillon asked.

"Yes, I've already got overseas service set up on my phone."

"Okay, I'll try to touch base with you this weekend, and let's plan on meeting Tuesday at the church."

"Oh, thank you. We're all looking forward to meeting you."

"See you then," Dillon said, and they disconnected.

He placed his Beretta on the bedside table and climbed into bed. He laid in the dark and thought long and hard about the Hickey family, losing a mother and father in the course of just a few months. That led him to the McGinns losing their daughter. For the first time in a long time, he thought, *'Does it ever end?'* Of course, he already knew the answer was no.

FORTY-EIGHT

Dillon was wide awake at 5:30 the following morning. Since he was officially in lockdown and, other than meeting Roberts for breakfast, was confined to his hotel room with nothing to do, waking up early seemed to be par for the course. He shaved, showered, and left his wet bathroom towels on the floor. He was dressed and looking out the window of his room before 6:00. Other than a guy jogging across the Hyde Bridge, Sligo Town appeared to still be asleep.

He thought for a half-second about calling Maggie O'Hara, maybe getting their flight number and meeting them at Dublin airport, but then decided that didn't make any sense. Besides, with the time change, it was midnight back in Chicago. He attempted to watch the news, but after fifteen minutes, he couldn't stand anymore. He clicked the TV to hotel music, settling on the classical music station while he stared out the window watching the town slowly come awake.

It was just a little after 8:00, and he was thinking he would head down to breakfast in twenty minutes when there was a knock on the door. He used the remote to turn down the music. Whoever it was knocked again.

"Who is it?" Dillon called as he stepped over to the bedside table and picked up his Beretta.

"Housekeeping, sir," a woman said.

"I'm sorry, I canceled housekeeping for today. I'm working."

"Oh, yes, we got that notice. I just wanted to change your bathroom towels, and I'll be gone."

'Oh yeah, the wet towels on the floor.' "Just a moment," he called and hurried into the bathroom. "Okay, I've got them here," he said as he stepped to the door. He was about to look out through the peephole when he caught himself.

"Sir?" the woman said.

Dillon stepped off to the side and jiggled the door-knob.

Boom! Boom! Boom! Three holes appeared in the center of the door in a tight little grouping.

Dillon dropped the wet towels and fired four rounds from the Beretta. Each shot moving ever so slightly in a horizontal line across the door. There was a noise, possibly someone groaning, from out in the hallway and then a thud against the lower half of the door, causing it to shudder. Dillon waited a long moment before he reached up and opened the bolt on the door. He unlocked the lock. Still standing off to the side, he held the Beretta in his right hand and turned the doorknob with his left. The door swung open.

As it opened, a dark-haired woman dropped into the room face down. Her head bounced once on the carpet.

Dillon pointed the Beretta at her in a two-handed grip. She didn't move. He kicked a small pistol away from her hand. A pool of blood slowly seeped across the carpet from beneath her. She was dressed in black slacks and a black top.

He peeked out into the hall and looked left and right. A cart with sheets, towels, and a plastic trash bag was pushed up against the wall. A guy three doors down peeked into the hallway. He was barefoot and wore red boxers and a t-shirt. "Call the Gardai," Dillon shouted, and the man disappeared.

The body on the floor hadn't moved. Dillon felt the neck for a pulse but couldn't find one. He grabbed a handful of hair and pulled to turn her head. Instead, he pulled off a wig. The hair below was short and auburn colored. The face belonged to Sinead Lynch, although when he recognized the face, Dillon immediately thought of the name he first knew, Amelia Maher.

He heard footsteps hurrying down the hall and then stopping. He looked out the door, and there was a middle-aged man in a black sports coat. He was standing wide-eyed, staring at the pair of legs extended out into the hall. One of her shoes lay upside down a foot away.

"I'm with An Gardai Síochána," Dillon said. "This person is not a hotel employee. She's wanted for murder. Check wherever they store the cart and linens. You may have an employee in need of medical attention."

"Is she going to be okay?"

"Don't worry about this person. Check on your housekeeping people. Do it now, damn it!" Dillon shouted. The man hurried down the hall and disappeared. Dillon stepped over to the desk, picked up his cellphone, and called the Sligo station.

"Gardai," was how the phone was answered.

"This is Marshal Jack Dillon. I'm in room four-twelve at the Glasshouse Hotel. I've just been involved in a shooting. The individual is unresponsive and appears to be dead," Dillon said and disconnected.

He set his Beretta on the desk, sat down on the edge of the bed, looked out the window, and waited. He didn't have to wait long. He heard a siren within a minute. It suddenly stopped, and he figured there would be officers coming down the hall in the next five minutes. It was more like two minutes, and during that time, he heard four more sirens.

The first two officers in the room were playing it safe and told Dillon to stand, face the window, and hold his arms out. They stepped over the body and quickly approached, handcuffing Dillon.

It wasn't lost on him that the officer cuffing him politely asked, "If you'd please bring your right hand back, sir. Good, thank you, and now the left, sir. Very good. Now, if you'd please sit down. Comfortable?"

"Yeah, fine."

"Are you armed?"

"My weapon is on the desk. It's that Beretta. I fired it four times."

"Your name, sir?"

"My name is Jack Dillon. I'm a US Marshal attached to An Garda Síochána Special Branch in Dublin. I've been working a case down here with D.I. Emmett Roberts.

"Sir," the officer's partner said, "we need to read you your rights now." He pulled out a card and began to read Dillon his rights. When he was finished, he asked, "Can you tell us what happened?"

"The victim on the floor is a woman who I believe is named Sinead Lynch. I also knew her as Amelia Maher. She's wanted in connection with at least eight murders that we know of. The two most recent were an American named Dennis Hickey and Detective Inspector Kevin Rafferty with Dublin's Special Branch. She identified herself as housekeeping and fired three rounds through the door. I returned fire."

"Did you recognize her?"

"I would prefer not to answer any more questions until I have representation," Dillon said.

"Understood, sir," he said.

One of the officers used a ballpoint pen and lifted the the pistol Dillon had kicked off to the side. The officer placed the pistol on the desk next to Dillon's Beretta.

A voice out in the hall suddenly said, "On my god." Two more officers stepped into the room. One of them looked at Dillon and said, "Aren't you Dolan from the newscast last night?"

"It's Dillon," the officer who read Dillon his rights said.

Dillon was taken to the Garda station, his handcuffs were removed, and he was placed in an interview room. Twenty minutes later, an officer stepped in with a steaming mug of tea and set it down in front of Dillon. "LT Madden just got off the phone with your man McCabe in Dublin's Special Branch. They're sending a team down right away. Hopefully, they'll be here shortly after lunch. Is there anything you need in the meantime?"

"Thanks, I'm fine. Any word from the Glasshouse?"

"Afraid I'm not at liberty to say."

"Did they check on the housekeeping staff? The woman who attempted to kill me had a housekeeping service cart. She had to get it from somewhere."

"Like I said, I'm not at liberty to say, sir."

His use of the term 'sir' seemed to be more than just an automatic reply, and Dillon feared Sinead Lynch might not be the only body at the Glasshouse Hotel.

FORTY-NINE

Dillon was thinking it had to be close to dinner time when he finally heard voices in the hallway. The door opened a moment later, and four men stepped in. Along with files, one of them also carried a white paper bag that he set on the steel table in front of Dillon.

"Marshal Dillon, my name is Michael Bennett. I'm here with Thomas Killen," he said, nodding at a man who nodded over at Dillon. We just arrived from Dublin, and we're going to represent you. This is Timothy Scanlon and Devin Flynn. They'll be conducting the interview this afternoon. But first, Thomas and I would like an hour to get your version of the circumstances. Oh, and we brought you lunch," Bennett said.

"Lunch? It's almost dinner time, but I'll take it all the same. Thank you."

Bennett laughed. "I know it might seem like that, but it's just a little after 1:00."

"We'll be back in an hour," Scanlon said. "If you need more time, that's not a problem."

"Thanks, lads," Bennett said as Scanlon and Flynn left the interview room. "Help yourself," Bennett said, nodding at the white paper bag as he and Killen pulled out the chairs opposite Dillon and sat down.

Dillon opened the bag and pulled out a cheeseburger and sweet potato fries. He closed his eyes and inhaled the scent of the food as it drifted up, causing his stomach to growl loudly.

"Yeah, we heard you missed breakfast," Killen said, and they all laughed. "Go ahead and dig in."

Dillon unwrapped the cheeseburger and took a giant bite.

"We'd like you to tell us what exactly happened," Bennett said. "Please understand, you're in a good position. But it's important that we follow standard procedure here. You have us representing you. Scanlon and Flynn will assemble the facts and, God willing, give you the all-clear. So, in your own words, tell us what happened."

Dillon swallowed his mouthful of food. "Are you aware of what we know regarding Sinead Lynch? That she is basically an assassin for the Linnehan drug cartel currently headquartered down in Costa del Sol? That she is wanted in the murders of Dennis Hickey and Special Branch D.I. Kevin Rafferty on the M1? Not to mention six other individuals three months back, including an American couple in Desertserges, County Cork."

"Yes, we do know that. We have for quite some time. Just in case we were not aware, we were brought up to date by D.C.I. McCabe in Special Branch just this morning."

"Here are the facts. The murders of Hickey in Sker-ries and Rafferty on the M1 were an attempt to kill me. She mistook Rafferty for me. I met Sinead Lynch, inter-viewed her as an individual who had information on a suspect in the murder of the American couple in Cork. At the time, she was using the pseudonym Amelia Ma-her."

"So, how did she find you here in Sligo Town?" Killen asked.

"I spoke briefly at a press conference yesterday, fol-lowing the arrest of an individual who admitted to acci-dentally killing a young Sligo girl in Temple Bar. The press conference was on RTE along with a couple of other stations, and I'm guessing Sinead Lynch saw it, somehow found out where I was staying, and attempted to kill me."

"Why would she want to kill you?" Bennett asked.

"I'm not sure. I guess you'd have to ask her."

That brought a smile to Bennett and Killen's faces.

Scanlon and Flynn knocked on the door exactly an hour later. They interviewed Dillon, asked appropriate questions, and ninety minutes later thanked everyone for their time and for making the effort to comply with de-partment policy. They told Dillon he was free to leave and mentioned that, under the circumstances, the depart-ment had arranged a different room for him at the Glass-house Hotel. He'd have to check in at the front desk again. Everyone shook hands and left the interview room. Dillon was instructed to go up to the Homicide office and check in with LT Madden.

He said a quick thank you and goodbye to Bennett and Killen, who appeared to be in a hurry to drive the three hours back to Dublin.

Dillon walked down the hallway to Homicide and made his way to Madden's office. Roberts glanced up, caught Dillon's eye, and held his hands out suggesting, 'What's happening?'

Dillon smiled and flashed him the 'OK' sign with his right hand. He knocked on Madden's door and stepped inside.

Madden was on the phone and pointed to the chairs in front of his desk.

Dillon went for the chair Roberts had sat in the last time he was in the office. It felt solid and didn't creak or shift as he sat down.

Madden finished his phone call, hung up, and looked at Dillon. "You okay?"

"Yeah, thanks for asking, sir. I'm a little tired, but it went okay. I guess I'm on desk duty for a couple of days?"

"Officially, but consider it more as time off after all you've been through. I've cleared it with D.C.I. McCabe, so relax, take it easy. You've more than earned it. Now that it's over, I wanted to tell you the interview was just a formality. That said, should there ever be any questions, all our t's are crossed, and the i's are dotted."

Dillon nodded.

"I think it would be best if you kept a low profile for the next few days. Stay out of the pubs and just keep your head down."

"Happy to do that, sir. There is one thing I'd like to do."

"What's that?"

"Dennis Hickey, the American killed in Skerries a couple of weeks ago. His family is coming over here to bury him and his wife in a village called Geevagh on Tuesday. I'd like to attend the funeral and meet them if at all possible."

Madden seemed to think for a moment and said, "I don't see that as a problem. In fact, I think it sounds like a pretty good idea. Enjoy, if that's the correct term for a funeral," he said and extended his hand, signaling their conversation was finished.

Dillon shook his hand, thanked him, and stepped out of the office. He walked over to Robert's desk.

"How'd it go?" Roberts asked.

"Fine. No problem. I've been instructed to maintain a very low profile for the next few days. So I won't be coming in here. Madden told me to stay out of the pubs, so I'm going to be even more boring than usual. I'm meeting up with a family burying their parents in a village called Geevagh in a few days. You know where that is?"

Roberts shook his head and said, "Never heard of it. You interested in dinner tonight?"

"I just told you, Madden told me to stay out of pubs. I'm guessing that means restaurants too."

"Yeah, that's why I was thinking of cooking dinner."

"Oh, yeah, that sounds good. I have to check into the Glasshouse. They've given me a new room. Give me your address and tell me when you want me there. Can I bring some wine or a dessert or something?"

"How about you just keep a low profile and show up," Roberts said and laughed as he wrote down his address and handed it to Dillon.

FIFTY

oberts gave Dillon a ride back to the Glasshouse Hotel. "You want me to come in with you just to make sure everything is okay?"

"No need. I do have one question. Were there any hotel employees harmed by Sinead Lynch?"

"Fortunately not. They don't begin the cleaning rounds until nine o'clock. Apparently, she picked the lock on the supply room and wheeled the housekeeping cart down the hall to your room. She must have been in a hurry to take her second chance at getting you. By the way, the cleaning staff uniform is a black dress with a white apron, not slacks."

"Well, I guess I'll go and check in. Hopefully, they won't kick me out."

"I think they transferred you to a small room down in the basement next to the furnace," Roberts said and laughed.

"Not funny," Dillon said, but then he smiled. "Hey, I'll see you tonight, and thanks in advance."

"Don't be late," Roberts said as Dillon climbed out of the car. He waited until Dillon stepped into the hotel before driving away.

Dillon climbed up three steps, entered the lobby, and headed for the front desk.

"Oh, Marshal Dillon," the man at the front desk said as Dillon approached. Dillon had never seen him before. "Let me just bring your room up. We've taken the liberty of transferring your belongings to a new suite." He was typing as he spoke and then said, "Yes, here we are. We've moved you to a deluxe suite. King-sized bed, bathrobe, slippers, private outdoor area. I'll just need your signature here, sir," he said and pulled a sheet from the printer.

Dillon glanced at the invoice. It was billed to Sligo Town An Garda Síochána. *'God Bless them,'* Dillon thought as he signed the invoice and slid it back across the counter.

"Very good, sir. Here are your key cards. We've taken the liberty of placing some pastries and a bottle of one of our better red wines in the suite, sir. A pleasure meeting you, sir, really," he said and held out his hand to shake.

Dillon shook his hand and then asked, "How did you know who I was? I don't believe we met before, and yet you knew who I was as I approached."

"Oh, sir, believe me, the entire staff knows who you are. You are in deluxe suite number six-oh-two. Just take the elevator up to the top floor. If you need anything, please feel free to call."

"Thank you," Dillon said. He stepped onto the elevator and pressed the button for the top floor. He thought for a moment as the door closed and then pressed four. Force of habit, he glanced left and right before stepping off the elevator on the fourth floor. He headed down the hall to his former room, 412.

The blood-stained carpet had been removed. A four-foot by two-foot section of carpet had been torn from in front of the door, exposing the concrete floor. The door itself was gone, and in its place was a sheet of plywood covering the entrance to the room. Interestingly, instead of the normal blue and white An Garda Síochána tape crisscrossed over the door, there was a standard yellow tape with black letters, 'DO NOT ENTER!'

Dillon glanced at the wall around the door. It was coated with white primer paint. He glanced across the hall. There was an area about two inches in diameter that had been freshly plastered, which suggested that having shot four times, he may have missed at least once. He didn't see anything else that suggested the mayhem of the morning, and he walked back to the elevator.

Up on the sixth floor, the deluxe suite was just that, deluxe. A plate of chocolate covered pastries rested on the glass top desk against the wall. A bottle of wine stood next to the pastries with a card. Dillon opened the card. The words 'Thank you' were hand-written in the center of the card and surrounded by multiple signatures. He counted the signatures, fifteen total.

On the far wall was a door that led out to a narrow 'L' shaped porch overlooking the river and Hyde Bridge.

Dillon looked up the street beyond the bridge and could see the blue front of WB's Coffee House.

The bedroom featured a king-sized bed, upholstered chairs, and a couch. Dillon's suitcase rested on an attached counter next to the kingsized bed. He peeled off the shirt, reminding himself he'd have to return it to Horgan at some point. He stripped down and headed into the bathroom. The door was in the middle of the bathroom with the shower and a large tub on either side. Behind the tub was a heated towel rack. The black tile floor was heated. Body soap, shampoo, and skin cream were in small containers on a shelf.

Dillon turned on the water to fill the Jacuzzi. He eventually climbed into the steaming tub, settled back, and closed his eyes. He'd been in there for close to a half-hour when he suddenly came awake. He climbed out, dried off, and changed into his jeans and a reasonably clean t-shirt.

He made his way down to the underground garage, input Robert's address on the GPS system, and headed to dinner. Along the way, he stopped to purchase a bottle of wine, kicking himself for not grabbing the one resting on the coffee table in his suite.

Robert's home was a two-story attached white stucco structure in a neighborhood of identical units. His car was parked off to the side of a paved parking area. Dillon pulled in next to it and climbed out. The front door opened before Dillon stepped around the Mercedes.

"Any problems finding me?" Roberts asked.

"No, the GPS saves me all sorts of headaches," Dillon said as he stepped into the house and handed Roberts the bottle of wine.

"Oh, you didn't have to do this but thank you. Come on into the kitchen. Can I pour you a wine?"

"I'd love one," Dillon said and followed Roberts into the kitchen area. The house was pretty much a carbon copy of Dillon's with the exception of wall colors and white kitchen cabinets as opposed to Dillon's oak. Dillon settled onto a kitchen stool, there were two, and Roberts slid a glass of wine across the counter to him. They raised their glasses, clinked, and took a sip.

Over the course of the evening, they avoided talk of the arrests and the shooting of Sinead Lynch that morning. They spoke in general terms about growing up, failed relationships, and funny things that had happened in their lives. Dillon was back in the deluxe suite just a little after 9:00. He opened the wine bottle on the coffee table and poured himself a glass. He was in bed by 10:00, and the wine glass remained untouched.

He spent the next two days in the hotel, venturing out only once a day to walk along the river and quietly sip a coffee at a back table in WB's Coffee House. He did purchase a white shirt and a tie in a shop next to WB's. He phoned Jimmy Hart, the man in charge of the cemetery at St. Joseph's Church and coordinated some plans with him for the Hickey funeral. He phoned Daniel Sexton, the bagpiper he'd met following Kevin Rafferty's burial in Glasnevin cemetery.

Sexton answered on the second ring. "Dan Sexton."

"Hi Dan, this is Jack Dillon. I don't know if you remember me, but we met—"

"Oh yeah, after the Rafferty burial. Of course I remember. You were all over the news a few days back. What's up?"

Dillon gave a brief explanation of the Hickey funerals the following day and said, "So, I'm hoping you might know a piper out this way I could call to play at this funeral."

"I got a better idea. Why don't I drive over and play?"

"Dan, it's a three-hour drive over here. The funeral is in the church in a little village. It's probably just going to be me, three family members, and a priest."

"All the more reason," Sexton said.

"You sure?"

"Yeah, I'd be honored. You said the funeral's at 11:00?" Sexton asked.

"Right."

"I'll be there an hour before, get the lay of the land, and warm up the pipes. Looking forward to seeing you and glad you're okay after everything."

"Thanks, see you tomorrow," Dillon said and hung up.

He received a call from Roberts later that afternoon. Dillon was finally off desk duty, and he could come in, retrieve his Beretta, sign some paperwork, and be ready to check out of the Glasshouse the following morning.

FIFTY-ONE

Dillon was up early the next morning and the first person in line for the breakfast buffet. He ate a leisurely breakfast, then packed his bag and took the elevator down to the lobby to check out. The same man was working the front desk, and after checking Dillon out, he asked if he could take a selfie with Dillon. They stood while the man, with his arm around Dillon's shoulder, actually took three. He thanked Dillon and promised a discount the next time he checked in.

Dillon climbed into the Mercedes, set the GPS for the village of Geevagh, and drove out of the underground parking lot. It was a forty minute drive to the village. He brought up a list of classical music and listened to that on the way. He turned off the main highway and made his way toward the village on country roads that seemed to narrow a bit more every few miles. Eventually, he entered the village, and the GPS directed him to take a right-hand turn.

He drove past the Prisoner's Memorial, honoring 8 working men from back in 1908. Just beyond the memorial was St. Joseph's Church. The church was a two-story structure of white stucco, with a slate roof and large stained glass windows. He pulled into a parking spot across the street, one of two cars. Apparently, the Hickey family had yet to arrive. He crossed the street and was about to head into the church when he heard voices coming from behind the church.

He walked toward the voices and saw three men standing in the graveyard. Two of them held shovels and stood next to a small pile of dirt. Dillon walked over. As he approached, they stopped their conversation and watched him.

"Jimmy Hart?" Dillon asked when he was just a few feet away.

The man without a shovel smiled and said, "You wouldn't happen to be Jack Dillon now, would you?"

"Yes, nice to meet you," Dillon said and extended his hand.

"This is your man on the news," Hart said, shaking Dillon's hand. "We're all set. Both cremated, they'll be buried here next to your woman's parents."

Dillon glanced over at the small gravestone listing Donal and Ciara Gowan, Maggie O'Hara's grandparents. No dates were listed, which made sense since the cost for the gravestone would be based, in part, on how many letters had to be engraved.

"I checked around," Hart said. "There are a few people who remember the daughter, Maureen. They'll be here at the service. I met with the children. They arrived yesterday, staying at a B&B on the edge of the village, nice people." He glanced at his watch. "They should be here shortly."

"That's nice there'll be a couple of other people here. Folks who knew their mother when they were youngsters."

Hart gave Dillon a look but didn't say anything.

They heard a noise from out in front of the church, and suddenly, a bagpiper stepped around the corner playing the scale.

"Oh, Jaysus," Hart said.

"I lined him up. He drove over from Dublin," Dillon said.

Sexton gave a wave and headed toward them. "Oh, Dillon, thought I'd beat you here. Hi, I'm Dan Sexton, the bagpiper," he said to Hart.

"Never would have guessed," Hart said, nodding at his uniform.

"Is the burial going be here in this cemetery?" Sexton asked, looking around.

Hart said, "Two cremations. They'll be buried just next to that headstone," he nodded at the small Gowan headstone a few feet away.

Three people stepped around the corner of the church, two women and a man. They looked to be in their mid-thirties. One of the women, a blonde, waved at Hart and headed in his direction.

"Oh, here's the family now," Hart said.

Dillon watched as they approached. He guessed Maggie O'Hara, the woman he'd spoken to on the phone, was the blonde in the lead. "Hi, Jimmy," she said. "Thanks for doing this." She glanced at the piles of dirt and the two small holes. "This will work just fine. We placed the urns up at the front of the church. The priest showed us where. He said we're to sit in the front pew?"

"Yes, there'll be quite the crowd, and people will be giving their condolences to you's. Oh, I should introduce, this is your bagpiper," he said, raising a hand toward Sexton.

"Hi, Dan Sexton. I'll be leading you out here at the end of the service."

All three siblings nodded and introduced themselves, Maggie, Molly, and Mike.

Dillon said, "Maggie, I'm Jack Dillon. We've spoken on the phone."

She grew wide-eyed, wrapped her arms around Dillon, and hugged him tightly. "Oh, thank you, thank you, thank you," she said and started to cry. Her two siblings suddenly had tears running down their faces.

"Are you okay?" the brother, Mike, asked. "We heard about you on the news, but they just said seven shots were fired, and they never said if you were hit."

"Thanks for asking. I'm fine. Everything okay at your B&B?" Dillon asked, changing the subject. They nodded.

Maggie hugged Dillon even tighter and whispered again, "Thank you," then pulled away. "Oh, look at me," she said. "We'd better get cleaned up before people start arriving. Talk after the service, okay?" she said.

Dillon nodded and said, "Yeah, go on and get organized. You've got a lot to do."

Maggie and her sister suddenly grabbed Dillon and gave him a long kiss on his cheeks. "Thank you so much," Molly said.

Maggie sniffled, rubbed her nose, and they hurried back around the corner of the church.

"You should probably head into the church, too, Dillon," Hart said. "Take the second pew on the left-hand side. You'll be seated just behind the three of them. It's going to be crowded."

"Crowded? I thought you said there were just a couple of people who remembered the mother as a little girl?"

Hart laughed and said, "Aw, you're daft, man. Folks will be coming to get a glimpse of you."

"Me?"

"I told you. You've been on the news the past few days. That's big out here in the back of beyond. Off with you now, get in that pew before someone steals your seat."

FIFTY-TWO

Hart hadn't been kidding. The church was full. Maggie's brother Mike gave some brief remarks about his parents, ending with them being 'together forever and the rest of us will join them soon enough.'

As the line of people headed toward the altar for communion, Dillon was painfully aware of people glancing his way. At the end of the service, the priest gave a final blessing, and then Mike and Molly each picked up an urn with the ashes. Dillon recognized the urn with the brass plate on top holding their mother's ashes as they walked past, and he immediately thought of Kevin Rafferty. They followed the priest outside and around the corner of the church to the cemetery. Dillon noticed the three news cameras outside filming the crowd as they headed to the gravesite in the far corner.

As they stepped outside, Dan Sexton fired up his bagpipes and played a mournful tune that caused a lump in Dillon's throat. He continued playing until the crowd had assembled in the cemetery, and the priest gave him a nod.

The priest gave a short blessing, led everyone in prayer, and mentioned there would be an informal get-together in Paddy's Pub. Once the prayers were finished Sexton fired up the pipes once again and played an up-beat tune as he marched away from the gravesite. Dillon remembered Sexton had told him he was leading the devil astray. People waited in line to give their condolences to Maggie O'Hara, her brother Mike and sister Molly.

Dillon made his way to the opposite corner of the cemetery where Sexton had just finished playing. "Dan, I just wanted to thank you for coming all the way out here and playing. What do I owe you?"

"You gotta be kidding, Dillon. I'll be on three different news channels tonight. I couldn't buy advertising like this. I gave my card to all the news people. Two of them interviewed me, and I told them you hired me to come out here and play and that we met at the Rafferty funeral. No, I should be paying you."

"Listen, I arranged a gathering at Paddy's Pub. You probably saw the place when you came into the village. They're going to have session music and a cash bar, but it'll give you a break before you head back to Dublin. I'm heading down there in a bit."

"Thanks for inviting me. Yeah, I'll see you there," Sexton said and shook hands with Dillon.

EPILOGUE

The crowd gradually left the cemetery and headed down to Paddy's Pub, a short five-minute walk. Since it was a nice, sunny day, that seemed to be what most people did. There was session music in the back room of the pub, locals playing Irish tunes, two fiddles, an accordion, a tin whistle, a set of uilleann pipes, and a bodhran drum.

Dillon hadn't been there five minutes when Sexton came up to him and said, "Thank you, man, I really mean it. Oh, and thank God that slapper didn't make good on her second chance."

"Yeah, you got that right," Dillon said.

Maggie O'Hara came up with her siblings. They thanked Sexton for playing and asked if they could have a private word with Dillon.

"Not a problem. It just so happens there's a young lady at the bar who looks like she may be interested, so if you'll excuse me," Sexton said and headed toward the bar.

The siblings looked at one another, and Mike nodded at Maggie. "Umm, Marshal Dillon, we just wanted to thank you again for all you've done. We know it hasn't been proven yet, but we believe the woman you shot is the same person who murdered our father. When we heard on the news she was with this Linnehan gang, it reminded us of a story our mother would tell. Her folks, our grandparents, were killed in a car crash. It was always suspected that one of the Linnehan's ran into them and killed them. Our grandfather owned a small grocery store here in the village, and apparently, the Linnehan's wanted a percentage."

"He wouldn't pay them," Mike said.

Maggie nodded. "So they were killed in a car crash. No one was ever arrested or held accountable. We'll never really know for sure, but when she came after you the other day, well, you paid all of them back. What goes around comes around," she said, then reached up and gave Dillon a kiss on the cheek. "Thank you."

THE END

Thank you for taking the time to read <u>Second Chance</u>. If you enjoyed the read please take a moment and leave a review. Even if it's just a word or two, it really helps.

Don't miss this sample of <u>Payback Brother</u>, the next book in the Jack Dillon Dublin Tales series.

PAYBACK BROTHER

PROLOGUE

Dillon opened his eyes on the second ring and looked into the deep brown eyes staring back at him. Unfortunately, the deep brown eyes belonged to Lucifer, his dog. Lucifer gave him a look suggesting something along the lines of *'Are you going to answer the damn thing?'*

Dillon rolled over in the opposite direction and pulled his cellphone from the bedside table. Special Branch calling. It wasn't quite 6:00 AM on Saturday. This couldn't be good. "Marshall Dillon," he said.

"D.I. Bennet, Marshal Dillon, sorry to wake you."

"Not to worry. I've been up for a bit," Dillon lied. "It can't be good news if you're calling at this hour on a Saturday."

"A shooting, sir, in Finglas. Your presence was requested."

"Is it an American?"

"I've no idea, sir, just that your presence was re-quested." Dillon's phone suddenly indicated an email coming through. "I sent you what little information we had just a moment ago."

"Has D.I. Suel been notified?"

"No, sir. You're the only one from Special Branch, at least at this time."

"And you said you sent me the information?"

"Yes, sir. What little we have, basically the name of the officer in charge and an address of the scene. One victim shot."

Dillon exhaled. "I'm on it. Appreciate the call," he said, meaning anything but. He disconnected and rolled out of bed. Lucifer was already back asleep and breathing heavily. So much for a leisurely Saturday. He went down to the kitchen, turned on the coffee, and took a dog biscuit from the cookie jar, clanging the lid as he did so. He eventually heard Lucifer hop off the bed. A moment later, Lucifer peeked around the upstairs newel post.

"Come on. Biscuit, outside," Dillon called and waved the biscuit. Lucifer bounded down the stairs, and Dillon opened the front door. He tossed the biscuit out onto the drive, and Lucifer leaped off the front stoop. Dillon closed the door and headed upstairs to shower.

Showered, shaved, and dressed in clean jeans and a black sweater, he checked the address on his email and the victim's name, Patrick O'Shea. It didn't ring a bell. He filled his travel mug with coffee, slipped on a black leather jacket, and opened the front door. Lucifer hurried inside, headed to the kitchen, and started in on his bowl of food. Dillon locked the door behind him and drove over to the address in Finglas, a mere ten minutes from his home and a completely different world.

He turned onto Deanstown Avenue and could see the scene from two blocks away. Three squad cars, an EMT van, white tape with blue letters blowing in the wind, warning people in English and Irish not to cross the line. He pulled to the curb and climbed out of his car.

He flashed his warrant card before one of the two officers at the gate had the opportunity to tell him to stop. "Who's the officer in charge?" Dillon asked, although he'd read the name Seamus Mullen in the email.

"D.I. Mullen," one of the officers said. Both men sat on the three-foot wall running across the thirty-five-foot property. Their arms were crossed, and they didn't make the slightest effort to stand, nod, or smile. Dillon figured they'd probably been there for hours and were now working overtime.

"Thanks, lads. Enjoy the day," Dillon said. He pulled a pair of latex gloves from his jacket and slipped them on as he headed for the front door.

ONE

The houses, there were actually six of them, were attached, two-story units with slate roofs, all exactly the same. Dillon had lost count of the number of times he'd been in similar layouts. The first floor would feature a sitting room with a coal-burning fireplace that had originally been the source of heat for the room. The kitchen and dining area would be just behind the sitting room with another fireplace. The entryway was actually a small hall leading back to the dining area. The staircase to the second-floor would be maybe six feet beyond the front door. There would be a landing twelve steps up where you'd make a ninety-degree turn and take two more steps to the second floor hallway. Two or possibly three bedrooms and the bathroom would be on the second floor.

Dillon walked up the driveway, past the dark blue Mercedes Benz E300. According to the license plate, it was a 2021 model. He peeked inside through the driver's window and studied the comfortable-looking blue leather interior for a moment. He stepped on the stoop, glanced once more at the Mercedes, opened the door, and stepped inside.

Voices were coming from the back of the house. He listened for a moment before heading into the sitting room. A couch was positioned opposite the fireplace, with a coffee table in front of the couch. A wine bottle and two wine glasses were sitting on the coffee table, each wrapped in an evidence bag. One of the wine glasses had lipstick on the rim. Dillon headed toward the conversational noise coming from the kitchen.

As he stepped into the room, the conversation stopped, and all three individuals, one wearing white protective gear and a face mask, looked at Dillon. There was a sliding glass door leading out to a back garden. The glass was mostly shattered, with three bullet holes in the remaining upper portion. Outside, a gurney with a black body bag was positioned on the edge of a brick patio. Two men, probably medical examiners, were outside in white protective gear. One was photographing a pool of blood and splatters on the steps leading into the house. The other was filling out a form on a clipboard. Behind them was a patio dining set, a glass-topped table with six wicker chairs. The table was empty, and the chairs were all pushed in against the table, suggesting it hadn't been used recently.

"I'm looking for DI Mullen," Dillon said.

"You got him," a man with thinning brown hair and a mustache said with a nod.

Dillon guessed he might be forty, maybe forty-five. He wore jeans, a blue flannel shirt, and a wrinkled navy-blue sport coat. He was maybe six feet tall. His chest and squared chin suggested a muscular build. Possibly an athlete as a younger man.

"I'm Marshall Jack Dillon, Special Branch. I got a call about forty-five minutes ago directing me here."

Mullen extended his hand in a latex glove, and they shook. "Appreciate you making the time, Marshal. We've got a victim shot multiple times. Appears to be an American. We've found a passport." Mullen turned and sorted through a half-dozen evidence bags on the dining room table. "Yeah, here we go," he said, handing Dillon the bag. The passport in the bag was opened to the page with the photograph and basic information. Dillon looked at the image, a younger red-headed man named Patrick Joseph O'Shea. The date of birth was April third, 1997.

"I don't recognize him," Dillon said, looking at the photo. He turned the bag over to check the cover just to make sure it was an American passport. It was. "Was he living here, visiting, going to school?"

"Apparently, he owns the house. It was purchased by a Boston Company, Bridge Street Capitol, although Patrick O'Shea is also listed on the title. He moved in two years ago. Thus far, no sign of employment that we've been able to determine. We'll be making calls later in the day."

"Any idea of the time of death?" Dillon asked.

"Sometime after 3:00 this morning. A next-door neighbor phoned in a report of gunshots maybe ten minutes after 3:00. We've got a recording. Didn't say anything about your man being shot, but then at that hour, well…."

"Is he, or rather, was he the owner of that Mercedes parked out in the driveway?"

"Again, it's registered to Bridge Street Capitol at this address, with O'Shea also listed. We'll double-check just to be sure, but as of this moment, yeah, he's the owner."

"Nice set of wheels for anyone, let alone someone in their mid-twenties."

"Like I said, no word yet on employment, although we're just getting started. Who knows, maybe he was living on one of your American trust funds."

"Or maybe self-employed, is there an office? Could be he was a computer guy or someone working from home."

Mullen gave a slight shrug. "Possibly. We're really just getting started on going through things. Nothing to suggest an office upstairs, but you're welcome to have a look. I should mention I got your name from a friend of mine, Paddy Suel. We went through the same training class together when we first signed on."

Dillon smiled. "Paddy and I are partners, although he'd seldom admit to that."

"Well, he said he'd be joining us, but knowing Paddy, he probably rolled over and went back to sleep."

"Sounds like you know him well," Dillon said, and they both laughed.

"Paddy mentioned you've got a contact at the American Embassy."

"Yeah, Eric Bergman. If you'd like, I'll give him a call. It would probably be best to wait another hour or two. I'll call him maybe sometime after 9:00 if that works."

"Works for me," Mullen said.

"I noticed on the wine glasses out in the sitting room one of them had lipstick on the rim. Any idea who that might be?"

Mullen shook his head. "I only wish. No idea if she was here when your man was murdered. Did she run out the door, hide upstairs, or behind the sitting room couch?"

"Or, was she the shooter?" Dillon said.

"Yeah, that too," Mullen replied and shrugged.

"Have you been upstairs?" Dillon asked.

"Only for a quick look around. Didn't see anyone. Feel free to take a look. Just don't touch anything. We'll be up there soon enough, taking pictures."

"If it's all right, then I'll take a peek."

"You find your woman hiding under the bed, let us know," Mullen said and set the bag with O'Shea's passport back on the table.

Dillon walked into the sitting room again and looked around. He made a mental note that there wasn't a TV anywhere in the room. He glanced in the fireplace. It was swept clean, with no ashes. There wasn't any wood stacked in the room to burn. It seemed unlikely someone would have cleaned out the fireplace last evening. The wine bottle in the evidence bag was half-full. With two glasses on the coffee table that suggested both parties each had one glass of wine. He wondered if they may have been interrupted.

He made his way up the staircase, being careful not to touch the stair rail on the way up. There were two bedrooms and a bathroom on the second floor. The first bedroom, the larger of the two, had a double bed, a dresser, and a white wardrobe. A flat-screen rested on the dresser. A lamp and a TV remote were on the bedside table next to the bed.

Although the duvet on the bed was pulled up, both pillows appeared to have been used and flung haphazardly. It didn't suggest anyone was trying to hide something. He thought of it more as someone climbed out of bed, tossed the pillows against the wooden headboard, and maybe wandered into the bathroom.

He opened the double doors on the wardrobe. Hanging shirts and jerseys, all mens, filled the upper area. Four drawers and a rack holding eight pairs of men's shoes and boots were arranged along the bottom. He closed the doors, gave another quick look around the room, and headed into the second bedroom.

Almost immediately, he mentally labeled the second bedroom as a guest room. There was a small antique chest of drawers and, next to that, a wooden folding luggage rack. The single bed had a flower-patterned bed-spread and one pillow. He pulled open the three drawers on the antique chest of drawers. They were all empty.

He stepped into the bathroom. There was a toilet, sink, and shower. The glass on the shower was spotted, and Dillon guessed it hadn't been cleaned or squeegeed in quite some time. The small shelf in the shower had two white plastic containers, one labeled 'Body Wash' and the other labeled 'Shampoo.' A gray towel hung haphazardly on the towel rack. The mirror above the bathroom sink was bolted to the wall. The lower righthand corner of the mirror was cracked. The white bathroom sink could do with some cleaning. A tube of toothpaste, a toothbrush, a shaving razor, and a can of shaving cream rested next to the sink. Three drawers, one on top of the other, were on the right side of the bath-room cabinet. The two bottom drawers were empty. The top drawer held a box of cotton swabs and three wrapped condoms.

Nothing in the bathroom or the bedrooms, including the almost empty roll of toilet tissue, suggested any long-term presence of a woman.

"Dillon, you up here?" Mullen called as he came up the stairs.

"In the bathroom," Dillon replied.

Mullen appeared in the doorway a moment later. "Come up with any ideas?"

"Yeah, just looking around. I don't think there was a woman living here. He might have had the occasional overnight guest, but I'm sure they would have fled the scene come morning."

Mullen chuckled at that.

"Hello, anyone home?" a voice called from downstairs.

"That would be Suel," Dillon said.

TWO

Dillon followed D.I. Mullen down the stairs. Suel was standing in the entryway carrying a white bag and a tray holding six paper cups with plastic lids.

"Hi, Paddy. Just on the way home from last night?" Mullen asked.

"I only wish," Suel said. "I've some scones and teas for you lot and a coffee for my crabby partner."

Mullen laughed and said, "Come on back to the kitchen."

"You get your beauty sleep?" Dillon asked.

"Are you kidding? I waited in a bleeding line for the teas and coffee for almost a half-hour. Now be nice, or there'll be no scone for the likes of you." Dillon placed a thumb and forefinger on his lips and pinched them. "Much better," Suel said and headed for the kitchen.

He set the tray of cups and the bag of scones on the table and stepped over to what remained of the sliding door. The gurney with the body bag was gone, along with the medical examiners. "God bless, this looks like a number of rounds fired. How many times was your man hit?" Suel asked.

"Four that we know of," Mullen said. "All in the chest. Initial examination suggests death was immediate and sometime between 3:00 and 3:30 this morning. Close range shots, I'm guessing at maybe a distance of five or six feet."

"So he's outside at that hour? Was someone in the back garden trying to get in?"

"Obviously, someone was in the back garden," Dillon said. "The time suggests that maybe Mr. O'Shea heard someone. Maybe they caused the motion detectors to turn on the lights. How was he dressed?" he asked Mullen.

"Jeans, a short sleeve six nations jersey, and barefoot. No wallet on his person. We haven't found one in the house yet. From what we can determine, he was unarmed."

Dillon shook his head. "The bed upstairs appears to have been more or less made. If you were jumping out of bed because someone was prowling in your back garden, I don't think you'd adjust the pillows and straighten the duvet."

Mullen pulled a paper cup from the tray and opened the lid. Steam rose from the cup. "Any Milk?"

"In the bag with the scones," Suel said. Mullen pulled out a small container holding no more than a tablespoon of milk. Suel bent down and called through the broken glass to the two men taking pictures on the patio. "Tea and scones, lads." He stepped over to the table and handed a cup to Dillon. "Your coffee, sir, just as you requested, black and paid for."

"Well done, Paddy. I take back some of the things the others have been saying about you."

Everyone laughed. Suel took a tea from the tray and pulled a scone from the bag. They chatted for fifteen minutes, discussing who may have been responsible and why. Nothing was known of the victim, Patrick O'Shea, except that, apparently, he was an American. No one had knowledge of a prior arrest. Other than the wine glass with lipstick, there was nothing that indicated interaction with anyone; no mail, no bills, no personal photos, nothing, and thus far, no phone.

Once they'd finished their tea and scones, Dillon, Suel, and Mullen went through the bedrooms and bathroom. Absolutely nothing unique was found other than the three wrapped condoms in the bathroom drawer.

"Why wouldn't he keep these in the drawer of that bedside table?" Dillon asked.

"Maybe he didn't have women here. Maybe he only participated in the event at their place," Mullen said.

"Yeah, maybe. Although based on the wine glass in the sitting room, he served wine to a woman."

"Yeah, and you saw how well that worked out," Suel said, and they all smiled.

Dillon and Suel left forty-five minutes later. They were in the Special Branch office in Phoenix Park before 10:00 and none the wiser on the death of Patrick O'Shea.

The first thing Dillon did was phone Eric Bergman at the American Embassy.

He was placed on hold for a half-minute before his call was sent through. "Hi, Jack, how are things?" was how Bergman answered.

"Morning, Eric, the usual, unfortunately."

"Oh, what do you have?"

"A shooting last night in Finglas. An American named Patrick O'Shea. Shot on the back steps of his home sometime between 3:00 and 3:30 last night. I've been in the house. There's just something funny about it. The place didn't seem lived in, although there were clothes in the wardrobe, food in the refrigerator, soap, and a toothbrush in the bathroom. Let me give you his passport details."

"Hang on for just a second. Okay, I'm ready. Go ahead."

Dillon read off the passport number, O'Shea's full name, date of birth, date of passport issue, and date of expiration.

"What do you know about him?" Bergman asked.

"Other than he was shot four times, not much. No idea of employment. No mail on the premises, no wallet, or any forms of identification except for the passport. Nothing like a U.S. driver's license or credit cards. Who can get by in today's world without a credit card?"

"I'm sure those will turn up. Let me see what I can find out."

"So this is the first you've heard of it? You haven't been officially notified yet?" Dillon asked.

"No official notification as of yet, but it's just before 10:00. I'm guessing we'll hear something around the noon hour or early afternoon."

"If you find anything out, let me know. I'd be interested in any travel information you can dig up on O'Shea. I neglected to page through his passport," Dillon said. They chatted for another minute or two, promised to get together soon, and hung up.

Suel looked over from his desk and shrugged. "Anything?"

Dillon shook his head as he headed over to Suel's desk. "I'm going into McCabe's office and give him an update. You want to join me?"

Suel shook his head. "No, you go ahead and deal with it. Let me know how it goes. I'll be on the line to a friend at the Bureau." Suel meant the National Bureau of Criminal Investigation, a team most recently investigating various relationships between serving members of the Gardai and criminals.

"You expect to learn anything?"

"No, it's more a case of just checking the box and giving a friend a heads-up. I feel as if that house in Finglas was staged. The clothes there, the bathroom, food in the refrigerator. If your man wasn't living there, I'd say it's a safe bet he was just staying there from time to time. No washing machine, no dirty clothes, no wallet, not so much as a bill or letter. How many twenty-five-year-olds do you know without a computer? The whole thing is almost too perfect. We're lucky they found that passport," Suel said.

"You know, as you say that, I'm wondering if your man O'Shea was planning on traveling somewhere. Let me bring McCabe up to date, and I'll check that out. I'll check with Mullen, too. I want to know where they found that passport."

Dillon knocked on DCI McCabe's doorframe. McCabe looked up from his computer screen and waved Dillon in. "Have a seat, Dillon. You were on site over in Finglas this morning?"

Dillon settled into one of the chairs in front of McCabe's desk. "Yes, sir. I was, although not an awful lot to see. A victim by the name of Patrick Joseph O'Shea, an American, was shot four times on the steps of his back door. At least seven shots were fired, possibly more."

"I'm getting the impression you're thinking there might be something wrong with the investigation."

Dillon shook his head. "Nothing's wrong with the investigation, sir. It's more what we didn't find." He went on to describe the lack of any personal information, no mail, cellphone, computer, or a wallet. Nothing that suggested a long-term residence. "It's as if someone cleaned the place out. But the initial response was just minutes after a 999 call reporting gunshots. The entire place just seemed to have a staged look to it."

"Did you contact the American Embassy?"

"I did, sir. Eric Bergman, we've dealt a number of times in the past. I trust him. If something isn't right, he'll let me know. He hadn't been informed yet and said that probably wouldn't come through until around the noon hour. I was able to give him the victim's name, Patrick O'Shea. It may take a while, but if he finds anything, he'll let me know."

McCabe seemed to think about that for a long moment then said, "Keep me posted. If I'm reading between the lines, you may be suggesting some sort of what? Possibly a governmental intelligence situation?"

"Mmm-mmm, that could be one of a number of options, sir. It might be some criminal enterprise, or maybe Mr. O'Shea is living on a trust fund, and he doesn't need a job. Maybe he just enjoys life. Or, God forbid, the poor guy just has an office somewhere, and he confronted a prowler who shot him."

"Let me know what you find out. Anything else?"

"No, sir. I just wanted to keep you up to date. Anything changes, either Suel or I will let you know."

"Very well, don't let me hold you up on your investigation."

"Thank you, sir," Dillon said and hurried out of the office.

THREE

It was after the noon hour before Dillon phoned DI Mullen expecting to leave a message. Instead, Mullen answered on the second ring. "Marshal Dillon, calling to tell me you've already solved our investigation?"

"I only wish. Actually, just checking in to see if you've come up with anything. I did phone Erick Bergman, my contact at the American Embassy. My call was the first he'd heard of the murder. O'Shea's name didn't ring a bell with him, which, on a certain level, is a good thing. He expected to receive official notification around the noon hour. I've not checked in to see if that happened. Anything new on your end?"

"Unfortunately not. Nothing that would suggest any personal information. I've one of our tech people searching the internet as we speak. We've come up empty-handed thus far looking for any sort of a business. A google search brought up everything from a painting company to doctors, solicitors, school teachers, athletes, and restaurants. Suffice to say Patrick O'Shea is a rather common name."

"Did you search the US?"

"Ireland, the US, UK, and Australia, trust me, it's a common name in every English-speaking country."

"Where did you find that passport?"

"That was another strange thing. One of the medical examiners was going to warm up their tea in the microwave. They opened it, and there was the passport just sitting in the microwave."

"Did you have a chance to look at the passport? There might be pages stamped from different trips."

"No, not yet, and I don't know when I'll get to it. We're investigating an assault at the moment. All the evidence from the O'Shea scene has been sent to the station. You know where we're located, on Mellowes Road?"

"Yeah, I know it. I'd like to swing by and take a closer look at that passport."

"I'll make a call as soon as we're finished. When you get to the station, ask for Sergeant Micheál O'Mara. He's in charge of property. I'll tell him you'll be stopping by and want to view your man's passport. We only sent a handful of items over, so he should have no problem finding it, even if things haven't been logged in yet."

"If you'd make that call, I'll head over there in the next half-hour," Dillon said.

"I'm on it. Ask for Sergeant Micheál O'Mara," Mullen said and disconnected.

Dillon touched base with Suel and then walked out to his car. He gassed up on the way over before he drove to the Finglas Garda station. The station was a contemporary four-story red-brick and stucco building on Mellowes Road. Dillon wasn't wild about the appearance but figured it had probably won some architectural award somewhere. He showed his warrant card to the officer and pulled into the secured parking lot. A car was just pulling out, and he was able to park near the door.

The front desk was another contemporary affair, only in more of a spiral design. Two uniformed officers watched Dillon as he approached. "How can I help you?" the younger of the two asked.

Dillon presented his warrant card and said, "I'd like to see Sergeant Micheál O'Mara, in the property room."

The officer examined the card, turned it over to look at the back, and then handed it to the older man, a sergeant.

"You're an American?" the sergeant asked.

"Yes, Marshall Jack Dillon assigned to Dublin's Special Branch. I report to DCI McCabe."

The sergeant nodded, seemed to think for a moment, and then handed the card back to Dillon. "You were involved in that incident out at the airport, terminal two. What was that, four years ago?"

"Closer to six, but yeah, that was me."

"Nice work, lad," the sergeant said. "Let me make a call, and I'll get someone to escort you down. Take a seat. It might be a few minutes," he said.

Dillon walked over to an area filled with five rows of black plastic chairs. Only one other person was seated, a middle-aged man wearing a gray suit. Dillon took a seat at the end of the row and pulled out his phone to look busy in the event the man thought about striking up a conversation. He noticed a framed item on the wall. At no real surprise, it was an architectural award dated 2009.

Five minutes later, a voice called, "Dillon." Dillon stood and hurried over to the uniformed officer holding the door open.

"Hi, I'm Marshal Jack Dillon. You need to see a warrant card?"

"No, you're good. Follow me. We're downstairs." They walked down the hall to an elevator. The officer pushed the down button, and a half-second later, the door opened. They stepped into the elevator, and the officer pushed a button labeled -1. Apparently, it was the only level below the main floor. There was no conversation during the brief ride. Dillon followed the officer off the elevator and down a hallway. They entered the second door. "Here's that American, Sarge," the officer said and then stepped behind the counter and disappeared behind a rack of metal shelving.

As he disappeared, another man stepped in front of the counter. He wore sergeant stripes on his uniform, and Dillon said, "Sergeant O'Mara?"

"Yes, and you're Dillon from Special Branch. I got a call from Ronan Mullen not twenty minutes ago saying you'd be stopping by."

"Yes. I was with him this morning at the O'Shea house. Apparently, they sent over a few items. One of them was an American passport. I'd like to take a look at it, see if there's any travel information."

"I have it set aside. Amazing the few things they sent in."

"Yeah, unless I'm mistaken, the passport was the only identification item. No wallet, no paperwork or mail. Absolutely nothing."

O'Mara nodded and said, "They did manage to grab the vehicle license, a Mercedes if I recall."

Dillon nodded. "Yeah, a dark blue car. An E300, I think. Could I look at that license too, please?"

"Coming right up. Help yourself to some gloves," he said, nodding at a box of latex gloves at the end of the counter. "And if you'd fill this in. I'll be back in just a moment," he said and slid a form across the counter to Dillon. Dillon checked the three boxes on the form, wrote down the number on his warrant card, and signed the form at the bottom.

He slipped on the latex gloves just as Sergeant O'Mara reappeared, holding two evidence bags, one with O'Shea's passport and the other was the vehicle registration document. The registration document had been in a holder attached to the bottom of the windshield on the passenger side of the vehicle. "You can grab one of those cubicles over along the wall," O'Mara said as he placed the evidence bags in front of Dillon.

"Thanks, this should just take a couple of minutes," Dillon said and walked over to the far wall. There were six white Formica countertops with a panel on either side, allowing for a degree of privacy. Dillon set the evidence bags on the countertop and turned on the light switch. A light in the ceiling came on, but it illuminated the chair rather than the countertop.

He settled onto the plastic chair, turned off the light, and glanced at the vehicle registration document. The car was a 2021 Mercedes E300 registered to Bridge Street Capitol and Patrick Joseph O'Shea. Dillon pulled out his cell phone and took a picture.

He opened the evidence bag and pulled out the passport. He studied the main page with O'Shea's photograph for a moment and then paged through. All the pages were blank, with one exception. The first page allowing for stamps was stamped in green ink with the date '04 JAN 20.' Dillon paged through the passport again to make sure he didn't miss anything. Apparently, at least based on this passport, O'Shea had arrived in Dublin on January fourth, 2020 and never left the country. Dillon took a photo of the page, took another photo of the page with O'Shea's picture and information, and placed the passport back in the evidence bag.

"That was fast," O'Mara said as Dillon approached the counter. "Find what you were looking for?"

"Unfortunately not. The guy looks to have been even more boring than me."

O'Mara laughed and said, "Well, better luck next time. Nice to meet you. Give my best to Ronan Mullen when you see him."

"I will. Thanks for your help."

"You can find your way out?"

"Yeah, not a problem. Thanks," Dillon said and headed back down the hall to the elevator.

FOUR

Dillon was at his desk the following morning when his phone rang. "Jack Dillon," was how he answered.

"Hi Jack, Eric Bergman, how's your morning going?"

"The way you say that, Eric, I'm thinking you've got either good or bad news. Which is it?"

Bergman laughed. "As far as I know, neither. I got the official call late yesterday morning on your man, Patrick O'Shea. Turns out he had dual citizenship, Irish and American. His parents were both born in Ireland and emigrated as a married couple in 1988. Father owned a bar and restaurant in Boston, Charlestown actually, at no surprise, a place called O'Shea's."

"Are the parents still alive?"

"No, they died back in 2019, supposedly a gas explosion in their home."

"You say supposedly. Is there some question about the explosion?"

"There was talk about the father, Emmett, owing money to some underworld types. Nothing ever really established. Anyway, Emmett and his wife, Aoife, died in the explosion along with two children."

"Doesn't sound good, and that happened in 2019?"

"Yeah, November fourth, actually."

"Interesting that the son Patrick arrives here two months later, and he has, or had, dual citizenship."

"Yeah, but that's a long process. His dual citizenship was granted in 2016, well before the parent's died."

"Any other family members?"

"An older brother, Sean, born in 1987. An army veteran, served as an officer in Iraq and Afghanistan, Special Forces. Left the army, and the last position on the information I read, he was a professor at Boston University."

"He sounds like the only one in the family who made it over the wall."

"Yeah, certainly looks that way. Maybe he was just the lucky one," Bergman said.

"I have the sense there's something that's not adding up with Patrick O'Shea. The dual citizenship adds some credibility to his basically unused US passport. By the way, they found it in the microwave in his kitchen."

"What?"

"Yeah, nothing providing any personal information in the house, no wallet, cellphone, mail, nothing, including Irish passport you mentioned, and then someone opens the microwave to warm their tea, and there's O'Shea's US passport."

"Yeah, you're right, that is strange. Very strange."

"I was over at Finglas Garda station this morning looking at the US Passport. The only stamp in the entire passport was from his entry into Ireland back on January fourth of 2020."

"Well, after losing his parents and two younger siblings in an explosion that may have been questionable, maybe he came over with the idea of never going back. That doesn't sound too far-fetched."

"You're right, it doesn't, but then why was he murdered? Seven or eight shots fired doesn't strike me as some potential burglar attempting to break into the guy's house. Based on what you've told me, I think we have to look at the possibility of a mob hit. It sounds as though there were at least rumors to that effect with the father. Maybe O'Shea was over here getting protection from someone or some group. Coming out of Boston, it's possible he could have had those sorts of connections here. Any info on the parents? What were their names, Aoife, and what was the father's name?"

"Father's name was Emmett. Owned a bar and restaurant."

"Anything else?"

"No, that about does it for now. If I hear of anything else, I'll give you a call."

"Thanks, Eric. I owe you a beer."

"I'll be sure to take you up on that, Jack. You hear anything, please let me know."

"Thanks, Eric," Dillon said, but Bergman had already disconnected.

Dillon glanced over at Suel's desk. He still wasn't in, and Dillon decided to head back over to Patrick O'Shea's residence in Finglas. He drove over and parked on the street. There was no sign of the dark blue Mercedes, which made sense. DI Mullen would have had it towed to a Gardai lot and had the thing searched. He sat drumming his fingers on the steering wheel for a minute and then climbed out of the car, and walked over to the unit next door, and rang the doorbell.

A heavyset woman opened the door a minute later. She wore a powder blue terrycloth robe and held a cigarette in her right hand. She clearly wasn't wearing makeup, not that it would have made much difference, and she was barefoot. He pegged her as maybe fifty or fifty-five.

"Hi, sorry to bother you. My name is Marshal Dillon. I'm with An Garda Síochána," he said, holding out his warrant card. "I'd like to ask you about the incident the other night at the O'Shea residence if you can spare a minute."

"Honey, for a man like you, I've got all the time in the world. What do you want to know?" she said. She took a long drag from her cigarette, crossed her arms over her chest, and exhaled a cloud of blue smoke up toward the top of the doorframe.

"Well, did you hear anything or see anyone coming or going the other night?"

"No, I'd been out with the girls at the Jolly Topper, lost count of how many glasses of wine. Thank God I wasn't driving. I can't even remember coming home. All I know is there were four or five Garda cars out on the lane when I woke up the next morning, and that was just before noon."

"So you never heard any shots fired?"

"Even if I had, I wouldn't have known what it was. I was out of it, honey. Besides, little Paddy O'Shea pretty much kept to hisself. Believe me, we all would have enjoyed a piece of the lad, but he didn't seem that interested. Every so often, there was a young slapper coming around. You ask me, they probably enjoyed each other's company if you get what I'm saying."

"You know what he did for a living?"

She chuckled for a moment. "No idea. That was always the question. He had that fancy car, but he never seemed to leave for a job. He'd maybe be gone a day or two, but no idea where he went."

"Let me give you my card. If anything comes to mind, feel free to call me," Dillon said as he handed his card to her.

"If you have any more questions, you're always welcome here. Stop by, you never know what I might come up with," she said and raised her eyebrows.

"Thanks, I'll keep that in mind," Dillon said and headed back down toward the street. He knocked on the next two doors but got no answer. He walked up to the next place, four doors away from O'Shea's and knocked.

An older man answered, maybe seventy or so. "Whatever it is, we're not interested. Good day," he said and started to close the door.

"An Garda Síochána," Dillon said quickly. "I'd like to ask you some questions if you have a moment."

"This about that dreadful event the other night? The O'Shea lad, was it?"

"Yes, sir, it is about the event the other night, and it was Patrick O'Shea."

He nodded and said, "Please come in. Sorry if I sounded rude earlier. Hopefully, you can understand. We've all sorts of knackers pounding on the door day and night, one worse than the other, and half of them I can't decipher what in God's name they're saying. Please, please come in," he said, stepping to the side as he held the door open.

"Thank you, sir. My name is Marshal Dillon. It's a pleasure to meet you."

"Eoghan Walsh, can I talk you into a tea?"

"Yes, that would be lovely," Dillon said and followed him into the kitchen. The layout was exactly the same as O'Shea's. Down the short hall, past the staircase, and through the door into the dining area. Instead of a sliding glass door leading outside, there was a wooden door with a yellow frosted glass window, no doubt original to the place. A gray-haired woman sat at the dining table reading the paper.

"Kiera, your man's with the Gardai, here to ask about the other night," Walsh said to the gray-haired woman reading the paper.

She nodded, smiled, and then folded the newspaper.

"Good morning, ma'am. Sorry to interrupt your morning. My name is Marshal Dillon. I'm with An Garda Síochána. Trying to see if you might have something to add to our investigation."

She smiled, and her blue eyes seemed to sparkle. "Well, we don't wear our hearing aids to bed, so we slept through the entire event. Didn't know anything was going on until Eoghan stepped out to get the newspaper, and there were all these Garda vehicles down the lane. That's the first we learned of the incident."

The kitchen was suddenly filled with the sound of water boiling in the kettle. The Walsh's remained quiet for the better part of a long minute as if a low flying plane was going over and conversation just had to stop. Once the kettle came to a boil and Eoghan began to fill the cups, Kiera said, "Now your young man's name was O'Shea?"

"Patrick O'Shea, nice neighbor, we never heard so much as a sound coming from the unit. Drove a nice car, a fancy-looking Mercedes," Eoghan said as he set a mug in front of Kiera and then Dillon.

Kiera added a drop of milk and two sugars, stirred the mug, and said, "Eoghan, don't forget the biscuits, dear, and serve them on a plate, please." She flashed a smile at Dillon, suggesting wasn't it amazing she had to tell her husband about the biscuits.

Eoghan brought over a small plate piled with chocolate-covered wafers referred to as biscuits and sat down. "So, do you have someone in mind for this?" he asked and dipped a biscuit into his tea mug.

"We're still in the preliminary part of our investigation," Dillon said. "Trying to learn as much as we can about Mr. O'Shea and any contacts he may have had."

"Well, I think it's fair to say there never seemed to be any noise coming from the place. Nothing along the lines of a wild party or people coming and going," Kiera said.

"Oh, you'd think the lad was a hermit. In all the while he lived there, we only saw the same girl come and go, pretty young thing."

"Nothing inappropriate, maybe there for an hour or so. Never late at night that we were aware, but of course, we're in bed before ten almost every night."

"She was over quite a bit. But, as I say, it wasn't every day, maybe once or twice a week," Eoghan said and took another biscuit off the plate.

"She drove a red car," Kiera said.

"A Toyota Corolla," Eoghan said.

"Oh, of course, he'd know. Never misses a thing," Kiera said.

"Can you describe her? Was she young, old? Maybe her hair color."

"I'd place her around your man's age. Of course, I'm seventy-six, so anyone under forty-five looks like a child to me."

His wife smiled. "I'd say no older than twenty-five and probably closer to twenty, maybe even younger."

"She had that spotty hair," Eoghan said.

Kiera smiled again. "Dark hair, blonde highlights. Always nicely dressed, although like all the young ones, the dresses were way too short. I'd say she paid attention to her figure."

"And she was there twice a week?" Dillon asked.

"At least that often, almost since the day he moved in," Kiera said, and they both nodded.

They talked for a few more minutes. Dillon gulped down his tea and hoped he didn't make a face because he was not a fan of the stuff. Finally, he smiled, stood, and thanked them for their time.

"Do you have a card? We may come up with something else, and we could call you," Eoghan said.

"Yes, of course," Dillon said, thinking for half a second they could join him with the large woman in the blue bathrobe. He reached into his pocket and pulled out two business cards.

Eoghan read the card. "Special Branch, and you're an American. Are things that bad here?"

Dillon smiled and said, "No, just a long, ongoing, working relationship."

"Hmm-mmm, interesting," Eoghan said. He walked Dillon to the door. They shook hands, and Dillon walked back to the street. He knocked on the next two doors, but no one answered. As he walked back to the opposite end of the block, a squad car pulled up and parked behind Dillon's car. A uniformed officer stepped out of the car, watched Dillon for a moment, and then stepped between the vehicles, as Dillon approached.

TO BE CONTINUED . . .

Thank you for taking the time to check out the sample of <u>Payback Brother</u>, the next book in the Jack Dillon Dublin Tales series. Things are about to get complicated.

Check out the list of books by Mike Faricy on the following page.

BOOKS BY MIKE FARICY
CRIME FICTION FIRSTS

A boxset of the first four books in four crime fiction series:

Russian Roulette; Dev Haskell series
Welcome; Jack Dillon Dublin Tales series
Corridor Man; Corridor Man series
Reduced Ransom! Hot Shot series

The following titles comprise the Dev Haskell series:

Russian Roulette: Case 1
Mr. Swirlee: Case 2
Bite Me: Case 3
Bombshell: Case 4
Tutti Frutti: Case 5
Last Shot: Case 6
Ting-A-Ling: Case 7
Crickett: Case 8
Bulldog: Case 9
Double Trouble: Case 10
Yellow Ribbon: Case 11
Dog Gone: Case 12
Scam Man: Case 13
Foiled: Case 14
What Happens in Vegas… Case 15
Art Hound: Case 16

The Office: Case 17
Star Struck: Case 18
International Incident: Case 19
Guest From Hell: Case 20
Art Attack: Case 21
Mystery Man: Case 22
Bow-Wow Rescue: Case 23
Cold Case: Case 24
Cash Up Front: Case 25
Dream House: Case 26
Alley Katz: Case 27
The Big Gamble: Case 28
Bad to the Bone: Case 29
Silencio!: Case 30
Surprise, Surprise: Case 31
Hit & Run: Case 32
Suspect Santa: Case 33
P.I. Apprentice: Case 34
Rebel Without a Clue: Case 35
Puppy Love: Case 36

The following titles are Dev Haskell novellas:
Dollhouse
The Dance
Pixie
Fore!
Twinkle Toes
(*a Dev Haskell short story*)

The following are Dev Haskell Boxsets:
Dev Haskell Boxset 1-3
Dev Haskell Boxset 4-6
Dev Haskell Boxset 7-9
Dev Haskell Boxset 10-12
Dev Haskell Boxset 13-15
Dev Haskell Boxset 16-18
Dev Haskell Boxset 19-21
Dev Haskell Boxset 22-24
Dev Haskell Boxset 25-27
Dev Haskell Boxset 28-30
Dev Haskell Boxset 1-7
Dev Haskell Boxset 8-14
Dev Haskell Boxset 15-19
Dev Haskell Boxset 20-24
Dev Haskell Boxset 25-29

The following titles comprise the Jack Dillon Dublin Tales series:
Welcome
Jack Dillon Dublin Tale 1
Sweet Dreams
Jack Dillon Dublin Tale 2
Mirror Mirror
Jack Dillon Dublin Tale 3
Silver Bullet
Jack Dillon Dublin Tale 4

Fair City Blues
Jack Dillon Dublin Tale 5
Spade Work
Jack Dillon Dublin Tale 6
Madeline Missing
Jack Dillon Dublin Tale 7
Mistaken Identity
Jack Dillon Dublin Tale 8
Picture Perfect
Jack Dillon Dublin Tale 9
Dublin Moon
Jack Dillon Dublin Tale 10
Mystery Woman
Jack Dillon Dublin Tale 11
Second Chance
Jack Dillon Dublin Tale 12
Payback Brother
Jack Dillon Dublin Tale 13
The Heist
Jack Dillon Dublin Tale 14
Jewels To Kill For
Jack Dillon Dublin Tale 15
Retirement Scheme
Jack Dillon Dublin Tale 16
The Collector
Jack Dillon Dublin Tale 17

Jack Dillon Dublin Tales Boxsets:
Jack Dillon Dublin Tales 1-3

Jack Dillon Dublin Tales 4-6
Jack Dillon Dublin Tales 1-5
Jack Dillon Dublin Tales 1-7
Jack Dillon Dublin Tales 6-10

The following titles comprise the Hotshot series;
Reduced Ransom! Second Edition
Finders Keepers! Second Edition
Bankers Hours Second Edition
Chow Down Second Edition
Moonlight Dance Academy Second Edition
Irish Dukes (Fight Card Series)
written under the pseudonym Jack Tunney

The following titles comprise the Corridor Man series:
Corridor Man
Corridor Man 2: Opportunity knocks
Corridor Man 3: The Dungeon
Corridor Man 4: Dead End
Corridor Man 5: Finger
Corridor Man 6: Exit Strategy
Corridor Man 7: Trunk Music
Corridor Man 8: Birthday Boy
Corridor Man 9: Boss Man
Corridor Man 10: Bye Bye Bobby

Corridor Man novellas:
Corridor Man: Valentine

Corridor Man: Auditor
Corridor Man: Howling
Corridor Man: Spa Day

The following are Corridor Man Boxsets:
Corridor Man Boxset 1-3
Corridor Man Boxset 1-5
Corridor Man Boxset 6-9

THANK YOU!

Contact the author:
- Email: mikefaricyauthor@gmail.com
- Twitter: @Mikefaricybooks
- Facebook: Mike Faricy Author
- Website: http://www.mikefaricybooks.com

Published by

MJF Publishing